Remembering Elinore Pruitt Stewart
June 3, 1876 — October 8, 1933

A remarkable woman of self-reliance, courage, and
optimism

Waiting for Hope

Karen J. Hasley

ISBN-13: 978-1497553828
ISBN-10: 1497553822

Chapter 1

Sad to say, all my childhood memories are connected in some way to The Sanctuary. I regret that truth, not because of what The Sanctuary was, but because my mother and I took up residence there when I was six, and thus all the years of my life prior to that move are irretrievably lost.

I cannot recollect any home other than that handsome red brick building although Mother and I must have lived somewhere before she and Ellie Fontana struck up the commercial relationship that brought us to the most famous bordello on the northern California coast. Noted in *A Gentleman's Guide to San Francisco*, Sanctuary, as it was familiarly known by both boarders and customers, was a narrow, three-story building with steps leading up to an imposing front door flanked by pillars entwined with sculpted ivy. As a child I thought the place elegant and beautiful, but I suppose if I saw it today I might consider its flocked wallpaper and ornate décor flamboyant, even tasteless. But through my child's eyes when the sun shone through the red half-circle window over the door and reflected a rosy light against the hallway walls inside, it was as if I'd been transported to a place of magic. Sanctuary was not a place of magic at all, of course— far from it—but it was the only home I can remember throughout my childhood.

I came to The Sanctuary a biddable, quiet, and ignorant child until The Professor opened up the world of books to me. A more appropriate name for the man would have been The Piano Player because that was what he did nightly at the parlor house, but his spontaneous quoting of Shakespeare and the fact that he always carried a book in an inside pocket earned him the affectionate scholarly nickname.

Entering Sanctuary's kitchen one quiet afternoon, I stopped in the doorway to stare at The Professor as he sat at the old oak table, his head bent over whatever small volume he had with him at the time, immersed in the story and oblivious to anything going on around him. I couldn't imagine what in that little book was able to hold his rapt attention and keep him so still. I was as engrossed in watching him as he was in the reading until, somehow feeling my eyes on him, he looked up.

"Here's a little Miss Mouse," he greeted, teasing. "I heard there was a kid around somewhere." He noticed my gaze fastened on the small volume on the table and asked, "Haven't you ever seen a book before?" pushing the book across the table toward me. "Here, take a look."

I came forward and picked up the leather-bound volume, handling it as if it were fragile.

"I can't read," I finally admitted regretfully. I put the book down on the table, conscious of an almost overwhelming sadness. At that moment I never wanted anything as much as I wanted to be able to read what was on those pages.

"A grown up girl like you? Well, that's not good." He studied my face soberly. "You've got your mother's eyes, Miss Mouse, but I see something else in that little face of yours. I'm guessing there's a bright mind there, too." Then, more to himself than to me, he added, "No need to follow in her footsteps if you can find a better way."

From then on, The Professor made it a point to arrive earlier than he was needed, and using the clever combination of good literature, newspapers, and the labels of common household items, he began to teach me my letters. I was very quick and loved reading from the start, and I believe he enjoyed his self-assigned role of teacher as much as I loved the printed word.

When I proudly read my first complete literary sentence to him unassisted, The Professor startled me by laughing out loud. I had chosen the book from several he had scattered on the table earlier in the week and had worked on the first page so diligently that I fell asleep at night clasping the novel.

"'It is a truth universally acknowledged,'" I began, "'that a single man in possession of a good fortune must be in want of a wife.'"

I didn't stumble over any of the words, even *acknowledged*, which had taken me a while to figure out, and I didn't understand what he found amusing in my reading. For a moment I hesitated, a child among adults all my life and having learned caution at an early age because of it, but his eyes remained kind. His had been the laughter of a quiet joke, not directed at me specifically and not mocking, so after another reassuring glance at his face, I bent my head and started reading again. I didn't understand everything I read, but I loved the rhythm of words and the sound of the story, loved, too, the puzzle of reading, putting the pieces together and making sense of it all. I was too young then to understand the irony of that particular sentence in our circumstances at The Sanctuary and why it must have struck the eccentric Professor as funny. I understand better now.

Besides reading, he taught me arithmetic and writing, both of which came easily and never caused me a moment's puzzlement or labor. With The Professor's encouragement I scribbled (as my mother always called it) from my early years, created stories and poems, wrote letters to imaginary friends, started the habit of maintaining a journal that I continue to this day. His was the only schooling I ever had, but it was more than enough. I never knew the man's real name, and by the time I was nine, Ellie did away with the piano entirely, so I never saw him after that and didn't have the chance to thank him for what he gave me. But because of The Professor, I discovered the "better way" he mentioned and didn't follow in my mother's footsteps. To this day I wish there were some way I could let him know how those few hours a week so many years ago changed the course of my life.

My mother, who was indifferent to both reading and writing, never knew what to make of my predilection for learning. At times she would be weakly scornful, unsure of its attraction for me, perhaps wondering what changeling had been left on her doorstep, who could lose herself for hours in the printed word. At other times she would show me off to the girls in the house.

"Look at my Hope," Mother would say. "That girl has more brains than all of us together." Pride was clear in her voice but something else, too, something more ambiguous and harder to interpret. Perhaps emphasizing my intellectual accomplishments allowed her to ignore the fact that I was growing up and filling out in other ways and she was growing older.

I spent most of my early years trying to stay one step ahead of my mother, trying to love and understand her and in the way some children reverse the roles, trying to protect her. I couldn't explain why I thought she needed my protection. She was sixteen when I was born, no longer a child in either years or experience, and she was beautiful. As a very little girl I can recall her straight, smooth, golden hair fanning out about her shoulders on the pillow. I can see myself tracing the line of her perfectly arched brow with my finger as she slept, surprised when she awakened, those brilliant green eyes laughing at me, perhaps loving me. I was never quite sure of that.

Mother was mercurial at best, often despondent and at other times so brilliantly gay her presence lit a room and made lamps unnecessary. Because morning was the only time I had any real freedom and she of necessity slept well into the afternoon, my time with her was limited. Although we usually lunched together, I never knew what to expect from day to day and so learned to be quiet and watchful until I could take a cue from her. Was she lethargic and exhausted, requiring me to be very quiet and speak only when spoken to? Or perhaps she would be brittle and short-tempered, letting me know in her special way that nothing I said or did pleased her. The very good days saw her happily pleased with herself, satisfied and content with whatever had happened the night before.

My mother never struck me or even raised her voice to me, but I would have preferred those actions to her way of coldly ignoring me if I did something to displease her, whether I was aware of my fault or not. She was all I had in the world and her censure, whether open or implied, stung. Being plainspoken and straightforward by nature, I found the times almost unbearable when she disregarded my presence as if I were invisible, cheerfully talking to others in the room and disavowing any knowledge of a daughter as I sat before her in plain view, mute, furious, and resentful. Eventually the incident would pass and she would once again speak to me, never sharing whatever I had done to make her unhappy and always assuming she had taught me a lesson by her silence. She had but not the lesson she intended.

On the rare occasions when Mother talked about her childhood, usually when alcohol made her voluble, she painted a dismal picture of a northern California farm, endless drudgery, long days of field work, too many mouths and not enough food to feed them, not enough love or attention either, although she never said that in so many words. She left the farm at the age of fourteen with a traveling actor of so little consequence to her that she never mentioned his name and I doubt could remember it. It was he who had brought her to San Francisco. Sometime after that arrival she met up with a woman named Ellie Fontana and the rest of the story I knew. Ellie was an up-and-coming businesswoman, one of the most elegant and successful madams in San Francisco, and it didn't take either of the women long to decide that they could form a flourishing and successful business relationship using Mother's beauty and Ellie's brains.

To Mother's credit, she worked out an agreement with Ellie that permitted me to stay with her. I know now how rare and infrequent such an arrangement was. But my mother insisted that she would reside at Sanctuary only if I resided there, too, and Ellie eventually agreed to it. Ellie Fontana knew her fortune was tied up with my mother in those days because it was my mother's ability to charm both in the parlor and in the bedroom that first brought the influential and powerful men of the city to the house. Over the eight years I was there, Ellie added many more women to The Sanctuary, all young, attractive, and well mannered, but my mother was always the queen bee and her clients requested her by that name: Queen Bea.

The Sanctuary was a house for men, equipped with every luxury and extravagance necessary for their comfort. Growing up as I did, surrounded almost exclusively by women, I wondered what it was men did that was so arduous and trying they must be pampered and indulged with fine wines, soft furniture, and even softer women. I could gaze down from my third-story room and catch glimpses of the men who frequented

The Sanctuary, men who looked well-dressed and well-fed, hardly men who had borne the rigors of the elements and grueling, hard work. Why should so much be at their disposal and dedicated solely to their wellbeing?

When I asked my mother that question, she was in one of her good moods and responded very seriously, "The world was made for men, Hope, and everything in it is at their disposal. Do whatever you must to stay on their good side. Never forget that." Just as she said, I never forgot her advice, but I never followed it, either.

Mother could have become a wealthy woman. She was often requested by affluent customers, who would have only her, but she loved beautiful things and fine food, and so it seemed we were always poor. She periodically reminded me that I was a great part of the reason we stayed in debt. There was a charge for my stay at The Sanctuary—exorbitant, I'm sure, as all of Ellie's charges were. My room and board and all of my clothes came out of my mother's percentage of the business as well as her own personal expenses. Later I discovered that Ellie encouraged my mother to buy beautiful and overpriced gowns and hats from several local dressmakers and milliners. By prearrangement the merchants put the cost on Ellie's account so that my mother remained forever in Ellie's debt. No doubt Ellie Fontana received kickbacks from the dressmakers as well. Such practices were all part of the business, commonplace and accepted.

The rules that applied to the early years of my life were simple: be neither seen nor heard; be invisible. Sometimes I picture myself as a ghost child in that big house, a silent phantom drifting quietly up the back stairs to my little room as soon as the bell on the front door tinkled and Ellie called out, "Company, girls."

For Ellie I held the danger of notoriety. She kept a discreet and quiet parlor house, with only moderate alcohol, no excessive profanity, tasteful music and decorous dancing, polite conversation, and stylishly decorated rooms where her girls entertained their customers. Ellie would have feared the outrage of some respectable, reforming San Francisco matron if it were discovered that a little girl lived on the premises of a brothel. The notoriety would have ruined her business had The

Sanctuary been splashed across the newspapers. What respectable man of any prominence or importance would risk being seen there after such scathing publicity? And prominent, important men, respectable men, were Ellie's bread and butter. So I was made to understand very clearly that I must never be seen on the premises by any of the guests.

My mother had other concerns. I believe she felt a certain fear for my safety, knowing there were men who would have preferred a child to any woman they were offered, but I think, too, that mother was not a role the Queen Bea often felt like playing. She was much more at home as the beautiful, flirtatious, charming courtesan, able to make any man feel he was king in whatever role he chose to act out. Motherhood did not fit the part and could hardly be expected to act as an aphrodisiac for her or her clients, so I must be carefully hidden from view. Sometimes one of the maids was allowed to take me on a walk in the park, and I could spend as much time as I wished in the kitchen with Cook, but "Company, girls" always sent me scurrying up the back steps.

If it had not been for the books The Professor brought me, I might have believed that life at The Sanctuary was all a woman should expect and followed unquestioningly in my mother's footsteps. But once books opened other worlds to me, I knew I wanted something different, something more. Even at so young an age, I began to plan for a real home of my own.

My mother never shared who my father was. Now I think that was because she wasn't entirely sure, but as a child I imagined something more glamorous or tragic, a heroic father lost at sea or gone on some romantic excursion to China or India, never to return. It never crossed my mind that my mother may have had so many partners she could not identify with any certainty the man who fathered me. I led a strangely sheltered life in the midst of such sin and indulgence and peculiar as it may seem, it wasn't until I turned fourteen that I began to make sense of my surroundings. Until then, Sanctuary was the only life I knew. Protected by the women, the dressers, the bouncer, The Professor, and the day help, I never felt threatened or fearful and was disturbed only infrequently by noises that reached my top story. Once I was awakened by the sound of gunshots, but because no other sounds followed, I thought it had been a dream and promptly went back to sleep. In the morning, except for several lamp globes missing in the first-floor hallway, nothing seemed the worse for wear and no one mentioned anything untoward.

Another time, one of the new girls, a pretty, plump thing named Lottie, came down to lunch with a fresh bruise along one side of her face. She sat forlornly at the table, unable to stop crying, but when I approached Lottie to offer some comfort, my mother sharply forbade me to address the weeping girl or acknowledge her tears.

"She has to learn that once the door closes, her wishes are unimportant. Lottie had to learn a hard lesson last night, and she won't soon forget it. Let her cry." It was the closest my mother ever came to telling me what her life was like, and I remember thinking at the time that when I grew up, I would never allow myself to be trapped in a place where my wishes were unimportant.

Except for those two occasions, I don't recall anything that made me uncomfortable or afraid. My childhood was queer and solitary but not unhappy. Those were times that preceded today's civilized San Francisco, times when the city was extravagantly unrestrained. How could I, a child, have known to be ashamed of the activities at The Sanctuary when the adults in my world accepted them as commonplace?

Through the early years my mother aged gracefully, growing into a woman of great beauty and voluptuous figure, but some time between my tenth and fourteenth birthdays her health began to falter, the decline taking a toll on both her face and figure. Too much laudanum perhaps or some illness associated with her trade.

After I turned fourteen, my familiar, carefully constructed existence collapsed. One late afternoon I slipped downstairs to retrieve my journal that I'd forgotten below in the kitchen. Returning up the narrow back steps to my room, I met a man coming down. Such an occurrence was rare but not unheard of, and I did what I had been taught to do years ago: lower my head and not make eye contact, hunch my shoulders so I would appear as small as possible, and move sideways quickly to slide past him. The man smelled strongly of alcohol and as we passed, he put both hands on my shoulders and pushed me hard against the wall, almost causing me to lose my balance and tumble down the stairs. I gave a little cry and fell against him.

"Well, what's Ellie been keeping from me?" the man asked, lifting my chin with a finger to stare at my face. His arrogant and drunken tone and his manhandling of me both frightened and infuriated me. I had never felt so angry.

"Leave me alone," I demanded with disgust. "You're drunk," and reached up to push him away. He said something foul and bent to kiss me. As I struggled and cried out, Ellie came to the foot of the stairs, then hurried up to where we stood.

"So this is where you are, Marcus. Lottie is waiting for you in the parlor. I wondered where you'd gotten to." She talked to him in a friendly, almost motherly, tone and pulled him gently away from me and down the steps as if I really were invisible. I was angry that Ellie hadn't chastised him for his behavior, and I was revolted and appalled by the man's smell and sound and touch. So *this* was what my mother tolerated night after night after night. I truly had had no idea.

The next day Ellie, Mother, and I met in the front parlor. Ellie Fontana was a stout, handsome woman of indeterminate age with a prominent nose and dark eyebrows over black eyes. She was as much a part of my childhood as my mother, but that morning she observed me with cool detachment as if seeing me for the first time.

"Hope is turning into a beauty," she remarked to my mother. "We need to do something with her." The two women eyed each other without speaking until my mother finally looked away. Then Ellie turned to me

"You're old enough to understand the business we have here and the services The Sanctuary provides, aren't you, Hope?"

"Yes," I replied, although I had only the most rudimentary knowledge. My mother never spoke to me of the more intimate details of her profession. All I knew I picked up from oblique references by some of the other girls, and they were always careful not to say too much in my presence.

"Does it hold any interest for you?"

Before I could answer my mother said, "Absolutely not. I will not have it, Ellie," with great vehemence. She was usually so lethargic in her speaking that I was taken aback by her forceful tone

Ellie, ignoring Mother and examining me with dollar signs just behind her eyes, spoke to me again. "Hope?"

I looked at Ellie Fontana squarely, remembering the man from the night before and the uncomfortable combination of anger and fear and helplessness I had felt.

"I'd hate it more than anything else," I told her bluntly. "You'd have to force me."

Ellie nodded, unsurprised. "There are some places that would do just that but not in my house." Then she added, "So what are we to do with you?" speaking more to herself than to Mother or me. "You're too grown up to stay here any longer."

When I looked over at my mother she wore a curious expression of relief mixed with sadness. Had she been concerned for my well being or only worried that as she grew older and more worn by time, I might pose some kind of threat or competition because of my youth? It was a disloyal thought, but sometimes I understood her better than I wished. I would never be a beauty like my mother, but youth has its own attraction and perhaps she feared the comparison.

Finally Ellie said, not unkindly, "Hope's a good girl, Bea, smart and quiet, even-tempered and strong. She can go into service. It's time she got out into the world, anyway, and discovered what life is all about. I know people who know people. I'll find a place where they'll treat her well."

My mother hesitated only a minute. "All right," she said, and the matter was settled.

When the time finally came for me to leave The Sanctuary, I received a small, tearful farewell from nearly everyone in the house. Some of the girls there were hardly older than I and astonished that I could possibly prefer working as a servant to their own choice of profession. I only laughed and asked them not to think me too crazy. They had come to The Sanctuary to escape a harsh world, I told them, but I had yet to experience the world, harsh or not.

These were not bad women, just girls like myself using what they had been born with to survive in a world unkind to females, but I had known for a long time that their choice was not the choice for me. From books I had discovered that somewhere was a life different from The Sanctuary, a life better, and I was determined to find it, determined to have a home of my own someday where I would be subject to no one's whim or caprice, neither man's nor woman's, a life dependent on no one but myself. I believed I could take care of myself, believed there was nothing I could not accomplish if I only planned well and worked hard.

In my journal I had written the words from the book *Jane Eyre* as a reminder: "I can live alone if self-respect and circumstances require me to do so. I need not sell my soul to buy bliss." I wasn't sure what a real home would look like, but I knew I'd recognize it when I saw it, and I was single-minded in my purpose to have a home someday without having sold my soul in the process. I was fourteen and all my dreams lay before me like a paved road extending as far as I could see into the distance, into the future.

On my final morning at The Sanctuary, my mother sat with me in the front parlor, one hand folded into mine, neither of us speaking. She looked drawn and thin, and the sudden surge of tender protection I felt for her nearly brought me to tears. She sat next to me on the overstuffed sofa, now and then stroking my hair away from my face in the common gesture of mothers everywhere. Finally she turned me to her and put a palm against my cheek.

"Listen, Hope," she said, her tone both urgent and sad. "Be prepared for the worst. People are unkind and men are not to be trusted. Don't tell anyone who your mother was or where you came from or how we lived. People will hold that against you. It's not fair but that's just the way it is. Make something of yourself. You have more of a head on your shoulders than I ever had, and the times are changing." She drew me against her and hugged me hard. "Make something of yourself, Hope," she repeated.

Then the doorbell rang, and I heard a woman's voice asking for me. Ellie came to stand in the parlor doorway.

"Are you ready, Hope?"

I nodded, speechless now that the moment of departure had really come, picked up my small bag, and stood up.

Ellie pressed a little pouch of coins into my hand as I passed her.

"Hold onto this," she whispered, "and never be apart from it. A woman may need a stake when she least expects it."

I thanked her and turned to wave a small goodbye to my mother, who smiled weakly in return. Ellie had called me a woman, but I didn't feel grown up then, only nervous and excited and more than a little apprehensive about the future.

When the door closed behind me, I went down the walk with my new companion and I never looked back.

Chapter 2

*T*he years I spent in service at the Gallaghers' Nob Hill mansion were sometimes monotonous to the point of numbing boredom, sometimes frustrating, physically tiring, and tedious. To be fair, however, they were as equally educating, enlightening, and necessary. From the beginning I knew there were things I needed to learn in order to be independent some day and have a home of my own, things I could not learn in a brothel. I needed to know the everyday activities of living that most people took for granted, cooking and sewing and cleaning, housekeeping activities that most women learned from their mothers but which I had never been taught. All of that is what I learned in the Gallaghers' house.

For me, the worst part of those years was the loss of reading time. The household staff started its day before sunrise and worked until well after supper, often until dark. The long, leisurely, unencumbered days I had enjoyed at The Sanctuary disappeared. Thus, as determined as I was to save money, I allowed myself one extravagance from my small earnings: an oil lamp that allowed me to read or write in my journal after I was supposed to have gone to bed. At the time I imagined my literary activities to be a well-kept secret shared only by my roommate and me, but now I believe all the servants in the house knew about my habit and indulged me.

When I arrived at the huge house in San Francisco's most affluent neighborhood, I met the other live-in staff: Pansy, a girl close to my age and Mrs. Paine, the housekeeper. Besides Bertha, the day cook, I spent most of my time, whether waking or sleeping, with those two women. I soon realized that I had a lot to learn about taking care of others and of myself, much more than I expected. Mrs. Paine, a gray-haired widow with a constantly weary expression, discovered that although I was always willing to do whatever she asked, I usually didn't know how, so she wisely and patiently started me on basic chores.

My first year there was just prior to Mr. Gallagher installing indoor plumbing, so dumping the slops in the back latrine was a nasty but easy job to learn and my first official assignment. I must have been observed more than I knew, for after the first few weeks of handling that chore along with washing dishes and scrubbing floors, Mrs. Paine called me to her. She had pale, almost colorless eyes that I found disconcerting, but they warmed when she smiled.

"Hope," she said, putting a hand on each of my shoulders and smiling then, "I think it's time for you to learn some other tasks. Bertha has asked if you may help her in the kitchen. She believes you may have a flair for cooking."

I had passed a test of some kind, and after the first month the work never seemed that hard again.

Several weeks later, Pansy, with whom I shared a room for all the time I lived at the Gallaghers', asked, "Don't anything bother you, Hope? Don't you never get upset or mad or anything like that?" It was night and we were both in our narrow cots in the top-floor room we shared.

I answered thoughtfully, "A lot of things bother me, Pansy, more than I let on, but what good would it do to let my feelings show? I can learn from everything that happens to me and put it to good use later. Someday I'll have a place of my own and none of this will matter." From my first day there, I believed that with all my heart. Whatever a home was, a real home, I knew in some deep and private part of me that I would one day have it. I just knew.

For a long time my employers, the Gallaghers, puzzled me. Mr. Gallagher, a prominent San Francisco business man, went off to work every morning except Sunday dressed in a three-piece suit and a dark derby hat. On Sundays he left for church dressed exactly the same. The only difference I could find in his Sunday departure was the destination.

"He speculates. Gold and silver and commodities," Pansy told me, having overheard that information from someone else, and because neither of us had any idea what it really meant, we could only wonder about our employer's daily activities—speculating ourselves, as it were.

Ralph Gallagher always presented a self-satisfied and proper appearance, sure of himself and his place among the city's financial and social leaders. Privately I found him haughty and unattractively smug, but I am certainly not complaining about his character. In exchanges with other servants I quickly realized how fortunate I was to be in a household where I didn't have to fear that the head of the house might catch me alone and unprotected and make an advance that would outrage me, disappoint him, and embarrass us both. Mr. Gallagher would never have stooped to a dalliance with any of his servants, even if we'd all paraded around stark naked. It was not his wife that absorbed his affections but commodities, and whatever commodities were, they apparently supplied all the affection and activity he needed in his life.

Perhaps for that reason, Irene Gallagher was one of the unhappiest women I have ever known. Nothing pleased her, not her beautiful home or the bowls of lush hothouse flowers that fragranced every room or satin dresses of gemstone colors that rustled when she walked or all the leisure time a woman could want. Lines of discontent were already etched into her face when I first met her and they only deepened as the years passed. It took me over a year before I realized how profound her unhappiness really was and why.

One evening I stood in the shadowed doorway of the drawing room, holding the Gallaghers' outer garments over my arm as they both descended the stairs on their way out to some evening's entertainment. He walked briskly down the steps ahead of his wife, she speaking as she trailed behind him, trying to catch her husband long enough to place a hand on his arm.

"Did you remember, Ralph, that today is our twentieth anniversary?" she asked, a desperation and a longing in her tone that were as tangible as tears.

I watched his reaction covertly, knowing he had heard her words because I did, and I was farther away. Mr. Gallagher took his coat from my hands, not noticing me any more than if I'd been a wooden coat tree, and without responding to his wife at all, as if she hadn't spoken and didn't exist, walked out the front door and down the porch steps.

I turned to see Mrs. Gallagher come to an abrupt stop with her eyes fixed intently on the now empty doorway, watched the grief and anger gather in her face and realized the exact moment that she became conscious of my quiet presence. I met her look soberly and with a pity I could not hide, not mistress and servant at that moment but two women in a grand hallway, she knowing that she was unloved and well aware that I knew it, too. The lines that ran from her nose to the corners of her mouth became more pronounced and without a word, her face suddenly like stone, she turned her back to me and slid into the cape I held for her. Then she followed her husband out the front door where a carriage waited for them.

In books I had read about homes where love existed and true affection bound husbands and wives, but since I had never experienced anything even remotely close to such a description, I considered that the idea might be just a liberty of fiction. Certainly most of the men who visited The Sanctuary had had wives at home but still preferred to spend intimate moments with my mother and women like her. Could any of them have really loved their wives if that were the case? Not all the books in the world could help me understand the contradictions in the lives of men and women.

The Gallaghers had lived together for over twenty years as man and wife but acted as strangers, often passing in the hallways of their luxurious mansion without a nod or a word. I never saw them touch each other even in the most casual way during any private family time that I witnessed. At meals, even an informal breakfast, they sat at the long dining table cool and proper, distanced from each other in both space and emotion, and at least in front of the servants never indulged in any conversation that was either warm or personal. Their laughter always seemed contrived and perfunctory. The two Gallagher sons, who made dutiful but infrequent visits home, were both at school in the East by the time I came to their house, and I thought the absence of her sons must have increased Mrs. Gallagher's loneliness. She radiated a discontent in her tone and posture that was always obvious to me.

When I commented about my observations to Pansy, my roommate gave a snort of disdain and disbelief. "You're crazy to think that with all she's got, Mrs. Gallagher is anything but satisfied and thanking the stars she was born under. Sometimes, Hope, I don't know what to make of you. Lonely indeed! The woman's hardly ever home and when she is, it seems we're setting a table for half of San Francisco."

But in a way difficult to explain, I recognized that Irene Gallagher and my mother were not very different, despite their outward circumstances. They had both made trade-offs that did not satisfy them but somehow must. I often told myself that I would never do that, would never sell my soul to buy bliss. I would have what I desired on my own terms and without compromise.

The staff was usually given time off on Saturday night after supper and for a few hours on Sunday afternoon following Sunday services. Mrs. Paine, Pansy, and I were expected to attend services at the Episcopal Church every Sunday, where we sat in the back pew reserved for the household staff of each family who sat up front. I learned to treasure that time, one of the few occasions when I could simply sit, think, reflect, and plan. The service always included fine music and wonderfully literate phrases from the Book of Common Prayer spoken sonorously from the pulpit.

"Yea, the sparrow hath found an house," we would read from the Psalms, and I would think of myself as that sparrow ready when the time was right to find my own nest.

"You're the strangest girl, Hope," Pansy once told me, her voice sounding as if she were describing a freak from the circus, but her teasing always so good-natured, just like her, that I never took offense. "I believe you'd prefer church to stepping out with that fella from the telegraph office, who keeps making eyes at you. You didn't even notice him, I guess."

Pansy was my opposite in temperament and appearance, short, plump, and brown, like a sparrow herself, with a talkative chirp to her voice, playful dark eyes, and an unabashed appreciation for the young men who crossed our paths.

"Of course, I noticed him," I retorted, "but I think it's you he's making sheep eyes at, not me. His name's Eddie and he asked what your name was."

"He never!"

"Yes, he did, and I told him it was Pansy and you were unattached. So next time you should be a little bolder and talk to him." My telling Pansy to be bolder was like telling the temperature to get hotter in July, an inevitability. She attracted young men like bees to clover, something honeyed in her eyes and expression that I couldn't sense but that the opposite sex certainly recognized. Pansy was good natured and uncomplicated, everything about her written across her face for all to see. I think she was as fond of me as I was of her, but she found me too serious and too bookish and never knew what to make of me.

Every other Sunday afternoon I spent time with my mother. After my first return trip to The Sanctuary, she told me never to come back there and we began meeting on a bench in Golden Gate Park. I thought she had grown too pale and drawn, but she was always gay when we were together and curious about my life. She knew of the Gallaghers but made no other comments about them. I shared every new skill I mastered: baking bread, sewing, quilting, planting, harvesting and preserving, spinning and weaving, the things a girl of my age and my position should know.

"These things don't bother you, don't make you wish you could run away?" she asked once. The suggestion was so completely opposite the way I felt that my amazement must have shown on my face, for she laughed and answered her own question. "What an odd girl you are, Hope! I believe you enjoy all that dreary work." I didn't know how to explain that enjoying it or not never crossed my mind. For me, all my chores were a means to an end and I could tolerate everything with equanimity.

"How is Ellie?" I asked and because I had been accustomed to reading my mother's expression all my life, I caught a furtive look cross her face.

"Fine."

"And everyone else? Is Lomira doing all right with her rheumatism?"

"They're all fine, Hope. Some things don't change." But from her tone I knew something had changed, although I didn't know what.

I was eighteen the last time I saw my mother. Early fall brought a cool breeze off the ocean as we sat together on our usual park bench, but the sunshine still held considerable warmth and enough glow to burnish a nearby statue. Mother appeared weak and weary and seemed to have grown smaller, but perhaps it was only that my figure had filled out, and with all the physical work I was doing, I felt strong and healthy. Her usual finery had been replaced by common, too-worn clothing that didn't become her.

By then, I had been with the Gallaghers four years and was comfortably situated. I hadn't needed to spend any of the coins Ellie Fontana had slipped to me years before, and I kept the pouch, stuffed with tissue paper to keep it from rattling, pinned securely to the inside of my skirt, a talisman of sorts for me, a promise of a hopeful future. In addition, except for the small reading lamp I'd purchased or some special treat for Pansy or Mother, I spent very little and had hoarded enough from my scant pay to open a small bank account of funds. My future seemed bright and hopeful.

"What are you going to do with that money?" my mother asked. Like the day I had left The Sanctuary years before, I sat with her hand folded in mine, conscious that she was smaller than I remembered and sadder, no glowing spark of wit or gaiety about her any longer.

"I want a home some day, a place of my own." I thought she might laugh at such grandiose plans, but she said nothing, only reached into her purse and brought out a yellowed paper that she unfolded and handed to me.

"Here, maybe this old deed will help you find your heart's desire." The phrase she used, "heart's desire," was unusual for my mother, who was not given to poetry or fanciful language. The paper was a land deed dated 1877, seven years before I'd been born, for 160 acres outside of Laramie, Wyoming. The stamp and signature of the recorder of the general land office were faded but legible and made the document appear official. Someone had blackened out the original owner's name and replaced it with my mother's full name printed carefully, even boldly, as if the writer wanted to make sure there would be no challenge to the change. Next to the name *Beatrice Birdwell* were the scrawled initials *CM* and the date of June 1, 1884.

"How did you get this?" I asked.

"The year before you were born, I met a man who fell in love with me. He was older than I was by several years and he was a drifter, but I grew fond of him. My, he was a handsome man, fair haired with brown eyes, and he always knew how to make me laugh." She paused, remembering something that brought a faint smile. "Didn't have a cent to his name, though. He'd had some unfortunate experience years before that he couldn't quite get over, and he told me I was the only woman who could help him forget his foolishness. Charlie gave me this deed to a property he said he'd never go back to. He won it in a card game, he said, but the place was lonely and too cold to sleep alone."

"Charlie?"

"His name was Charlie McKinney. He up and left one day, and I don't know what ever happened to him, but he gave me this to pay for the companionship, and I've kept it all this time, almost twenty years now. You should have it."

I held the document as if she had given me gold bullion. Whatever she saw on my face caused her to put her arms around me and begin to cry in small, gulping, wrenching sobs that hurt me to hear.

"What's wrong?"

"You're the only right thing I've ever done in my life, and all I have to give you is an old piece of yellow paper for land in some god-forsaken place. What kind of life can you have with a whore for a mother?"

I was shocked at the word I had never heard her use before.

"That doesn't matter. No one knows and even if they did, why would they care? It's a new century and things are different now."

"There's nothing different," she replied bitterly, wiping her eyes and pushing away from me. "The world was made for men. It's too hard for a woman all alone."

"It doesn't have to be. You'll see. I know I can make it on my own."

She softened a little, standing up and linking her arm in mine as we strolled toward the street. "Perhaps you can," was all she said.

We said goodbye outside the gate, and I, fearing I would be late back to Nob Hill, didn't turn to wave goodbye as I usually did. I wish I had. Even now I can't bear to picture her with her hand raised, waiting for me to turn with a final good-bye that never came.

But that day I was too hurried and preoccupied to turn around, too caught up in my own life, too busy planning for tomorrow and next week and next year. That afternoon was the last time I ever saw my mother.

On our next scheduled Sunday, I waited for Mother in our usual place, but she didn't come. I knew instinctively that something terrible had happened, so I took a great risk and went to The Sanctuary. When I knocked, a woman I didn't recognize opened the door, and when I asked for my mother, she looked at me strangely.

"No one here by that name."

"Don't be silly," I said abruptly. "Queen Bea. She's always been known as Queen Bea. Tell her Hope is waiting outside. She'll see me no matter what instructions she gave you to the contrary."

"No one here by that name, girl," the woman repeated. "Now you'd best leave before I have to call someone to see you off the property."

Behind her Ellie Fontana said, "It's all right, Martha, let her in." Ellie had hardly aged a day, no gray in her dark hair and no lines creasing her face. "I haven't seen you in a long time, Hope."

Four years." I stepped inside as the woman Martha closed the door behind me. "Hello, Ellie. I'm looking for my mother."

"Come in here." We stepped into the parlor, and Ellie shut the double doors. "Your mother isn't here, Hope."

"Where is she then?"

"I've lost track of her."

"What do you mean?"

"Your mother stopped being good for business," Ellie responded coolly. "She grew too fond of opium and used laudanum indiscriminately. She drank too much and became unreliable. Our clients no longer found her attractive and they stopped requesting her. I had to ask her to leave."

"You were friends."

"She was just one of my girls, Hope. I have few friends, and your mother was never one of them." Ellie's flat and unemotional tone took my breath away for a moment. "As it was, I took a loss when she left. She owed me a great deal of money."

"I'd venture to say she made you a great deal of money as well, but apparently you've forgotten that," I snapped back.

"Your mother was a weak woman who always chose the easy way. She made a great deal of money for a few hours worked and despite opportunities to leave the business, even some marriage proposals, she stayed because she liked her luxuries."

"Which you were only too happy to provide in exchange for the excessive profit you made off her services."

"It was an agreement about which she never complained."

I was stiff with anger. "Where did she go?" Ellie looked at me with sympathy.

"She went to the south side, to a place called the Red Candle run by a woman named Margery Plantain. Not The Sanctuary, but not a bad place. She didn't stay there very long, though, and the last I heard she had a crib on Morton Street with a loafer named Ivan Fletcher."

Tears stung my eyes. Why hadn't Mother told me? To have fallen so far, to be displayed and hawking her services to men off the street in the heart of the red-light district! My beautiful mother! How it must have humbled her! With trembling hands I lifted my skirt and unpinned the small pouch of coins I had carried there for the last four years.

"Here." I tossed Ellie the bag, which she caught by reflex. "Money is so important to you, you must have regretted this gesture as well. Put it toward my mother's account." Then I turned and left.

Mother was ill, I thought, that's all, ill from the rigors and degradations of her life, and since she could not come to me, I would find her. I had enough money put away that I could afford to find her a small room at a quiet hotel. She could rest while I made plans for the both of us. I'd think of something.

The next Sunday I went to Morton Street.

"I'm looking for Bea Birdwell," I said to every woman I could find that looked as if she might know my mother. Women from the streets carry a look about them that can't be mistaken, but it was only when I said the name Ivan Fletcher that I saw recognition on someone's face.

"You'd best stay away from that one, honey. He's bad clear through."

"I need to find him," I insisted stubbornly and listened for directions to a beer hall where he might be. I think now I was somehow possessed, so focused on finding my mother that I didn't realize how precarious and truly dangerous it was for me to be standing outside the door of a beer hall in such a rough part of town. I was sensible enough to know it would be unsafe to go in, though, so I stopped someone about to enter and asked him to see if there was an Ivan Fletcher inside.

"And what will you give me if I do that?" asked the man, unkempt, bearded, and leering.

I showed a coin. "This," I told him sternly, "and don't try to take it from me. I'll scream bloody murder, and they'll cart you off to jail for accosting an innocent young woman who got lost in the wrong part of town. Just find Mr. Fletcher for me and it's yours." I held little hope of his success so was surprised when he returned followed by a swaggering young man with dark brown hair and a pencil-thin mustache.

"Are you Ivan Fletcher?" I asked.

"Who's asking?"

I tossed the coin to the other man, who disappeared.

"I'm looking for my mother, Bea Birdwell. I'm told she works for you."

He stepped too close, his breath smelling of beer and cigarettes, and looked me in the face.

"You look a little like her, but she was a tired old whore without much meat left on her bones."

"She's my mother and I want to know where she is." I found the man repulsive but because I needed something from him, I didn't let my feelings show.

"She's not here." He was enjoying himself at my expense, with his nasty breath in my face and a grin of yellow teeth.

"Where is she, then?" I asked, my tone still calm and deliberate.

Fletcher grew tired of the game. "Dead, darlin'. She went to sleep and never woke up. I knew she was a mistake from the moment I took her on, and she never did bring in the money. I told her I was through with her, and the next morning she was stone cold."

"Where did they take her body?"

I had somehow known this all along and would not let him see how grieved and shaken I felt.

"How should I know? What do they do with old whores? I dropped her corpse out in the street, and the next time I passed that way, it was gone. Maybe they dumped her in the Bay."

I knew he was right, that the city authorities would have done what prostitutes feared and put her in an unmarked pauper's grave somewhere. I would never find her body now. When I turned to leave, he took hold of my arm.

"She left me holding some debts, and as you're her next of kin maybe you and I could figure out a way for you to pay them off." He reached up to touch my hair with his other hand. "That hair and that face will get any man's attention." I hit him full across his mouth with the flat heel of my hand, causing his head to fly back and a trickle of blood to appear along his upper lip.

"You disgusting excuse for a human being! If I were a man, I'd kill you and mark my words, if you ever touch me again, I will and I won't need a man to do the job for me!" The fury and the passion of my tone startled him enough for me to break free.

I turned and ran away as fast as I could, from him, from that terrible place, and from the great sadness that had been my mother's life and death. When I reached the Gallaghers' neighborhood, I stopped to catch my breath and compose myself, and it was only then that I realized I had been weeping the whole way home. For a long time afterwards, the thought of my mother continued to stir a confusing combination of guilt and tenderness and grief deep inside me, and to this day I regret that I didn't turn and wave goodbye to her that last Sunday in the park.

The final two years I spent with the Gallaghers were difficult for me.

Pansy spent more and more time with the young man from the telegraph office, and she spoke of getting married as soon as they could set aside enough money to live. She was making plans for her future and was full of Eddie this and Eddie that. I didn't begrudge her happiness, but I missed the times at night when we would lie in our beds, giggling and talking foolishness. She had serious dreams now that occupied her thoughts.

Mrs. Paine found another post and was replaced by a new housekeeper, who was pretentious and unkind. Worst of all, try as I might, I could not escape the hovering, threatening presence of Ivan Fletcher, who somehow tracked me down for ominous reasons of his own. I had opened a Pandora's Box when I met him, and he made it clear that he would never forgive me for striking him and drawing first blood.

Six months after my trip to Morton Street I was coming back from the meat market when out of the blue Fletcher fell into step beside me. I recoiled and picked up my step.

"Walk as fast as you want," he called from behind me, "you won't be able to lose me," and he was right. I couldn't. He would appear when I least expected it, and he knew my weakness. "I'll bet that fine family you work for would be surprised to know about your mama and where you were raised. I'll just bet they would."

Usually I ignored him, but one day that repeated threat caused me to turn to face him and state calmly, "Don't threaten me, you bully. Tell them anything you want. They won't care. It's your word against mine anyway."

"And if they do any investigating, what will they find, eh? It won't take long for them to figure who's telling the truth. And I might just have to tell a little more than the truth. Like mother, like daughter, after all, and do you think a fine society family like that would have a whore working in their house?"

As much as Fletcher took pleasure in trying to torment me, I refused to show him how both he and his threats alarmed me.

"Tell them anything you want," I repeated. "You don't scare me."

But, of course, he did, in more ways than one. I felt he resented me and wanted to do me harm, calling me and my ways "uppity." For some reason it bothered him that I wouldn't be discomfited by him or act frightened. But his resentment was easier to bear than the venal look of dissolute speculation that was present more often than not when he looked at me.

"Do you have a beau, Hope?" asked Pansy, once seeing Fletcher and me together.

I shuddered. "No. He's a man who's been bothering me and won't leave me alone."

Pansy was indignant. "You should report him to the police. They'll make him stop."

But I couldn't risk having him speak to anyone about me, so all I could do was pretend his presence didn't really trouble me and take good care that I wasn't caught outside alone. The situation forced me to curtail my walks and any expeditions I might make during my few free hours, whether to the park or to the library, and the resulting time I was forced to spend in my room made me irritable and angry. I don't know how long that situation would have continued because something unexpected happened to change my circumstance, change my whole life and future, in fact.

Ralph Gallagher died suddenly. He left for work one November morning as usual and mid-morning a messenger from his office came pounding on the front door with the terrible news. Mrs. Gallagher turned so white I thought she'd faint, but instead she put a hand on the banister for a moment of support and then told me to call the carriage around. She was gone most of the afternoon, and when she returned she called all the household staff together to tell us that her husband had clutched his chest and fallen in the doorway of his place of business, dying on the spot. She was dry-eyed as she relayed the information.

The funeral had to wait a week to allow the Gallaghers' sons to come home from school, and the eventual service was followed by a large gathering of mourners at the house. We had draped the door in black crepe, covered Mr. Gallagher's portrait in black silk, and all of us wore black armbands out of respect. Despite the animated tone and conversation of the wake and the presence of dignitaries, it was ostensibly a house in mourning.

Mrs. Gallagher never shed a tear for anyone to see during all the public amenities of bereavement, but one night I heard her behind her bedroom door sobbing harshly, gasping for breath from grief. Perhaps her heart had been broken. He had not loved her, but I thought that for all her rectitude and propriety, she might have felt quite passionate about him. Maybe she grieved her husband's passing or maybe something even worse, the irreversible finality of knowing that he had gone to his grave uncaring and oblivious to her affection for him.

It seemed unspeakably sad to me that one could love another human being, and no force on earth could make him reciprocate. Surely living alone was preferable to that painful arrangement. Two weeks after the funeral the regular household staff was called into the front parlor. The family's attorney was there with an announcement. It seemed that in complete contradiction to the kind of man I thought Ralph Gallagher had been, he'd left everyone on his household staff a sum of money in his will. An extraordinarily exorbitant sum of money. One hundred dollars each. A collective but silent inhale of breath followed the news. Such a gesture was not unheard of but the amount was, and while we controlled ourselves so as not to give the impression that we were thrilled to profit from Mr. Gallagher's death, it didn't keep Pansy from throwing her arms around me once we were back in our room.

"Hope, do you know what this means? Eddie and me can get married. A hundred dollars." Pansy spoke the words like a prayer. "Who would have thought Mr. Gallagher had it in him?" She was the happiest I'd ever seen her, already stretching that hundred dollars into a thousand.

As for me, I took it as a sign and that night got out the land deed to examine seriously. All things happen for a reason, I thought, and for me the reason now included Wyoming and my own home.

I waited for Pansy to marry and on the day after her wedding, with my cash in a belt around my waist and all my worldly goods in one small suitcase, I boarded the train for Laramie, Wyoming. I had never been outside the city limits of San Francisco, but that didn't matter. While my stomach was a little fluttery with excitement and apprehension, the far greater part of me—heart, mind, and soul—knew I was doing the right thing. I was twenty years old, and it was time to really belong somewhere, time to find a place of my own.

Chapter 3

*B*ecause I was determined to be as frugal as possible with my small savings, I purchased the least expensive train ticket available, which meant I spent the entire trip in close and crowded quarters with other people similarly circumstanced. That didn't matter. Over the hundreds of miles I read, wrote, slept, and fell in love with the increasing beauty and wildness of the terrain. Every time we stopped, I stepped outside to breathe deeply of the cold March air and make mental notes of anything I thought worthy to be transcribed into my journal. Every mile that passed put the sad history of my mother and the distasteful threat of Ivan Fletcher farther and farther behind me. On the cool, blue-skied afternoon I finally arrived in Laramie, Wyoming, I wasn't even tired.

I stepped off the train onto the platform, spread out my arms for a good stretch, and took a long, decisive look around me. Laramie was larger than I'd expected, with several streets, an assortment of commercial buildings, and considerable traffic, both horse and human. The Union Pacific Hotel and Depot looked respectable enough, and from where I stood I could see that young trees lined the street. Not San Francisco, but not the sleepy, shabby little town I'd anticipated, either. I began to turn full circle, people's chatter and the train's puffing all around me, and came face to face with the mountains. The sight brought me to a standstill, literally open-mouthed. They sat at a distance, white tipped against the western horizon, unassailable royalty presiding over the otherwise flat plains. My eyes and my heart couldn't get enough of them, and at that first glimpse I knew I had come home.

After acquiring directions to the Albany County Clerk's office, I stopped there to confirm that the property described in the deed I held was really mine. Truth be told, I had a secret fear that my mother's offering would turn out to be a mistake, a forgery or a joke of some kind, but it wasn't. The man sitting at the desk next to the cast-iron stove in the middle of the cavernous office hauled out a large book of maps and traced a section with his finger.

"It's right here," he said, pointing to the paper as if I could appreciate what he showed me.

I couldn't, of course, since I hadn't any notion of where the property was compared to where I was standing, but I tried to listen intelligently. He wrote down my name in his book and initialed the land deed before he gave it back to me. Then he smiled.

"Don't look so worried. It's all yours, young lady. Are you by yourself?"

"Yes."

I thought he would ask how the land had come into my possession but he didn't. Instead he said, quite kindly, "We've had a thaw, and there's not much snow on the ground, but it's muddy. You'd best stop by the store and get yourself a good, sturdy pair of boots. What you're wearing won't last long here. And if there's shelter on that land of yours, it's bound to be run down after all these years. I'd say you've got your work cut out for you." I appreciated that he wasn't scornful or patronizing.

"I'm not afraid of work," I said, smiling back at him, "or of being cold either, but thank you for the advice. Which way to the store?"

He walked with me to the door and pointed down the street. "You can't see it from here, but just keep walking. You'll cross Grand and Garfield, and then it'll be on the right down by Lovejoy's. You can't miss it. Look for the sign that says *Moss Dry Goods and General Store.* Anything you want, they've got. Best think about a good, warm bedroll, too. George Moss will help you out. Tell him Amos sent you down."

Moss's was a large store, almost a city block long, full of goods and tools, fabric, groceries, even clothing on the rack. Because several people waited in line ahead of me, I had time to browse and make a mental list of what I might need until I could speak to the short, bald man behind the counter.

"Yes, young lady. What can I do for you?" His sharp, dark eyes peered at me from behind rimless glasses.

I put out my hand to shake his. "My name is Hope Birdwell, and Amos sent me down here because he said you could help me." I took out the land deed and spread it on the counter. "I'm a greenhorn to Wyoming, but I'm also your new neighbor. This is where I'll be living. Besides a good pair of boots and a bedroll, I'm thinking I should get a frying pan, some matches, and probably some canned goods. What else do you think I need?" Something in my manner made him laugh out loud.

"Young lady, you've got your work cut out for you if you plan on homesteading, but I like your spirit. You might consider a small line stove. In my opinion that would be the best thing for you. A little more expensive but you won't regret it. Then you should have a good knife, a lamp, some utensils, maybe a small ax." He began to gather up items and stack them on the counter.

I was dismayed at the growing pile of goods on the counter because the total would be more costly than I'd expected—I hadn't considered half of what he was suggesting—but what he said made sense, and I didn't think he was taking advantage of me. When Mr. Moss gave me the total cost, I took a deep breath before I turned my back to him and counted out the money from the belt where I kept it.

"Now," he continued, "how are you going to find your way out to your place and carry all these things along with you?"

I allowed myself a moment to savor the phrase 'your place' before speaking. "I thought I could hire someone to transport me to my property. Do you know anyone who'd be willing to do that for a reasonable price?"

Mr. Moss shook his head. "No need for that, Miss Birdwell. I saw the Davises in town and they've got the place right next to you, about six miles north of the Wildflower."

Somehow the place "right next" to me sounded like it should be closer than six miles, but I was still thinking in city terms.

He went to the door of the store and called to a boy in the street, "Ricky, I'd guess Lou Davis is still in town. She's probably down by the church. Go find her and ask her to come by and see me before she leaves." He returned to the counter and began to load the items I'd purchased into boxes. "Have you thought about getting yourself some kind of transportation since you're going to be out of town a distance?"

"I was considering a bicycle."

He nodded his approval. "We've got our share of them in Laramie, and I imagine I can find a used one for you. Bicycles don't work all that well in the spring mud, but they'll carry you well enough the rest of the year. 'Course you can't ride them with those skirts of yours. Better be sure you've got your bloomers ready. A few years ago I recall one young lady getting her skirts so wound up in the rear sprocket that she couldn't move. Mighty embarrassing for her."

"Oh, I don't embarrass very easily," I said, smiling at him, "and I'm more careful than that."

"We'll see. Sometimes the best plans don't work out."

"My plans will," I responded confidently.

He raised his eyebrows at me, looking a little surprised by my positive tone but didn't comment further, only asked, "How about if I send word when I get hold of a bicycle for you?"

We were still speaking when I heard the door open behind me and a woman's voice say, "George, you caught us just in time. Ricky said you were looking for me."

Mr. Moss introduced us as I turned to face the woman who had just entered the store. "Lou, this is your new neighbor, Miss Hope Birdwell, who just got into town. She's got the property southeast of you, where Wildflower Creek flows. I thought the two of you should meet."

I liked the newcomer instantly but would have been hard-pressed to explain why.

She was at least twenty-five years my senior, tall for a woman and slim. Her chestnut hair, with a dramatic streak of silver showing at the temple, was loosely plaited down her back, exposing a long white hairline scar in conspicuous contrast to her sun-browned skin. She wore a man's blue shirt and a split skirt, tall boots, and a heavy brown coat that fell not quite to her knees.

Her face invited a second look, although a person couldn't have described her as pretty, not in the way I'd been raised to think of pretty, nothing girlish or soft or pink about her. Dressed in working clothes, fine lines of age fanning out around her eyes and lips when she smiled, with her height and tanned face and a mouth that seemed just a little too wide, she should have given the impression of an ageing and unrefined woman, not attractive enough for even a first look. But somehow that wasn't the case. Instead, the impression she radiated was of a woman genuine and vibrant and warm, casting an inviting glow around her as if she drew from an inner fire of joy and kindness. I thought both men and women would always turn to take an admiring, perhaps envious, second look at her, and she would always be oblivious to their attention. I felt comfortable with her immediately, as if I'd known her for years, and mentally searched for the right word to describe her, a word more descriptive than beautiful and more suitable. After glancing at her face once more, I had it. Luminous. This woman seemed luminous, inside and out.

Mrs. Davis put out her hand, her dark gray eyes smiling and friendly. "Welcome, Miss Birdwell. I'm Lou Davis. My husband and I run the JL. I'll be pleased to have a woman living so close."

Behind her, a man pushed open the door and stepped inside to stand next to Lou Davis, who gave him a quick, sideways smile. Even with her height, the man stood taller and his lean, weathered face, deeply lined and roughened by time and the elements, made him seem considerably older than she. His close-cropped silver hair and sparse silver beard that traced his cheeks and jaw line added years, too.

"This is my husband, John. John, meet Hope Birdwell. She'll be settling the land around Wildflower Creek."

Mr. Davis took off his hat and nodded at me, his deep-set, very blue eyes examining me carefully. Although nothing in his glance appeared disapproving or threatening, I still found him intimidating, an austere and stern man with no share of his wife's warmth, so much her opposite that I wondered how the two of them had ever come together.

George Moss said, "I thought since you two were on your way home, you'd be willing to drop Miss Birdwell off along the way. She'll be camping a while and could use some help carting these goods."

"Of course, we'd be happy to do that. I know there's some kind of shelter by the Wildflower that's been used on and off as a line cabin by the herders passing through, but I don't think it's in very good shape. Miss Birdwell, it's late in the day. Why don't you stay with us tonight and we could send someone over tomorrow to help put your place in order?"

Lou Davis's offer was tempting, but I had my heart set on sleeping on my own property for my first night there. I stumbled a bit in the explanation, thinking I must sound childish, but she nodded.

"I understand about having a home of one's own," she said softly and then added in a brisker tone, "so we should load you up before it gets too dark for you to see anything once we get there."

I was surprised that no one questioned whether I was capable of such a venture, that no one made disparaging remarks about my intentions, called me foolish or odd or warned me of failure. Such matter-of-fact acceptance left me feeling exhilarated and unexpectedly powerful.

I rode next to my boxes of goods in the back of the Davises' wagon and changed into my new boots as I did so. The ride was rough because of the muddy ruts in the road, but I was so entranced by the surrounding country that I hardly noticed the bouncing. Patches of snow still dotted the landscape but just enough spring green showed through to make a cheerful contrast with the blue sky and the white caps of the mountains in the western distance. The eastern horizon showed several layers of high hills dark with trees as a backdrop for flat, brown grassland that occasionally dipped into ridges.

As we jolted along I thought that this was exactly where I was meant to be. I had waited for twenty years to find where I belonged, and I knew without a doubt that this wild place was it.

We followed a rougher, smaller road east off the main thoroughfare and finally stopped at that road's end.

Lou Davis turned to me and announced cheerfully, "Here we are!"

Her husband handed her down to the ground as I scrambled out of the back of the wagon. The shelter Lou had mentioned, an old log cabin that tilted a little to the south as if the north winds had blown so hard and so steadily that the whole structure had shifted to escape them, stood before us. The walls were weathered black from time and the elements. A decrepit covering connected a small shed to a sidewall of the cabin, and several yards behind the shed stood the privy. Beyond the little grouping of buildings a stand of trees rose from a shallow gorge, and in the distance as far as the eye could see dark foothills backed up against even darker foothills.

I was thankful for the new boots as I walked up to the ramshackle house through the combination of snow, mud, and dry grass that made up the front yard. The cabin had two rooms, a large windowless front room with a fireplace and a surprisingly dry dirt floor and a smaller back room, also windowless. Lou Davis frowned a little as she looked around inside, and her husband seemed to have disappeared completely.

"Are you sure you won't stay with us tonight, Miss Birdwell?" Lou asked again. "This place needs some work to be habitable, and you're bound to feel the cold."

"Thank you, but I know I'll be fine. I don't mind the cold and I'm used to work. By tomorrow night you'll hardly recognize the place."

She gave me her glowing smile. "Then let's unload what you have. I hope you remembered a lamp and oil but if you didn't, just make a list of anything you need and we can help get it for you."

John Davis joined us as we carried in the last two boxes. Her glance asked him a wordless question, and he nodded at her.

"Everything looks all right," he told her.

"John scouted around a little and checked the out buildings to be sure there weren't any problems close by that might alarm you," she explained. "You may be cold tonight, but you'll sleep safely enough, Miss Birdwell."

"If we're going to be neighbors, I wish you'd call me Hope, and I'm not in the least uneasy about being here by myself tonight."

John Davis proceeded to set up the small stove for me and bring in some dry brush.

"I wouldn't use the fireplace and the chimney until we have a chance to be sure it's not stopped up," he advised. "Otherwise you might find yourself smoked out of your own house."

There was something comforting and reassuring in the way both of them concerned themselves about me. No one had ever treated me like that before.

As they got ready to leave, Lou Davis took off her warm barn coat and handed it to me. "Here, use this for extra warmth tonight."

"Oh, I couldn't take your coat! Really, I'll be fine."

"I'll reclaim it tomorrow. You can have our daughter Becca's coat. It'll run long on you, but it's warm and heavy. I'll send it over in the morning, and you can send this one back then."

"I can't take your daughter's coat, either," I protested.

"Becca's married and not at home any more, and she's certainly not interested in that old coat. I've just kept it around for emergencies, so you might as well get some use out of it. John Thomas can come over in the morning with a couple of the hands and help put this place in order for you."

At that comment I noticed her husband turn and give her a thoughtful, almost speculative, look.

"You can spare them in the morning, can't you, John? We don't get a new neighbor every day."

"I don't see a problem," he replied, but I caught a lighter tone in his voice, almost a hint of laughter, although I didn't know what it was she said that would have amused him.

"I don't feel right about taking your coat," I protested again more feebly. "You'll be cold."

"No, I won't, but if I am, it will just give me an excuse to sit very close to my husband the whole way home."

As John Davis handed his wife up to the wagon seat, he asked mildly, "Since when have you ever needed an excuse for that?"

They shared a quick, smiling look, and then Lou Davis turned back to me to say, "I've wanted a telephone system ever since Becca moved to Laramie, and now I wish we had one even more. Then I could call and check on you. The only thing I can do now is send smoke signals, and I don't think I'd be very good at that."

"I wouldn't be very good at reading them, either," I responded, laughing. "We'd only confuse each other, especially if it just turned out to be supper burning over on the stove. Thank you both for all your help. I really will be fine tonight."

Lou Davis looked down at me from the wagon seat, her left side pressed close against her husband.

"I believe you will, Hope. You watch for John Thomas in the morning. We're not that far after all, only a few miles northwest, and I wouldn't be surprised if on a clear day you couldn't see the smoke from our chimneys."

I held her coat over my arm and watched them as they drove away. They had hardly gone any distance when John Davis pulled up, took off his own coat, and put it over his wife's shoulders. Although warmed, Lou didn't move away from him on the wagon seat, so I thought it must be something other than the cold that caused her to sit so near her husband.

I expected to feel apprehensive, even frightened or anxious, my first night in that run-down cabin in the middle of a Wyoming plain with no other human beings around for miles, but I didn't experience one troubled moment. For a woman who had been surrounded by buildings and people all her life, it seemed I would take to homesteading like a duck to water.

After boiling melted snow for tea water and opening some tins of food for supper, I lit my lamp and wearing a heavy nightshirt and Lou Davis's coat, crawled into my bed roll to spend some time commemorating the day in my journal, blowing on my fingers to keep them warm as I did so. Then after putting out the lamp, I lay there in the cold, thick darkness for only a moment before falling soundly and dreamlessly asleep.

I awoke the next morning with only the tip of my nose cold and lay there a moment, still amazed that I, Hope Birdwell, was sleeping in my own house. Maybe it had a dirt floor and maybe chinks of light shone through the walls where the logs didn't quite touch each other and maybe there was a rustling in the chimney as if some creature had taken up housekeeping here ahead of me, but it was still my house. That reality would take some getting used to, and I thought to myself, *Isn't life something?*

Outside, the morning air was cold enough to show my breath, but a bright rising sun that held the promise of coming warmth was peeking over the hilltops. At the rear of the cabin, behind the stand of trees, murmured Wildflower Creek, a convenient stream that flowed from the foothills in the distance, ran through my back yard, then meandered west until it was lost out of sight amid the tall grasses. As far as I could see were rolling hills of meadow grass merging into the high dark hills that stretched into the distance. The view took my breath away.

"Thank you." I spoke aloud to no one in particular. Then I stopped and looked up and said it again, only louder. "Thank you, wherever you are."

I couldn't have said who it was I was thanking, whether God or my mother or a man I'd never met named Charlie McKinney, but someone deserved a thank you for this good fortune of mine.

After morning coffee and oatmeal, I decided my first project would be to patch up all the openings between the wall logs. They had let in too much cold air last night, and because I had a natural and plentiful supply of mud, I thought I could improve insulation easily enough.

In the middle of that chore I heard a man's voice call, "Hello," and thought that must be the company Lou Davis had promised. A man with a large gray moustache and curly gray hair was driving a wagon accompanied by two men on horseback. I wiped my hands on my old skirt and stepped outside to wait for them.

One of the riders dismounted and came toward me. He looked so much like John Davis that he had to be the older man's son. He carried himself with the same formal dignity as his father, was about as tall with the same lean face and serious expression, only he had black hair and skin still unlined by time and his eyes were his mother's, dark gray like smoke.

He took off his hat when he met me, obviously surprised. "Are you Miss Birdwell?" he asked, his tone slightly incredulous.

"Yes. I'm the only person here so I must be." I felt suddenly self-conscious, aware that I was a mess, my hair escaping its kerchief, my smock spattered with mud, and I asked quickly, "Do I have mud on my face?"

"What?"

"I thought I must have something smeared across my face the way you were staring at me. Pardon me if I do." A small smile lit up his face.

"As a matter of fact, you do have something streaked across your forehead,"—I reached up to rub it off—"but that's not why I seemed to be staring. My mother described you a little differently, a little older, so I was just surprised. I'm John Thomas Davis."

I reached out a hand to shake his, then drew it back apologetically. "I'm insulating," I said by way of explaining my dirty hands. "I had too good a view of the stars last night, so I thought I could make it a little cozier with some well applied mud. Goodness knows I have enough of that."

He laughed as he turned to loop his reins around the saddle horn. "It's the season for mud, at least until the next snowfall and freeze."

"You mean there's a chance there'll be more snow?"

The gray-haired man on the wagon seat gave a hoot. "There's three seasons in Wyoming, winter, July, and August. You can count on more snow."

"Then all the more reason for me to get snug before it comes."

John Thomas said, "That's Curly on the wagon and Tony behind me. My mother sent some things over for you and said you might need a little help getting settled."

I looked into the wagon and gasped. "She must have sent over half your house! I can't accept all this."

He ignored my protest and reached for a box, saying as he did so, "Miss Birdwell, we've all learned this early on so you might as well, too, if you're going to live in the neighborhood: Don't argue with my mother when she sets her mind on something."

The men unloaded a small iron bed frame with a straw-stuffed mattress, a sturdy little table with two chairs, a box of foodstuffs that included eggs, butter, and a loaf of fresh bread, a large stack of old newspapers, another box of assorted household items, and a variety of clothes, including the coat

Lou Davis had promised. They unloaded firewood, too, and stacked it under the lean-to roof.

That finished, John Thomas stood back to examine the cabin from the outside. "Is it just me or does the place tilt a little?"

"I'm tempted to say I don't notice a thing just to see your expression, but I'm afraid you're right. It does list to the south. Unless the hills in the background are crooked."

He looked at me quickly, caught my expression, and smiled in return, the nicest smile I'd ever seen, warm and slow and reaching his eyes in a way that gave my stomach a flutter, as if I'd swallowed a butterfly.

"Well, we'll see what we can do. We'll tighten up the roof, put the doors on straight with good hinges and latches, and clean out the chimney so you can use your fireplace."

"Yes, I think I had some kind of furry companion in there. I heard it rustling around during the night."

"I hope that didn't bother you too much."

"I've learned not to let most things bother me," I replied, "and creatures whose only fault is their desire to escape the cold are in that category."

The three men worked all morning, eventually chasing a long, brown creature with black eyes and feet out of the chimney.

"A ferret," remarked John Thomas with surprise. "I never knew one to be so far above ground. It wouldn't have hurt you."

I thought so, too, watching the poor little creature scamper away. We could have shared the warmth easily enough. It had been here first, after all, and should have some rights.

By mid-afternoon they were done. John Thomas Davis stood in front of the cabin, from his expression clearly not completely satisfied.

"The place needs more work, but I think this will get you through until summer."

"It's a wonderful improvement!" I exclaimed. "I don't know how to thank you!"

The building seemed like a new cabin to me, with a fire burning in the fireplace and the little bed and table real furniture. For a moment tears of happiness pricked at the back of my eyes, and I turned away so he wouldn't see them. All my life I'd been considered an odd girl and realizing that was so had never bothered me before, but for some reason, I didn't want John Thomas Davis to think of me that way.

Outside Curly and Tony had already started off, but John Thomas held back for a moment.

"Please thank your mother for me and return this to her," I requested, handing him her coat from the day before. "She was much too generous with everything. I'm very obliged. And thank you, too. This must be the western hospitality I've read about."

"Do you really think you're going to make it here all right? Wyoming's not always bright and blue-skied like today, you know. And you ought to have a rifle with you, just to keep the coyotes away." I looked at him in amazement.

"I wouldn't know what to do with a rifle if I had one. I could probably figure out which end to hold and which end to aim but that's about it. I'm not sure I could shoot anything, either."

He adjusted his hat and pulled himself into the saddle. "I'll come back and show you sometime. My mother and both my sisters are good shots. It's something you ought to know, too." Then he gave me that surprised, quizzical look he'd had upon first meeting me. "You're not what I expected, Miss Birdwell, I'll say that."

"I can't comment since I don't know what it was you expected, but I hope I'm not a disappointment. And please call me Hope."

"Disappointment is the last word I'd use," he replied seriously before he rode away.

The good weather held for several days, long enough for me to finish patching the holes in the walls and then nail up some of the old newspapers for wall covering. Mrs. Gallagher's dining room had been covered in flocked wallpaper of a large floral print. In contrast, I had the *Laramie County Times, Laramie Boomerang,* and *Cheyenne Daily Leader* on my walls, which, while not nearly as ornamental, did serve the double purpose of insulation and reading material.

The only thing I missed was some kind of covering for the dirt floor. Eventually I planned to lay down straw and then top that with a rag rug or two, which would make the room warmer and more comfortable all around.

My mind was already picturing a garden as soon as the ground was tillable and a laying hen or two and maybe a goat for fresh milk. Sooner or later my savings would be depleted, but by then I might be able to sell produce from my garden, or eggs, or maybe take in sewing or laundry, anything to earn enough money to live on. I'd have to learn what crops grew in the area because, although I'd never seen a field of anything in my life before my recent train trip, I surely possessed enough land to plant, harvest, and sell something. I was so busy settling in that first week that I didn't have the time or the energy to consider how I would survive the next winter, let alone plan for the long term. As short-sighted as it might seem, for the time being it was enough that I was there.

On my fifth day of residence I was awakened in the early morning hours by a terrible racket that seemed to come from just outside my door. Roused from a deep sleep, I was at first startled and a little confused, unable to understand the cacophony of sounds: bells and bleating and barking and over it all a droning noise so loud and harsh that it could only be announcing the Day of Judgment. Grabbing my cooking knife, I marched outside and around to the back.

As far as I could see in the moonlight—from the rear of my house down the small gully and up onto the hills on the other side, past the trees and surrounding the stream—were sheep. Sheep everywhere. At least that explained the bleating and the bells, but that other sound, that raucous blaring, continued to blast into the night. Outlined against the slowly lightening early-morning sky was a small enclosed wagon, its horse unhitched and munching contentedly on dry grass. Next to the wagon stood a large figure holding and blowing into an unwieldy bag that seemed to be the source of the discordant sound I heard.

I nudged my way through the sheep and toward the man, a dog nipping at either my or the sheep's heels, I couldn't tell which. Intent on his musical task, the player remained oblivious to my approach for some time allowing me to get quite close before he finally looked up and saw me. The bag he held deflated and the sound faded away into the night. My visitor was a large man, appearing even larger because of the layers of coats he wore, with a bushy beard and wild unkempt hair, but for all that untamed appearance I wasn't frightened. He was playing the bagpipes, I had figured out, and there's something inherently trustworthy about a man who serenades the night with bagpipe music. Speechless and with a dumbfounded expression, the big stranger watched me approach.

As odd as he appeared to me, I must have been as strange a sight to him, dressed in Becca Davis's oversized coat and a pair of heavy boots, my own thick hair as unruly as his, and—most alarming of all—brandishing my kitchen knife as if carrying a flag in a parade.

"It's very hard to sleep," I called when I was within distance, "with all this racket going on. Not that I begrudge you your right to keep sheep or play whatever music suits your fancy, but I'd prefer you didn't do it in my backyard."

"Your backyard?"

"Yes. That's my house and this is my land and you're in my backyard."

"Since when?"

"This will be my sixth day as a homesteader."

"Lassie, I've been coming this route every year for the last ten, and this is the first I heard this place belonged to anyone." His voice held an unmistakable Scottish burr.

"It's belonged to someone for a long time," I answered reasonably, "only he never took up residence. Now I have, so I'd greatly appreciate it if you could forebear the music for whatever's left of the night. I'd like to get a little more sleep."

He had a wide white grin that showed through his beard. "Aye. I could do that."

"Good. Then after sunup if you have a notion for it, I'll put on eggs and fresh cornbread and coffee, and we can talk a bit. At a civilized hour, mind you. Over breakfast."

"Yes, ma'am." He appeared to have recovered from his astonishment at my sudden appearance in the middle of his flock. "I'd like that."

Chapter 4

*H*is name was Fergus Campbell, and by the time we sat down across from each other at my little table for breakfast, he'd made an obvious effort to wash his face, remove several layers of old coats, trim his beard, and smooth down his hair. He looked almost respectable.

"I take the same route every year," he explained, "and I always stop here first for lambing. Then all the sheepherders in the area gather for shearing, and we ship the wool east from Rock River. By then the weather is starting to warm, and I move the creatures north over by the Chugwater River for the summer."

"Have you no real home, Mr. Campbell? Such a nomadic life must be lonely."

The man shrugged. "Sheep need fresh pastures, so I've really got no choice about it. I have the dogs and my bagpipes." He paused to give me a quizzical look across the table. "And what about you, lassie? What's a pretty lass like you doing here all by herself? I can't imagine your family is at ease with this venture of yours."

"I don't have a family, so that's not an issue. I'm not like you, Mr. Campbell. I couldn't move around from place to place and be happy. I need to be settled somewhere, and I've decided this place will suit me very well. I have a house and a stove and I'm getting a bicycle. That's all I need."

Fergus Campbell could have been anywhere between forty and seventy with brown hair and very nice brown eyes under shaggy brows.

"I doubt that's all you'll need. I'll wager that once the newness wears off, you'll find that a house and a stove and a bicycle"—he gently mimicked my tone—"aren't nearly enough."

"If you've learned to make do with the life you have, so can I."

"I'm not a pretty young lass with emerald eyes and hair like sunshine."

I looked at him seriously. "That's very true, Mr. Campbell. You're nothing of the sort." He laughed at that.

"But you've not taken the risk of asking me into your home for breakfast just to make conversation, I think."

"I didn't consider it a risk. Should I have?"

"For sure you've nothing to fear from me. And by and large the folks around here are good people. During the years of the trouble, this was one of the few places a man could bring his sheep and know his animals wouldn't be butchered in the night or his dogs set on fire. Your neighbors, the Davises, ran cattle like everybody else around here, but no matter how they felt about sharing their range with sheep, they wouldn't have stood for violence in their backyard. John Davis wasn't a man to trifle with when it came to protecting his own. But it's still remote country and you're still by yourself, and it might not hurt if you were a little more circumspect when a strange man appears at your back door."

"Unless he's playing bagpipes, don't you think?" His eyes lit with laughter.

"Aye, you can always trust the pipes. They won't do you any harm other than rousting you out of a sound sleep."

"Which they did, considering that you settled in my backyard." I put my hands in my lap and met his look with a sober one of my own. "What is it worth to you to eat my grass and drink my water, Mr. Campbell?" He gave me a half-smile.

"Are you trying to drive a bargain with a Scot?"

"A fair bargain, but yes, a bargain."

"What is it you're wanting then?"

"Wool to start with. Then sheep someday."

"And what would you do with the wool?"

"I can spin, card, weave, and knit, Mr. Campbell, and although I don't have the wheel or the loom yet, I thought you might be able to help me with the wool, another of the essentials I lack."

He put down his coffee cup. "And what if I decide to take what I need for my flocks and give you nothing in return?"

"I don't think that's what you'll do, but I admit I'm not an expert on men, and I suppose there's always the chance you could do exactly that. I suppose I'd contact the authorities, then, and have you rousted off. But I would be sorry to do that, especially since it's lambing time. The move would be pitifully hard on both the mothers and their babies."

I met his searching gaze with an innocent smile, and he gave a shout of laughter.

"Now you're threatening me!"

"I am not," I retorted indignantly. "I'm stating the facts."

"Miss Birdwell,—"

"Call me Hope."

"Hope, I think we can do business together, especially if you'll throw some of your corn bread into the deal." His comment gave me another idea.

"I can cook and do laundry, Mr. Campbell. Do you think anyone would be willing to pay for those services?"

"If we're on a first name basis, call me Fergus, and I think at shearing you might find men who would pay generously for a home-cooked meal and clean clothes."

"So will you take me with you when it's shearing time?"

"If my woolies can wander over your land to their hearts' desire, I will."

I stretched my open palm across the table where it was enveloped in his huge, rough hand. "It's a deal," I said.

The lambing started in earnest that very day. Fergus separated the pregnant ewes into what he called a drop band, and that breakfast was the last meal he spent apart from them for some time.

When I took dinner to him at midday, he was standing and cursing creatively, his shirt sleeves rolled up and his hands mucky and bloody.

A newborn lamb was tottering after a ewe, which was clearly oblivious to her offspring's hunger, the little thing trying desperately on its frail, spindly legs to catch up with its mother.

"What's wrong?"

"Och, it's that little bummer."

"That what?"

"See its mother there? She's a dry ewe, one of the stupidest creatures God put on this earth. The only thing she's interested in is the next patch of grass, not the care of her lamb."

"Will it die?" I stared after the newborn in dismay. The lamb was a pitiful sight, all skinny legs and loud blat, obviously hungry and baffled by its mother's desertion. Fergus turned to look at me speculatively.

"Not if I can help it. We're partners now, you recall, so there might be something you can do."

Which is how I found myself that evening crouched in the small shed next to my cabin nursing three lambs with a combination brew of ewe's milk, water, and molasses.

"They do not have permission to die," I told Fergus fiercely as one of the lambs stood unsteadily by my side, greedily suckling an old rag soaked in the liquid concoction Fergus had devised.

Apparently recognizing an authority in my voice that would brook no disobedience, all three little bummers made it through the week.

Lou Davis rode over to see me on my second Friday in Wyoming. She rode astride, which I'd never seen a woman do before, dressed in men's pants and a short, heavy coat, her hair hidden under a broad-brimmed hat.

"Hello, Hope," she called, sliding off her horse. "You've had a week to get settled. How are you doing?"

My pleasure at seeing her warm, friendly face was reflected in my voice. "Just fine. I haven't had a chance to thank you personally for your generosity. I've put everything you sent to good use." Lou waved my words aside.

"No, thank you for taking some of those old things off our hands. We used that little table the first years of our marriage but we outgrew it, and I've had it stored in one of the barns. There was too much sentiment involved for me to discard it altogether so I'm glad you could find a place for it."

At my invitation, she stepped toward the cabin but stopped at the sound of the lambs baaing in the shed next door.

"Poor little bummers," I explained, laughing at her surprised expression. "Do you know Fergus Campbell?" She nodded. "Well, he stopped down by the Wildflower for lambing, and I'm helping out. I'm learning a lot about the sheep business." I watched her face carefully for any reaction to my words. Fergus had talked about the animosity between sheepherders and cattlemen, and I wondered if, despite her kindness, she harbored bad feelings.

But I saw only a smile there as she observed, "Fergus Campbell is a good man." Together we walked down to the flocks.

"I haven't seen you in at least two years, Mr. Campbell," Lou said when she saw Fergus. "I hope everything's well with you."

He wore a felt hat that he removed out of respect. "Aye, Miz Davis. It's been a warm winter this year, and I can't complain. I trust you and your family are prospering."

"Becca's a bride and Katherine's off to medical school. John Thomas swears he'll die a bachelor, Gus is making plans for the university, Billy is still fiddling, and John and I are getting older but not necessarily wiser." She gave a soft chuckle. "If that's not prospering, I don't know what is, and like you, Mr. Campbell, I can't complain. I'll let John know you asked after him." She took a deliberate look around at the restive sheep. "I see you've enlisted Miss Birdwell's help."

"I can't convince her to roam with the flocks, though. She insists on staying in one place."

"A place to call home is very important to a woman. I imagine that's why there are so many solitary herders." A ewe's distinctive bleating interrupted her next words, and with an apologetic shrug, Fergus left us.

Later over tea, Lou invited me to her home for Sunday dinner.

"I could stop by and get you for Sunday services if you'd like, as long as the weather holds. John and John Thomas will be pulling calves, but the preacher's our son-in-law, so at least one of the family should make an appearance at church. Then you could come for dinner afterward. We'll be sure you get home before dark. With both of my daughters away, I'd welcome your company."

Lou Davis had a way of doing kind things and somehow making you think it was you who was doing her the favor. She reached across the table and put a hand over mine.

"Are you sure you're doing all right, Hope?"

I said, "Yes," and then was horrified to feel tears pooling in my eyes. I suppose it was because I couldn't remember another time when anyone had expressed the same heartfelt concern or asked me such a question without expecting something from me in return, but I was mortified regardless of the reason.

"Fiddle tears," Lou remarked kindly, sensing my embarrassment, and at my blank look smiled. "We've always called those sudden, quick tears you didn't expect and can't explain fiddle tears. As I recall, Uncle Billy inspired the phrase years ago, and now it's become part of the family vocabulary." She rose. "I've got to get back or they'll send out search parties. I'll see you Sunday, and if you need anything before then, Hope, you only have to ask. Just flag down one of our hands and send word."

All my bummers lived, and to Fergus's delight we found wet nurses for them.

"Och, this is a good year, I'd say. The best in a while. You must be the lucky charm, Hope."

"I wish that were true, but I don't think so. Fergus, I've been thinking."

He looked at me suspiciously. "I don't know why your saying those words raises the hair on the back of my neck."

I ignored his comment and continued undeterred. "It seems to me that my saving the lives of several of your lambs, sacrificing several nights' sleep, and being at your and their beck and call ought to be worth something to you."

"Such as?"

"Perhaps a lamb or two of my own. If it's such a good year and I really am your lucky charm, a couple of wee lambies would be a fair exchange, don't you think?"

"You are a woman to be reckoned with, Miss Birdwell. I'll give it some thought."

Sunday morning I put on the only respectable dress I owned, threw my warm but worn cape over it, and waited for Lou Davis. The face reflected in my small hand mirror was acceptable enough, but I wished I had lighter brows and a more fashionable bow-shaped mouth. Nothing about me resembled the women in the fashion magazines with their smooth, soft hair and elegant faces. I had a sprinkle of unladylike freckles across my nose, dark brows that contrasted too dramatically with my fair hair, and a broad, expressive, full-lipped mouth that never looked maidenly. My hair was a constant source of frustration, so thick and wavy that any hat I tried to wear only looked silly perched precariously on my head overpowered by hair that could not be held up by pins. I was inevitably forced to pull my hair back with a band or barrette and hope the curls would stay confined. They had a mind of their own, though, and invariably sprang loose. I had been told that I looked like my mother, but except for her final years I couldn't recall that she had been anything other than smooth, well-coiffed, and beautiful. Nothing like me at all.

We rode into Laramie in a fine buggy, Lou driving as if she'd done it all her life and perhaps she had.

"Do you think you could teach me to handle the reins?" I asked. "I've never had the chance to try my hand at it." At her inquiring look I explained simply, "I was in service as a housemaid to a wealthy family for several years and I learned a lot about keeping a house, but they had their own livery men, so I never got the chance to handle the reins. I think I should know how to do that."

"I think you're right, and you may take the reins the whole trip home. It's not hard."

I would have recognized Lou's daughter anywhere. Just as John Thomas resembled his father, so Rebecca Wagner was a younger version of her mother. When I saw the women together, I was conscious of a sudden, surprisingly sharp pang of plain, old-fashioned envy. The two were so obviously close and fond of one another that for the first time in my life, I wished I had known that kind of warm relationship with my own mother. I don't believe I ever appreciated that such a bond could exist.

Sitting in church beside them and later, seeing the affection and respect in which both women were held, I realized I could never tell them about my bastard childhood, my mother's life and occupation, or her sordid death. I was ashamed of my past in a way I had never experienced before. What confused and disturbed me even more was that I was ashamed of myself for feeling that way, ashamed of the sudden unspoken determination to keep my childhood circumstances and my mother hidden from my new friends. I knew I hadn't done anything wrong and yet I felt guilty and embarrassed. My one consolation was that there was no reason my new friends would ever have to know about The Sanctuary and my time there. Laramie was a new life hundreds of miles away from San Francisco, and I could make that new life whatever I wanted it to be.

True to her word, Lou sat on the passenger's side all the way home and acted the part of teacher as I took the reins. Once I realized I had to hold firm and show I was boss, I did fine.

"You have good hands, Hope, firm but gentle. You're a natural," Lou told me when we pulled into the Davises' yard. I was pleased at her words, considering them high praise.

The Davis home seemed a natural part of the generous Wyoming landscape, a big, sprawling, whitewashed log ranch house with a porch that wound around two sides and one wall nothing but a huge stone fireplace and chimney. Several out buildings, a large barn, and animal pens exactly like the ones I planned someday for my own sheep stood at a distance. I made a mental note to find out how they'd been built. I didn't see any reason why I couldn't stake out a small pen by myself. If my handiwork didn't end up looking quite as well made as the Davises', it wouldn't matter to the sheep.

Inside, when Lou would have had me sit as a guest while she prepared Sunday dinner, I found an apron instead

"Maybe I'm new to driving," I told her firmly, "but one thing I do know is how to cook."

I never enjoyed time in the kitchen as much as I enjoyed that first Sunday with Lou Davis. She was full of bright and funny stories of her first years as a wife and mother, the cooking catastrophes, messy babies and naughty children, a leaking roof, birds down the chimney, and calves in the kitchen. I thought there must have been sad and terrible times, too, and when I commented as much, she nodded.

"Our first years here were harder than I ever imagined anything could be. We were so isolated, and at the time the winters and the work seemed endless. We weren't spared grief and disappointment either. No one is." A shadow crossed her face and quickly disappeared. "There are proper occasions to remember those times, Hope, but today isn't one of them."

When the men came in, I was taken aback to see Lou go up to her husband in front of everyone and welcome him by kissing him lightly on the mouth. My experience with family life had been limited to the Gallaghers, and Mrs. Gallagher would no more have greeted her husband in that manner than appear at dinner in her nightdress, but here no one paid any attention to the gesture or acted as if it were anything notable or out of the ordinary.

John Thomas came in behind his father and caught my eye across the room. I smiled, smoothing back my hair, finding myself suddenly self-conscious with him there. So that young man was going to die a bachelor, was he? I asked myself. Well, that would be a waste and a surprise because he was good-looking and kind, and some young woman would be sure to snatch him up. A single man in possession of a fortune must be in want of a wife, after all, and while it might not be exactly a fortune, the Davises appeared to be doing very well for themselves.

I met Gus, Lou's younger son, who looked to be in his mid-teens, and was introduced to a round-faced man with straw-colored hair, who Gus and John Thomas called Uncle Billy. He was probably in his thirties, but he was simple-minded and so didn't act like a grown man. He bore no physical resemblance to anyone there, but I could tell the family held him in affection.

"It's because of Billy that I met John," Lou explained later, "so I'll always owe him more than I can repay. And we never could have made it our first years here without him, especially after the children were born. I couldn't help John like I used to then, and Billy became his right hand until John Thomas got old enough and we could afford to hire help."

Becca and her husband Ben arrived a short while later. Ben Wagner had one of those faces that would always look young, but after studying his features more carefully, I could tell he was older than he first appeared. The two just seemed to fit together as some couples do.

For a moment I stepped back and watched the scene in the kitchen: Becca and her husband good-naturedly teasing Gus about a new girl in town, Lou putting a hand on her older son's shoulder to say something in his ear to which he responded with a slow smile, simple Billy in the rocker by the front window grinning at everything and nothing in particular.

Seeing the family together, I couldn't remember why I had ever thought John Davis stern and intimidating. His eyes followed Lou around the kitchen with such affection and pride that he might as well have spoken his love for her out loud, it was that obvious.

This is what I've been looking for, I reflected, taking it all in. This is exactly what I want. The realization was so crystal clear to me that for just a moment I thought I'd spoken the words aloud, but I must not have because no one turned to look at me. I had caught a glimmer of something that told me maybe I had my priorities out of order, maybe a home was more than a building and a plot of land, maybe the people were as important as the residence, even more important when all was said and done.

Then my practical nature silenced those sentimental reflections. I had to be realistic. The Davis kitchen might look attractive and appear to be what I wanted, but somewhere and somehow what I observed must certainly have a dark side. My mother's thin, haggard face came to mind as I had last seen her, and I remembered her words: *People are unkind and men are not to be trusted.* I didn't know if I believed her sentiment wholeheartedly, but if nothing else, I had to be sure I could take care of myself. If I could provide for myself, I would not be forced to be dependent on anyone.

The idea hardly seemed probable or possible, but when I left the Davis house, when the door closed after me and it was just a man and a woman together, how did I know that Lou Davis's wishes weren't deemed as unimportant as Lottie's had been years before? What I knew of the lives of men and women didn't bode well for the women, and I wasn't prepared to take the risk, even for the tempting attractions of the scene in front of me. I was so lost in thought that I didn't see or hear John Thomas come up behind me.

"You're awfully quiet. We can be a rowdy family sometimes, and I hope we won't scare you off."

"Oh, no, not at all. I think you have a wonderful family. Didn't your mother mention you have another sister?"

"My sister, the rebel," John Thomas responded laughing. "Yes, my sister Katherine is away at Kansas Medical School learning to be a doctor. We have a long family history of suffragettes."

"I never went to school. A family friend taught me to read and write, so I think any opportunity to get an education should be prized. There was a woman doctor in San Francisco, and at first people made jokes at her expense, but she was so strong and competent that eventually they came around. She has a thriving practice now."

"Why didn't you go to school?"

"My mother didn't believe that education was important, at least for a woman." Then to steer the conversation in a different direction, I asked, "What about you?"

"School, you mean? My mother was the teacher in this house. All of us had lessons from early years, and she was as hard as any schoolmaster you could find. I think I was a disappointment to her although she'd never admit it. She wanted me to go to college, but I never had that strong a liking for school. I just wanted to be a cattleman like my father. Gus is the boy genius of the family. Next fall he'll be going to the University, and Mother's determined he'll be governor in twenty years."

Lou, overhearing the comment as she walked past with her hands full, gave John Thomas a nudge with her hip.

"Ten, not twenty. No reason Gus can't be the youngest governor in Wyoming history."

During dinner, conversation buzzed on all sides, a brief heated debate once in a while, teasing and laughter and an infrequent but surprisingly sharp and sometimes funny comment from Ben Wagner. The more I listened to him, the more I thought there was more to the man than first met the eye. I had never spent any time with a parson before so I wasn't sure what to expect, but I certainly never heard any message of fire and brimstone from him, just a self-deprecating wry humor. His tone grew sharp only at the mention of hypocrisy or unkindness. I could easily see what it was about the preacher that must have caught Becca Davis's heart. Ben Wagner clearly had a sincere concern for others, a personal belief in the importance of his vocation, and a great passion for good that I admired and she obviously loved.

After the meal the women cleaned up, and as all the men headed outside, Lou called, "John Thomas, come back in an hour or two so you can drive Hope home."

That will be a pleasant ride, I thought, and felt inordinately cheered at the prospect.

Lou gestured toward a small box filled with books that sat in a corner of the parlor.

"I thought you might want to take these back with you, Hope. We'll have at least one more snow, and these books will help pass the time. Becca brought some of hers along, too. You don't have to read them all, of course, but you can think of it as the Davis lending library and return them as you finish."

"One of my projects is to open a library in Laramie," explained Becca. "We could partner with Cheyenne. People have been asking for a library, and I know a lot of folks would use it."

"San Francisco had a large library. I spent more time there than I probably should have because I was late back to work nearly every time I visited. It was so easy for me to lose track of time when I was there. Thank you both. I'd love to have something new to read, and I promise I'll take good care of the books. Of course, I can always read my walls, too, because I'm using some of the newspapers you sent over for insulation, but books are much more appealing."

I found myself reluctant to leave when the afternoon began to darken. Lou Davis gave me a hug, and I felt I'd known her all my life, wished I had, in fact, wished I had known what it was like to grow up in a family like this one. She had packed leftover food in a basket, and John Thomas loaded both it and the books into the wagon as I thanked her.

"I believe," I told her quietly, "that you are the kindest person I have ever met in my life." The words made her flush a becoming pink.

"You haven't been in Wyoming long enough to find out that most people around here are neighborly and have learned through the years to help one another. If I read you right, Hope, you'll do the same when you get settled in."

At her response, I realized how much I wanted to fit in and be a part of this place and these people. I thought that as long as no one knew that I had been raised in a bordello as the daughter of a prostitute, I could be accepted simply for who I was and have a chance of really belonging somewhere for the first time in my life.

"Don't tell anyone who your mother was or where you came from. They'll hold it against you," Mother had cautioned years ago, and I felt that here I had a chance to take her advice and start a new life that need not include any salacious or sordid details from my childhood years.

John Thomas and I rode along quietly for a while until he finally asked, "So, do you like it here?" His voice held a hint of desperation, as if all the while he'd been trying to think of something to say to make conversation and could only find a bland question to break the silence.

"More than I can say. Have you ever gone some place and thought you'd been there before even though you knew you hadn't? That's how it was for me when we pulled up in front of that old cabin for the first time. I knew the place so well, knew what it would be like inside and out, that I felt I was coming back for a return visit."

John Thomas turned to look at me with a smile. "Those are the most words I've ever heard you say at one time. Are you always so quiet?"

"I never thought about it, but I guess I am. I've been on my own a lot and I didn't grow up with a big noisy family like yours, so it takes some time for me to get used to having folks around to talk to."

"What was your family like?"

"My mother raised me." I answered with thoughtful care. "I can't remember my father. He died when I was a baby, and my mother never got married. Again," I tagged on quickly.

"Is that how you got hold of your property, from your father?" John Thomas flushed a little and went on to say, "I'm sorry. I'm asking too many questions."

"That's all right. My circumstances probably do seem curious to you. My father gave the land deed to my mother before he died. I don't know how he got it, but my mother loved the comforts of the city and would never have considered living anywhere else. Then she passed the land on to me before she died." I congratulated myself on telling the smallest lie I could get away with. Except for the father part there was truth in everything I said, and for all I knew Charlie McKinney could have been my father.

We pulled on to the rough road that led up to my cabin.

"So you just up and came to Wyoming?"

"Something wonderful happened," I began and then choked back a laugh. "What an awful thing for me to say. I mean that a terrible thing happened that turned out to be wonderful for me. The man I worked for died and left each of his house staff a generous sum of money. I took the bequest as a sign, and so yes, that's exactly what I did. I just up and came to Wyoming."

We stopped in front of my cabin and just sat there for a moment. The hills were reflecting a rose-red color from the splendid sunset streaking across the western sky, and the sound of the sheep down by the stream seemed almost like a lullaby. It was very peaceful.

Then, just as John Thomas started to say something, Fergus appeared around the corner of the cabin. John stiffened, putting one hand on the butt of the rifle that hung in its holder on the side of the seat.

"It's all right," I said quickly. "That's Fergus Campbell. I think I forgot to tell you about the sheep."

"You're right," my companion responded dryly. "I think you did."

John got out and swung me down from the wagon seat, and for just a moment it seemed he was loath to release me, but then he did, and I thought I must have imagined his brief hesitation.

Fergus watched the two of us with undisguised interest until I interrupted his speculation by asking, "Fergus, do you know John Davis?"

Fergus answered my question by addressing John. "Aye, but you were a boy the last time I saw you. For sure you're not a boy any more. I've known your ma and pa for some years."

John Thomas gave the Scot a close, hard look as they shook hands. "I remember your name and that's about all."

As if in answer to an unasked inquiry, Fergus told him, "Hope has nothing to fear from me, lad. As much as I may regret it later, the lass and I are partners of sorts, so it's to my advantage to keep her safe and happy."

"Partners?"

"I have something Fergus wants," I explained, "and that's safe pasture and fresh water for lambing. And Fergus has something I want, so we struck a deal."

"You struck the deal, lass. I was at your mercy." His meek words made me laugh.

"Don't be silly. You're twice my size and hardly an innocent victim."

Fergus started to laugh, too, but he took a look at John Thomas's face, caught the laugh in his throat, and instead said, "Good to see you again, John. You greet your parents for me," before turning away.

"I'm learning the sheep business because I want the wool," I volunteered to John Thomas. "If I get a loom, I can spin and weave cloth that can be turned into vests, blankets, scarves, hats, all sorts of useful items. I thought people might pay money for the wool cloth I weave, especially if the winter is as bad as everyone says."

John Thomas didn't look like he was really listening to me. Instead, he wore an expression that reminded me of his father: stern, unsmiling, a little intimidating.

"I'm not sure it's a good idea for you to be out here by yourself."

His comment struck me as unattractively pompous and superior, and I answered mildly, "I appreciate your concern but with all due respect, I don't recall that I need your permission to live my life."

He looked surprised at my words, and I thought at first he'd take offense, but then suddenly he laughed out loud.

"You sounded exactly like my sister Katherine just now, and you're absolutely right. Excuse me. I should know by now that when a woman sets her mind to something, it's not my place to get in her way."

John Thomas went to the back of the wagon and carried the basket and the box inside for me. I stood in the cabin doorway as he got ready to leave.

"When will you be ready for your first artillery lesson?" He patted the rifle. "If you're serious about sheep, you'll need a rifle for the coyotes."

"Whenever you're ready to teach me, I'm ready to learn, but I doubt I'll be a very good pupil when it comes to guns."

John pulled himself up on the wagon seat. "I'll stop by the first chance I get this week and we'll see."

I watched him drive away, conscious of a new feeling inside, a warm anticipation that was a little bothersome for all the pleasure it gave me. Hope Birdwell, I cautioned myself, you had better be careful around that young man. There's no security in gray eyes and an attractive smile and security is what you want. But I thought about that smile and those eyes well into the evening, anyway.

Before I went to bed, I wrapped myself in a blanket and walked out to the flocks.

"Did you have a pleasant visit today?" I nodded in answer to Fergus's question and he continued, "The Davises are good people, and you could do worse than being taken under their wing. I'd say you've got an admirer in that young man."

"Really?" I gave the idea some consideration before responding. "He's inclined to boss me around, and I think he considers me an odd and too quiet young woman. John Thomas Davis may be curious about me, Fergus, but I wouldn't assume he's an admirer."

The night had grown very dark, and I couldn't see Fergus's face to read his reaction to my words.

"You can believe me or not, Hope, but the look on that young fella's face when he saw me come round the corner was not the look of a man who's just curious about a woman."

"I think you're wrong, Fergus. You're speaking from a lifelong bachelor's viewpoint."

"I never said I was such a bachelor, lass." His quiet words made me peer more closely at him through the darkness.

"I'm sorry. I just assumed you were. You've never mentioned anything to the contrary." I felt embarrassed at my unintended blunder.

"My wife Lorna was a bonnie girl, not afraid of anything. A lot like you, though not in appearance. Her hair was black as coal, but like you, everything was an adventure to my Lorna and nothing scared her."

"What happened?"

"She died birthing our first child, she and the bairn both."

"I'm so sorry, Fergus. I didn't know and I wish I wouldn't have brought it up."

"It's been years now, and the pain's gone from the memories. My Lorna made me a happy man." But his sad, wistful tone, incongruous to his rough appearance and size, belied his words.

"It's not fair, is it, Fergus?"

"What's not fair?"

"Life. Life's not fair. Most of the time it doesn't make sense, either. If you ask me, life ought to be fair and it ought to make sense." I spoke vehemently. "The people we love shouldn't leave us, and the people who love us should be happy. That's what life ought to be like." I wrapped the blanket more tightly about me, preparing to make the walk back up to the cabin, but before I turned away, I added, "I'm truly sorry, Fergus. I wish that hadn't happened for you. I wish I could give you back what you lost."

I walked back up the hill, unable to forget the loss and grief and regret that had colored Fergus's voice. Love held a part in that, too, I thought, a part that hurt, that stayed tender to the touch and never quite healed. Earlier, the look and the feel of the Davis kitchen had been powerfully seductive to me with the strong bond of family I'd seen there, the laughter and the conversation, and the deep respect and affection that everyone appeared to share.

But Lou Davis had admitted there'd been painful, terrible times, too, her eyes dimmed and shadowed by the memories, and it seemed to me that no matter how much attraction there was to loving and being loved, it couldn't make up for the kind of heartache and quiet desolation I'd heard in Fergus's voice or seen on Lou's face. There was no fair trade-off for that.

Chapter 5

*T*he predicted snow returned at the end of the next week along with fallen temperatures and a bank of heavy, pewter-gray clouds that lay low on the horizon. Fergus and I, with the help of his two dogs, spent the better part of a Friday crowding the more vulnerable ewes and their newborn lambs into the shed.

"Snow won't last," Fergus pronounced confidently. "The ground's too warm, but if it's a heavy snow, the little ones can get too soaked to move and the snow can suffocate them. Better to keep them inside for the night, but that means you won't get much sleep."

"They'll be music to my ears," I said, "and since I'll be up anyway, you can play the pipes all night if you want."

It hadn't taken me long to get comfortable with Fergus and accustomed to his presence around the place. Although a big bear of a man, he was wonderfully gentle with the animals, and except for an understandable streak of melancholy that showed only now and then, he was practical and cheerful, much like me. I guessed that after lambing, when he moved to new pastures, I would miss Fergus Campbell even more than I expected.

The snowy weather continued well into Saturday afternoon, fat, wet flakes coating the trees and frosting the buildings and Fergus's house on wheels. Because I was windowless, I stood in the open doorway, hugging myself for warmth, and watched the snow in its soundless fall. Even the sounds of the animals in the neighboring shed were muted. I had never experienced so beautiful a snowfall. In the city the rare snow quickly turned to dirty slush, discolored by the traffic, the horses, and the heavy residue from the smokestacks, but here it looked pristine and lovely.

I trudged down to the creek after the sky lightened, carrying the results of my morning's work. Where the sheep milled, soggy patches of ground had already begun to show brown through the snow.

"Is everything all right?" I asked.

"Aye." Fergus had apparently been out in the inhospitable weather because his beard and hat were streaked with ice and snow. "Most of the snow will be gone by tomorrow at this time."

"I brought you supper. Ham and potato pancakes, pickles and dried apple pie.

His eyes lit up. "You're a wonder."

"We should both thank Lou Davis for the ingredients. Next year I hope to be able to use the harvest from my own garden, but I don't know when to plant. By this weather I judge Wyoming must have a short growing season. When does summer come, Fergus?"

"There's those who would say summer never comes to Wyoming, that it stays spring until it turns into fall, but then they've never been to Scotland. Planting is still a good two months away, Hope, but you should ask at the store when you order your seed. George Moss can tell you better than I can."

"I need the money I'll make from shearing to buy the seed, so don't forget your promise to take me with you. I'll need to get some things ready. When do you think we'll go?"

"It won't be long now. We'll wait until the lambies can make the trip without risk. And I won't forget about you. I'm looking forward to showing up with a pretty girl on the seat next to me. That'll cause a stir. I wouldn't be surprised if you had a proposal or two before you were through."

"I hope you're talking about cooking and washing proposals because those are the only kind I'll consider," I retorted sternly.

"That's not enough for a lass like you, Hope. You're only fooling yourself. You'll have your own family someday, a husband and little ones of your own on your knees." I shook my head decisively.

"Not in the near future, Fergus. That's not part of my plan. I intend to have my own place and my own livelihood so I never have to be dependent on anyone. Never."

"Never is a long time."

"I know, but my mother—" I stopped.

"Your mother?" Fergus prodded gently. We had never talked about my past or background.

"Let's just say that she taught me the dangers of being dependent on the charity of men and not being able to take care of myself. That's not happening to me."

"Hope," he said quietly, "whatever those words mean, you're making a mistake to think that being dependent on another person is always a bad thing. It doesn't have to be."

"How can you say that when you've had such a terrible loss and still grieve?" Fergus put a hand on my shoulder, a rare gesture because he was always careful not to be presumptuous.

"You'll know someday and then you'll understand. In life there's joy and there's grief and with the right person there are no regrets for either. Everything's a balance. You'll see someday."

"No, Fergus. You're wrong. I'm not exposing myself like that," I responded firmly. "I'll forfeit the joy if it means I'm not at risk for the grief."

This time he shook his head at me. "Girl, we're all at risk all the time. You mark my words. Someday you'll be surprised at how much you're willing to hazard for the right person."

"Not me. Not ever." He laughed.

"The gods just heard you, lass. You've issued them a challenge they can't ignore. Don't say I didn't warn you."

"The gods have more important things to do than concern themselves in my little life, Fergus. You'll be the first to know when I change my opinion, but don't hold your breath waiting."

I was awakened that night by someone shouting and pounding at my door. I thought drowsily that it must be Fergus and that something was wrong, so without thinking I threw a shawl around my shoulders and opened the door.

The man who stood there, leaning against the doorway, looked vaguely familiar, but he certainly wasn't Fergus, and I felt the first mild stirrings of alarm. At second glance I remembered where I'd met him.

"You're Tony, aren't you, from the Davises' ranch? You helped me move in. Is something wrong?" I couldn't imagine why Lou Davis would have sent this man on an errand to me in the middle of the night, but I also couldn't imagine any other reason he'd be standing in my doorway.

Tony leaned toward me and muttered in a slurred voice, "You're the prettiest girl I've ever seen," except he said *purtiest* and gave a little hiccup at the end of the sentence.

"And you," I said disgustedly, finally realizing that his presence had nothing to do with Lou Davis, "are drunk and a nuisance. Go away." I moved to close the door, but he put a rough hand against it to push it farther open and then stepped inside the cabin.

"A woman shouldn't have to sleep alone on a cold night like this. She should have a man to keep her warm."

I refused to back up, putting one palm against his chest instead to hold him at a distance.

"Maybe she should, but that man sure isn't you. Now go away before I have to tell your boss about this and you end up losing your job."

"It would be worth it."

Tony smelled strongly of alcohol and smoke, and I guessed he was fresh from his Saturday night on the town. He looked a little older than I remembered and was certainly too large for me to handle on my own. I felt suddenly fourteen again, caught on the steps and frightened by a man the worse for drink and lust.

"Go away," I repeated more forcefully. "You'll be ashamed of yourself in the morning. Go sleep it off somewhere else."

"In the morning we'll both be happy," he said and put both of his hands on my arms to try to pull me close. I wore only wool socks on my feet so kicking did no good, but I brought up a knee to his groin hoping to inflict enough damage to break free. I wasn't frightened then, only annoyed and furious. My aim was off, though, and he was able to wrap both arms around me and start to plant kisses on whatever part of my face he could get to. That was the moment I became frightened, when I realized I wasn't strong enough to break free, when he stopped trying just to land a few kisses and started touching me in a way that was more intrusive and offensive.

I had both palms against Tony's chest trying to push him away when his arms slackened and his bulk was suddenly removed. Fergus had grabbed him by the back of the collar, yanked him away, and had begun to shake him violently. When, arms flailing, Tony tried to turn toward him, Fergus hit him along the side of his head once with his fist. Tony choked, staggered a little, crashed against one of the chairs at the table, then tried to right himself. With an open hand, Fergus shoved him forcefully backwards, and Tony fell with all his weight against the chair. I heard the wood crack under him, and the cowboy slid to the floor, groaning.

I took a deep breath. "He works for the Davises, Fergus, so please don't hurt him any more. He's had too much to drink, is all, and I'm not hurt, just aggravated. Can we put him on his horse and send him home without worrying that he'll fall off into the snow and freeze to death?"

Fergus looked like some kind of avenging angel. The moonlight through the open door gave him a fearful, dark face, nothing like himself at all. Without a word he dragged the intruder's sagging body out the doorway and through the snow to where a horse waited restlessly with reins trailing. Fergus heaved Tony's body over one shoulder, wrapped the horse's reins around his wrist, and still without a word threw the drooping figure into the saddle, much as if Tony had been a lumpy sack of grain. The cowboy scrambled to keep himself from falling off, then finally sat dazed and slumped forward feebly grasping the saddle horn with both hands.

Fergus, still holding the reins of the edgy horse, spoke at last. "You show your face around here again and you won't see summer." He tied the reins around the saddle horn and smacked the horse's rump.

Picking its way carefully, the animal moved off in the general direction of the Davis ranch, Tony able to hang on but tilting from one side to the other. I heard an indistinct moan even after he disappeared into the darkness. He would have multiple headaches in the morning, deserve each one, and still probably not recollect anything from the night's activities.

"Will he be all right?" I asked, staring into the night.

Fergus didn't answer but walked over to where I stood, taking my chin in kind fingers and turning my face so it caught a gleam of moonlight.

"Are you all right is more the question."

"Yes." My voice was shakier than I wished so I added more firmly, "I really am, Fergus. Just disgusted and angry. I'll get over it. Thank you for helping me. I know if you hadn't been here, the situation would have gone from bad to worse."

Inside the cabin I saw that one of the chairs was in pieces and—to Fergus's obvious surprise—the broken furniture immediately became the most distressing part of the incident to me.

"Do you think the chair can be fixed?" I asked sadly. "It's only on loan from Lou Davis, and I'll never be able to return it like this. What will she think when she sees it?"

Fergus squatted down next to where I was crouched over the broken chair pieces.

"Hope," he said gently but with a touch of impatience in his tone, "Lou Davis is not a woman to give a second thought to that old broken chair." Meeting my look, his expression softened and he continued, "I'll look at it in the morning and do what I can. And I'll go into town on Monday and get a lock for your door. You should go back to bed now."

I felt a lone tear trickle down my cheek. "I don't want anything to spoil this for me," I whispered, meeting Fergus's eyes so he'd know I wasn't talking about the chair. "I have my heart set on being happy here, and I don't want anything to ruin it." A look I couldn't read crossed Fergus's rough face.

"He was just a drunken cowboy, lass. Don't dwell on it too long. It's nothing worth spoiling your dreams."

We both stood up. I was shivering with the cold and he handed me the shawl that I'd dropped.

"Go back to bed, Hope. I'll build up a fire to take off the room's chill."

Giving myself a mental shake, I said more briskly, "No, I can do it. I won't sleep right away, anyway. You go back to your woolies. Did you check on our mothers and babies next door?"

"I was just coming up to do that when I heard that yahoo shouting. I'll go check now. Are you sure you're all right?"

"I don't usually let things bother me for too long." Then I added, "Fergus, you've been a better friend to me than I deserve. Thank you."

That same unreadable expression crossed his face, whether affectionate or impatient or something in between I just couldn't tell.

"You're wrong there. We're partners, remember, and we have a mutual interest."

He pulled the door shut behind him as he left, and I went to start a fire in the fireplace, thinking that people had often stepped into my existence through no effort of my own and ended up changing the course of my life. Charlie McKinney was one example, Ralph Gallagher another, Lou Davis most likely another, and now Fergus Campbell. I didn't know whether I was going through life making chance connections or whether those people had—in some way and as part of some master plan—been waiting for me to cross their paths. I sat in bed under the blankets with my knees drawn up against my chest, the shivering subsiding as I grew warmer.

Part of me hoped Tony got back to his bed safe and sound, but my other, more vindictive, self hoped he fell off his horse into a snow bank and froze to death. I began to tell God that I didn't really mean what I'd just wished, but I fell asleep and never finished the sentence. Later I found out that Tony got back to the Davis ranch just fine, so apparently God finished the thought for me.

Fergus had been right about the snow not lasting. By Sunday afternoon the temperature rose and the wet snow began to melt, revealing patches of new grass beneath. We let the new mothers and their lambs out of the shed to wander once more, and Fergus began repairs on the broken chair.

Monday it was warmer still and sunny, and while I washed clothes in a big tub over an open fire in the yard, Fergus continued to piece together the damaged chair. We shared a companionable silence until we heard a wagon pull into our lane. John Thomas Davis was driving, with something hefty in the back of the wagon.

"Fergus, here comes my transportation," I called happily, because I could see a bicycle strapped down inside the wagon.

"I think this contraption is for you," John Thomas announced, smiling at my expression as I came out to greet him. "George Moss told me you'd ordered it, and I knew you'd want to have it right away." He lifted the bicycle out of the back and set it on the ground. "But you'd better wait until the ground dries up a little, or you'll end up stuck in a hole somewhere."

"It's beautiful. Thank you for bringing it. You're right about the mud, though. I guess I'll just have to sit and admire my transportation for a few days until I can get around on it. But a bicycle is cheaper than a horse and it takes up less space, so I believe it's going to work fine."

John looked beyond me to where Fergus stood over the chair that lay on its side on the ground and was still missing one leg.

"Looks like you've had an accident," he remarked. The unspoken question in his comment started out innocent enough, but something in my face made him give me a more intense look, his gray eyes narrowing just a little and not wavering from my face.

After a brief, awkward pause, Fergus said bluntly, "One of your cowboys came bothering Hope two nights ago, and I had to persuade him to leave. The chair got in the way." John Thomas's whole body grew very still.

"What are you talking about?"

"It was a misunderstanding," I interjected hastily, trying to catch Fergus's eye and signal him to be quiet. "I wasn't hurt or anything."

Both men ignored me, and John Thomas stepped closer to Fergus.

"What are you talking about, Campbell?" he repeated, each word slow and deliberately spaced, the first Wyoming drawl I'd heard since my arrival.

"Well, lad, one of your hands"—Fergus emphasized the word *your* so John Thomas wouldn't miss the point—"showed up seeking warmth and comfort for the night. Didn't get invited in but came in anyway and didn't go when he was told to leave. If he hadn't been the worse for whiskey and making enough noise to rouse the dead, I wouldn't have heard him, and I don't like to think about what would have happened if that had been the case. He was after one thing."

An understanding passed between the two men, and John Thomas turned to face me. The earlier smile had disappeared, replaced by an emotion that darkened his eyes and smoothed his tone to something cool and frightening, a different man from the one who had pulled up in the wagon minutes before.

"I'm sorry for that. Were you harmed?"

I gave Fergus an irritated scowl before turning back to John Thomas.

"No. I'm perfectly fine. He was coming back from his night on the town, didn't know what he was doing, and took a wrong turn. Please don't make it seem more serious than it was."

"Did he lay hands on you?"

"Not—" I began, but at the look in John's eyes, admitted, "Well, yes, and I confess I was frightened for a moment, but Fergus took care of him and I'll bet he hardly remembers what happened, he was so many sheets to the wind. It's over now and the only thing worse for wear is your mother's kitchen chair, so can't we drop the subject?"

"How do you know he was one of our men?" John Thomas ignored my request and didn't take his eyes from my face.

"You brought him with you that first morning you came, remember? Curly sat on the wagon seat, and you rode over with the other one, Tony. He's the one it was."

John Davis spoke very formally, a cold anger flattening his tone, and I thought the emotion was directed at me. I recalled that he'd warned me I might not be safe alone and that I had responded to his solicitude by telling him to mind his own business.

But instead of an I-told-you-so, John stated simply, "I can't tell you how sorry I am that something like that happened."

"Honestly, John Thomas, I didn't encourage him. I only opened the door because I heard a loud voice, and I thought it was Fergus and something was wrong." John's expression lost some of its sternness.

"That thought never crossed my mind. You have every right to be here and to live unmolested in your own home. I apologize that you were bothered and that it was one of our crew who did the bothering. And I'm thankful that you have a strong Scot for a friend."

He gave a nod to Fergus, who only watched him wordlessly. Then John Thomas climbed back onto the wagon seat, picking up the reins.

"I hope you enjoy that bicycle," he said, but he didn't smile when he spoke, and I could tell his mind was somewhere else.

After he left, I said crossly to Fergus, "You didn't have to go and tell him all that. What will he think? What will his mother think? It will just cause trouble."

"I've known the Davises longer than you, Hope. They don't tolerate the kind of behavior you experienced, and they need to know if and when it happens. People around here live pretty isolated, and they can't afford to ignore anything that threatens their homes and families. Without a firm hand, it's too easy for rowdy actions to get out of control. Putting your head in the sand and pretending nothing happened doesn't help anyone. Letting that man get away with bad conduct only means he'll try it again with someone else who may not be as lucky as you. I don't mind saying I'm surprised at you."

It was the closest to a rebuke I'd heard from Fergus, and I wanted to explain that growing up, I had concluded that men acted that way only toward certain women, women like the girls at The Sanctuary, women bought and paid for. No male visitor to the Gallaghers' house had been anything but courteous and genteel when in the presence of women, even the women on the household staff. I had long worried that I carried more of my mother in me than I wished, and Tony's uninvited appearance seemed to confirm my fears. I felt troubled and ashamed that that might be true, that Tony might have seen something in me that made him believe I would welcome his attentions, something I didn't realize and couldn't recognize. The idea was deeply distressing. Until I had the chance to think through the situation, I preferred to forget what had happened two nights ago, and I wanted everyone else to forget it as well.

I couldn't reveal all that to Fergus, however, as much as I wanted to. We hadn't known each other long enough for that kind of sharing. Someday I might get up the courage to talk to him about The Sanctuary and ask him to explain some of what I didn't understand about men, but that time wasn't the present. All I could do was send Fergus another bad-tempered look and go back to the laundry without any more words.

The next day the chair was mended and so was Fergus's and my friendship. Neither of us spoke about what had happened, and I was relieved that we were back to business as usual.

A warm, early spring wind picked up, melted the last of the snow, and even began to dry out the ground. The red-orange spikes of Indian Paintbrush started to poke out from among the dried grasses, and small green leaves appeared on all the trees.

"Spring," I announced with delight to Fergus one morning. "I believe it's really and truly on the way."

"I believe you're right," Fergus responded, taking an expansive look around him. "We'll leave for shearing in a week, and you'll be back in time for Easter Sunday."

I felt excited about the upcoming trip and the chance to earn money and wool. Both commodities were necessary for me to live independently—money to buy seed, laying hens, and a loom and wool to spin and weave into fabric I was convinced I could sell through George Moss's store. Once the storekeeper saw the quality of my work, I knew he would be willing to buy from me and then resell to his customers. From all I'd seen, Moss was a fair man and would give me a fair price. If I could start my own flock and raise my own sheep, I'd eventually have a steady supply of wool. I could turn the back room of my cabin into a workroom and keep weaving through the long winter months until spring. Then I could plant and harvest through the growing months. I had thought the cycle of seasons through and couldn't imagine why the plan wouldn't work just as I envisioned. Next year at this time I pictured jars of my own produce stacked in the corner, heard my own sheep and chickens in the shed next door and the steady click of the loom in the house. Sometimes, lying awake at night, thinking it all through step by step, I'd get so excited I couldn't fall asleep. It seemed incredible that a girl with no formal education and only the experience of a hired servant should have such opportunity all around her. That was why I had told Fergus—fear catching in my throat—that I didn't want anything to spoil my plans. True happiness seemed right around the corner.

That week I had a visit from Lou Davis. I was in the middle of pressing the laundered clothes from the week before and had already grown impatient with my progress. Lou had included one of Mrs. Potts' famous sad irons in the box of household items she'd sent over, but I was used to the luxury of the Gallagher home where we were able to work through the household laundry without interruption by keeping at least a half dozen of the heavy iron bodies hot and ready on the stove. Having several irons allowed us simply to detach the handle from the cooled iron and reattach it to the next hot iron waiting in line. Frequently having to pause and reheat my one iron before I could continue made me impatient and restless because so many other tasks still waited for me outside. Lou's cheerful call was a welcome break from a tedious chore.

She came in with her usual combination of energy and generosity, holding a small woven basket in one hand, and smiled at the look on my face.

"I know," she told me, without having to ask. "Ironing is my least favorite chore, too. I'm not patient or particular enough. I'd rather scrub floors or dig post holes any day. John always made himself scarce on ironing days."

Without waiting for me to respond, she held up the little container she carried and continued, "John Thomas said he dropped off your bicycle, so I thought you could fix this basket onto the front and use it for carrying things. John gave me some old wire fencing you can use to attach it with. I saw a picture of a bicycle basket in a magazine and thought of you right away. I brought fresh milk, too."

"Thank you. I admit I do miss milk. I've been thinking about getting a goat so I'll have my own milk supply. I don't expect I can order a goat from the Montgomery Ward catalog, though. Is there someone who'd have one to sell and maybe a laying hen or two?"

"You should ask George Moss about that," Lou suggested. "Everything and everybody goes through his store. Ask him about getting you some canned condensed milk. That seems easier than bothering with a goat. The sheep will keep you busy enough. In another eight weeks you can get your garden in and have fresh harvest all summer and into the fall. This is a hard land to garden, Hope, but I've learned that while Wyoming makes us wait, it eventually rewards our patience."

I poured tea for the two of us and we sat companionably at the table. Lou sat in the chair that had been broken, and despite the good carpenter job Fergus had done on it, the chair did not sit as evenly as before. We both noticed the wobble right away, but when I started to explain, Lou interrupted me.

"John Thomas told me what happened, Hope, and I wanted to stop in to be sure everything was all right with you. I can tell you that Tony's conduct was not typical of the men in these parts, but this is still Wyoming and not Boston, so I can't say it's unheard of, either."

"I've been reading *The Virginian* that was in the box of books you sent over," I replied, smiling slightly, "so I understand what you mean, but it's different when something's really happening and you're not just reading about it. I don't much agree with violence, but if I'd had a weapon handy that night, I would have brained that cowboy without hesitation."

"John Thomas took care of that for you."

"I hope no one was hurt," I said with alarm. "I didn't mean to cause any trouble."

She looked at me as soberly as Fergus had before she responded, "Hope, this is still wild country, and you're not the only woman who's on her own a great deal. We have to act on that kind of behavior firmly or it puts all women at risk, all people, for that matter. I've never been able to abide a bully, and my husband is fierce and uncompromising about my safety and our daughters' well-being. John Thomas takes after both of us. Tony no longer works for us, and he's been told in no uncertain terms that he's not welcome in these parts any more. I heard he was a little done in by the time he packed up his kit and left."

"John Thomas has never tolerated purposeful unkindness, even as a child, which I consider one of his most endearing qualities." She gave her low chuckle. "Of course, I'm his mother so it's my duty to think my son overflows with endearing qualities." Then, more seriously, "My family knows how I feel about vigilante justice, but I agreed in this case that Tony needed to be taught a lesson about good manners." I must have still looked troubled because Lou rested her hand on my arm. "Laramie isn't San Francisco, Hope, but we're just as civilized. I wish the incident hadn't happened at all, but as long as you're not the worse for the experience, you can trust us to do what's right."

"I do trust you. You and your family have been more than kind from the moment I met you. I just want to fit in here and not cause any trouble," I repeated.

"I think you're fitting in just fine," was all Lou Davis said as reply and changed the subject to ask about my coming trip to shearing with Fergus. She said goodbye to me, but instead of leaving right away she rode down to the creek where Fergus was camped. I watched them talk together for some time and then waved to her as she rode off.

Later when I asked Fergus about their conversation, he told me not to be so nosey.

"I just wondered what you were saying, is all," I protested.

"If the conversation had been intended for your ears, we would have invited you to join us. I don't see any reason I can't have a talk with an old acquaintance of mine without asking your permission first."

I gave him a poke with my elbow. "I never said you needed my permission and you know it." After a pause I added, "I don't believe I've ever met anyone like Lou Davis before. She doesn't seem afraid of anything or have any doubts about herself."

"You could look in the mirror."

I turned to him in astonishment. "How can you compare me to her? I'm nothing like her at all."

But he just grinned and turned away.

That same week John Thomas showed up in my front yard, brandishing a lightweight rifle as if he were showing off a trophy.

"Have you got time for a lesson now?" he asked.

I was in the middle of some chore at the moment, but at the sight of him, I quickly lost interest in whatever I was doing. The younger John Davis sat a horse very well, and the bright, mid-morning sunshine gave his black hair a deep blue gleam like a crow's wing. I vowed at that moment to stop reading so many romances and settle for more Sherlock Holmes. Conan Doyle's stories might cause alarm, but at least they didn't turn my mind to unbecoming flights of fancy.

Those flights of fancy only increased as the morning progressed because in order to show me how to hold the rifle properly, John Thomas had to stand with his arms loosely around me in order to position the rifle butt against my right shoulder and show me how to extend my left arm properly.

I thought he had to feel my heart racing, but he directed matter-of-factly, "Look through the sight and squeeze the trigger gently. Don't jerk it. You'll feel a little recoil against your shoulder, but it won't be enough to hurt you. Go ahead. Try it."

He stepped away, and I attempted to follow his instructions, taking aim at an empty can he'd set on a stack of boxes. I resisted the impulse to shut my eyes and fire and instead focused carefully on the target and slowly pulled the trigger just as he'd told me. I still missed the can by a yard, but after I got used to the feel of the gun and its recoil, I found myself surprisingly comfortable with the experience.

I never did hit the target that day, but I grew more at ease with the idea and thought I might even practice on my own. John Thomas left an extra box of ammunition with me and showed me how to clean and load the gun before he left.

"A gun is not a toy," he lectured sternly, "and you're still an amateur, so be careful with it."

"Thank you for explaining that. Otherwise I'm sure I'd have shot wildly about the room and put holes in the ceiling," I replied, not bothering to hide the asperity in my voice.

"You don't have to take that tone with me. What did I say wrong?"

"Sometimes you talk to me as if I were a child," I responded ungratefully and too sharply, "and I don't appreciate being patronized."

John Thomas looked at me for a moment, then reached out a hand to my chin to tip my face up to look at him.

"I don't mean to patronize you, and there's no way I think of you as a child. No way at all."

For just a minute I thought he would kiss me, but then the moment passed, and he backed away from me as if he'd been as unsettled by the exchange as I had.

I knew a quick regret at his forbearance but managed to speak calmly. "I guess I'm too sensitive. You were kind to take the time to stop by, John Thomas. I'd like to pay you for the rifle and the ammunition if you'll tell me what I owe."

He shook his head, his usual self-assured equilibrium restored. "No. It's my way of apologizing for exposing you to the bad behavior of one of our hands. I should have used better judgment when I brought him along the other day."

"You can't carry the bad manners of everyone who works for you around on your shoulders," I replied practically. "That would be much too heavy a burden. There's no way you can predict how people will act under all circumstances, unless you've figured out a way to look into the human heart."

John gave me a half smile before he turned to loosen the reins of his horse.

"I wish I could do that." His murmured tone held regret and a certain wistfulness as he repeated, more to himself than to me, "Lately I've wished I could do exactly that."

Despite myself I colored at his words because, although I pretended I hadn't caught his remark, I had, and I knew for sure he wasn't talking about cowboys.

Chapter 6

*O*n the first fine morning of the next week I couldn't resist the lure of the bicycle. With Fergus's help I fastened Lou's basket to the handle bars, then squashed a broad-brimmed straw hat over my hair and waved back at him as I slowly wheeled down the bumpy drive. The trip was almost an unqualified success. The main road was broad and level enough so I could avoid the ruts, and with the sun on my face, it wasn't long before I stuffed the hat into the basket and just enjoyed the wind in my hair. Not quite a horseless carriage, but the bicycle still gave me a heady feeling of freedom and self-sufficiency.

I had to giggle to myself as I parked my transportation next to the wagons and horses hitched to the rail outside the general store. The bicycle looked an incongruous sight among its neighbors. Maybe the twentieth century was coming a little more slowly to the wilds of Wyoming than to some other parts of the country, but its arrival was inescapable, and I was doing my part to welcome in the new century.

"I heard you were on your way," said a grinning George Moss, coming to the door of the store. "How was the ride?"

"On a day like today, just about perfect." I followed him into the store's dim interior. "I'd like to settle accounts for the bicycle, and then I have a few things I need to take back with me. Baking powder, for sure, and a can of peaches, and Lou Davis told me you had canned milk that I could get. Oh, and I wondered about ordering a spinning wheel and a loom. How would I do that? How long would they take to get here? How much would that all cost?" Mr. Moss laughed.

"So you weren't scared away by the solitude and the cold. I remember outfitting two sisters just like I did you. Out they went and back they came within the week. Too lonely, they said. Too windy and cold, they said. Beats me what they expected. But it never does to predict who'll last and who won't. I'd have guessed you were too little a thing to make it, but it appears you're enjoying your stay in Wyoming."

"I am for sure. Sometimes I feel like there's nothing I can't do. I thought Wyoming would have that same effect on everyone."

"Only on the folks it doesn't drive away, and now I'm predicting that won't be you."

As Mr. Moss filled my order, Becca Wagner came into the store.

"I thought that bicycle might belong to you, Hope. Mother said John Thomas had delivered it. If I didn't love horses so much, I'd ask Ben if I could get one. How was the ride?"

She had the look of her mother about her as she spoke, her chestnut hair coiled in braids at the back of her neck and Lou's same open, friendly manner.

"I think I'll have to pad that seat a little more," I told her, laughing and lowering my voice, "but other than that the ride was fine. I wish I had your experience with horses, but they seem awful high off the ground, so I think I'm too old and skittish to stay on a saddle now. The bicycle will have to do."

"My father put me on a horse before I learned to walk, so riding is second nature for me, but I think my husband would rather see me on the bicycle as long as I forego the bloomers. They wouldn't go over well with the congregation at all. Much too improper. Why don't you come by for noon meal before you head home? Nothing fancy, but Ben and I would love the company."

Having seen them together, I thought they were probably as happy to be by themselves as to have company, but I accepted the invitation anyway. I wasn't a newlywed, so the idea of fresh faces in different surroundings was appealing.

"We live on the other end of town. Turn right onto Garfield Street. We're the big house next to the little church. I've always thought it should be the other way around, but Ben's predecessor was the decision maker, not us, so I'm not apologizing. Come down whenever you're done here."

After she left, George got out the Sears catalog and pointed to the shaft looms shown on the page.

"Are you thinking something like this?"

The larger one on the page was what I wished I could order, but I answered regretfully, "It will have to be the smaller one, I'm afraid, and I need a wheel to spin with and hand carders, too. All as inexpensive as I can get."

We looked everything up in the catalog, and he wrote down the page numbers and the cost, which was daunting. I would have to do very well with the shearers to start this venture.

"Everything comes out of Chicago," George told me, "so orders usually get here three to four weeks after they're placed. But we've waited a lot longer, and then other times things have shown up practically over night, so I can only give you my best guess."

I did the calculating in my head. If I placed the order by Easter, everything should certainly be in by the end of May. It would take me that long to scour the wool and have it ready to work with. If I worked all summer, I could have woolen fabric to sell by fall, just in time for the long winter when people would appreciate the warmth and I would appreciate the earnings.

"Can you order the carders now?"

"I can do whatever you like. I'll send word when they're in or, if someone's going out your way, I'll send them along. Sounds like you've got plans."

"I always have a head full of plans and not enough hours in the day. That reminds me, I need seed for the garden and Lou Davis said you could help me get what I need. And do you know where I could get a laying hen or two?" He shook his head at me.

"Miss Birdwell, talking to you tires me out. It's too early for seed, so we can talk about that next time you make the trip in on that machine of yours. As for chickens, when I next see the Haberdinks, I'll tell them you're interested. They have a big farm north of the Davises, and they have to pass your place when they come into town, but they don't make it in all that often."

"I'd be obliged if you'd ask them to stop by my cabin next time you see them."

I loaded my basket and wheeled down the street toward the church, more than ready to take Becca Davis up on her offer of a home-cooked meal.

"I hope you'll forgive eating in the kitchen," said Becca, holding a wooden spoon in one hand as she led me into the large kitchen at the back of the house.

"I eat in the kitchen every day, also in the parlor and in the bedroom," I responded dryly.

"When I was a little girl, our kitchen was smaller than this, and it was the only room we had to gather in. We did everything at the table——that's the little table you have now. We had all our lessons there. Mother cut out our clothes on it and balanced the accounts there. It's where my father would spread out the paper after supper and where he sat and listened to our recitations and where he let all of us beat him at checkers. We have a dining room here, but Ben and I never use it."

"Maybe you'll need to when your family grows," I suggested, but she shook her head with a smile.

"I hope not. The kitchen's the place for family."

I pictured the Gallaghers sitting at their big table in their bigger dining room, distanced in space and emotion, and thought Becca Wagner was probably right.

Ben Wagner came in with his shirt open at the neck and his hair a little rumpled.

"Wrestling with a text," he told me apologetically. He walked past his wife, rubbed her arm briefly as if he couldn't help touching her, and sat down at the table. Over the meal he asked, "No second thoughts yet, Miss Birdwell?"

I wanted to invite him to call me by my first name but thought that might not be proper for a parson.

"About coming to Laramie, you mean? Oh, no, far from it. Every day I'm here I'm more and more certain that this is where I'm supposed to be." He nodded.

"I know what you mean. I feel the same way." At my inquiring look he continued, "I was a city boy from Philadelphia and I arrived in Laramie not knowing what to expect."

"And he found me," said Becca, teasing.

"Yes, I did," Ben readily agreed. "I found a pearl of great price." They looked at each other across the table, and for a moment I wasn't there at all. Then he continued, "And gained a whole new family and a place with more joys and more problems than I thought existed in the world."

"No second thoughts, Pastor Wagner?" I asked. He grinned at my turning his words back on him.

"Far from it. Like you, I'm certain this is where I'm supposed to be."

When I left, Becca walked me out to the bicycle.

"We're glad you're here, Hope. I feel like I've known you forever, and I know my mother's already grown fond of you. Now that Katherine and I are both gone, Mother misses female company, so I'm glad you're closer to her. Even John Thomas speaks highly of you, so at least he's not completely a lost cause."

"What do you mean?"

"My brother had an unfortunate experience with a red-haired actress too old for him. He wouldn't listen to any of us, but it was as clear as could be that they weren't meant for each other."

"What happened?" I couldn't help myself asking questions even if I came off vulgar and curious.

Becca retold the story with a rueful shake of her head. "She came through with a traveling show, nearly thirty years old if she was a day, and John Thomas not even twenty yet! He really fell hard for her. That's John Thomas, though. He's warm-hearted, and he can never do anything halfway."

"I warned him she wasn't the settling down kind, but there are times you can't tell John Thomas anything. He and I actually had quite a falling out about it. When she left with the first flush salesman that came along, it was a terrible blow to my brother. Probably to his pride more than anything else because I don't think it was love in any real sense of the word, but he swore off women then and hasn't shown much interest since. Every girl in Laramie's tried to catch his attention, but he just keeps to himself. I was surprised and pleased to hear him say he admired you. For John Thomas, that was practically an oration."

I thought about Becca's remarks later. Being "admired" wasn't exactly a tender or extravagant compliment, but at least he didn't say he found me odd and gawky. I admitted to myself that I cared what John Thomas Davis thought about me, but if anyone else had asked, I would have pretended to be indifferent to his opinion. Why I felt the need to keep my interest to myself I didn't know, but I thought it had something to do with not exposing myself to ridicule or to the weakness of emotion, with not wanting to become unimportant once the door closed behind me.

If I would have gone straight home from the Wagners, the trip would have been an unqualified success, but I didn't. I stopped off at the newspaper office to pick up the latest edition of *The Laramie Boomerang* so I could keep up with the community, and as I left I literally ran into someone who was lounging just outside the newspaper office door. I recognized Tony, who had made himself so unwelcome a few nights before. My instinct said that he had been waiting for me to come out. A fading but still unsightly bruise ran under his eye and down the side of his face and made him look older and rougher than I remembered.

"You better watch where you're going, Miss Prairie Queen," he said. Anger and resentment were reflected both on his face and in his tone.

I was surprised he was still around after what Lou Davis had told me and said as much to him. "Why don't you just go away?" I concluded irritably. "Haven't you caused enough trouble already?"

"I have as much right to be here as you and the high and mighty Davises. What are you gonna do, go whining to them about me again?"

Any further dialogue would have been useless and frustrating, so I walked past him to my bicycle without another word.

Tony remained in the shadow of the overhang and muttered, just loudly enough for me to hear, "You'll be sorry you went crying over there. I won't forget it, and sooner or later I'll get you back."

Truly, he didn't scare me. I recognized a weak and aggrieved man that needed to take his resentful unhappiness and hurt pride out on someone, and I was the most convenient target. From his perspective the most vulnerable, too. Compared to the malevolent cruelty of Ivan Fletcher, however, Tony seemed no more threatening than a petulant, spoiled child.

I balanced the bicycle against my hip as I carefully folded the paper and fitted it into the carryall, then said calmly, as if he were nothing but a negligible afterthought, "Don't threaten me. I'd as soon turn you over to the constable as look at you, and I'll do just that if you put one foot on my property. I'm not threatening you, just stating a fact, plain and simple. You won't catch me by surprise again."

I didn't bother looking at him as I spoke, and I rode off without a backward glance.

For a short while, I remained more uneasy than frightened. Fergus had put a latch lock on the door, and I had the rifle for protection besides, but the exchange took a little luster off the day and added an unwanted worry to the back of my mind. Remembering Ivan Fletcher, I wondered why it was my misfortune to meet unsavory men that didn't like my attitude and held extended grudges.

That night when I took Fergus his supper, he asked about the town visit. I leaned against the wheel of his wagon, watching the stars appear across the sky as if someone were unwrapping them one by one and tossing them into the night.

"I like Laramie and I never minded big city living, but I like it out here better. I know there were sunsets in San Francisco, and I know the same moon that's above us right now was up in the sky there, too, but it's just better here. I can't quite put my finger on why that should be."

"Maybe it's the company," he suggested, teasing.

I looked around me with exaggerated interest. "All these sheep you mean? Who would have thought they'd make such a difference, but you could be right." I heard him chuckling as I turned to make my way back to the cabin.

"We'll leave Monday at daybreak for shearing," Fergus called as I walked up the rise to home. "You'd best get your beauty sleep before then. Knowing you, you'll be too busy to sleep once we get there."

In fact, we left Monday before daybreak, and once we got there, Fergus was almost right. Not quite too busy to sleep but as near to it as a person could come without staying awake around the clock.

Shearing was held a day's travel northwest toward the shipping point Rock River on the land of a man named Pershing Filbert, who owned more land and more sheep than all the rest of the herders put together. I had Fergus introduce me to Mr. Filbert first thing.

"Mr. Filbert, my name is Hope Birdwell. I plan on doing a little cooking and cleaning on your property, and I hope that doesn't cause you any displeasure."

He was a short man—on eye level with me—but barrel-chested, with a broad face and a beard that ran down both cheeks and met at a point in the middle of his chin.

"It causes me no problem, missy. If Fergus Campbell vouches for you, you'll get no argument from me." He looked around at the crowd of people, the miles of milling sheep, and the general hubbub surrounding us. "Once you get their attention you'll be kept busy enough. If you sold kisses, you'd be busier still." He laughed when he said that, and I took no offense.

There was no confusing the solitary herders with the shearers, who were a rowdy, brawny bunch, given to profanity, socializing, and gaming. Yet I never experienced a moment of disrespect or uneasiness with any of them. I was one of a handful of women there, the others wives of either herders or ranchers, and although I had good intentions to seek the women out and introduce myself, once word got around that my kitchen was open for business, I hadn't a moment to spare for anything except cooking and laundry. All the food I had prepared in advance was gone in three days, but I'd brought my little stove and there was always a line for fresh cornbread in the morning and at mid-day more than enough takers for whatever soup I'd concocted. I sold the former by the chunk and the latter by the ladle and invariably ran out of both commodities before I ran out of customers.

When I could spare the time, I watched the process and marveled. A good shearer handled around a hundred sheep a day, but that was just the beginning. After the sheep were shorn, poor naked things then, they were forced into a malodorous dip of sulfur, tobacco, and something medicinal to kill off any lice or ticks, then branded with a paint stamp and finally earmarked.

The lambs complained loudly about getting their tails docked, and I admit I winced at my first sight of that practice.

"Needs to be done," Fergus said practically, "so don't look if it bothers you." Planning on my own flock someday, I made myself watch and get used to the procedure. There was no place for refined sensitivities in my future. At the same time most of the male lambs were wethered.

"Makes better mutton," Fergus explained, "and keeps the flock strong by forcing the ewes to breed with only the best rams."

The days held an old familiar routine for Fergus, but for me everything was new and exciting. Someday, I thought, I'll be here with a flock of my own. I'll fit in and people will know me. This will be home to me. The idea was an exhilarating consideration.

I saw less fisticuffs and brawling and heard more bragging and vanity than I'd expected and in the evenings loud music, singing, and dancing to the concertina and fiddle. I had my share of invitations to join in the festivities but said no to every one of them.

"I can't stay up to all hours and then have breakfast ready at sun-up," I explained, but they were a good-natured lot of men, who respected my intentions and ended up swinging each other around as partners while the music played.

By the end of the eighth day, as things were winding down, I sat on the steps of Fergus's wagon with my knees pulled up and my head resting on my arms.

"Tired, lass?"

"Only a little. I've had the time of my life, and I almost hate for it to end. I have plenty of wool to take home to keep me busy. I know it'll card down to less than I think, but it's enough to start with. And I've made the money I needed to order the loom and the wheel with some cash to spare. You were a very good friend to bring me along, Fergus."

"Partners as I recall," was all he said, turning away, but his tone bothered me.

"You're more my friend than my partner, Fergus. I hope you feel the same."

"I don't see a reason we can't be both."

He walked away and I watched after him, a little troubled. I thought I must have said or done something to upset him but didn't know what it could have been. Since he'd been with his flock and I had stayed busy with my own projects literally from dawn to dusk, we had hardly talked to each other the whole stay. I figured something had occurred to touch that melancholy temperament he possessed and was relieved that by evening his gruff, terse tone and disquieting attitude were gone, and he was himself again.

We left for home two days later. Pershing Filbert sought me out to tell me he'd expect to see me next year and in fact offered to work out an arrangement to pay me by the day to feed the whole shearing crew.

"How does five dollars a day and the best bundle of wool sound? You're a worker—I'll say that for you."

I thought it sounded pretty good but held my tongue. Maybe I could get another two bits from him, and I didn't have to be in a hurry to respond.

As if reading my mind, Mr. Filbert's eyes began to twinkle and a smile tugged at his mouth before he remarked, "It's a fair offer and you can think about it for a while. Pass word to me through Fergus when the time's right."

Fergus and I had a quiet ride home. I was tired and Fergus withdrawn. Coming east over the last ridge and catching my first glimpse of the cabin put an unexpected lump in my throat.

"Isn't it good to be home?" I asked, not really expecting an answer from my companion.

Next to me on the seat Fergus surprised me by replying, "It's your home, Hope, not mine, but I know it's a welcome sight to your eyes," his tone even and expressionless.

"You'll always be welcome here, Fergus. Stay as long as you want or just pass through—that's up to you—but I wish you'd think of it as your home, too, since we're partners and friends." I used the two words deliberately. "It seems to me that everyone needs someplace to belong."

Fergus's response was ambiguous. "Lou Davis said a woman needs a home in a way different from a man." I thought about the words as we approached the cabin.

"I can't speak for all women," I finally replied, "but I think she's right. I know I have a longing to belong somewhere, to settle and stay. Don't you ever grow weary of wandering and just want to put down roots somewhere?"

Fergus gestured at the sheep milling ahead of us, the dogs nipping at their heels to move them along.

"The woolies don't give me a choice in the matter."

We pulled in along the creek and I climbed into the back of the wagon to unload all of my belongings, then made several trips with my arms full up to the house while Fergus settled the flock. By the time I was done, the sky had turned completely black and I started a fire in the fireplace to take the chill off the room.

Later, crawling into bed, I couldn't remember ever being more exhausted. My back, shoulders, and legs ached from bending over both laundry and cooking tubs for nine days straight, but it was the best tired I had ever felt.

I could order the loom before Easter and have it set up and running even sooner than I'd planned. If the hand carders were in, I could scour the wool, a strenuous and time-consuming job in itself, then card it and have it ready to be spun. I had gathered a pile of rags that needed to be washed, then woven into a rug for my floor and I planned to weave a special blanket for the Davises as a thank you for all their kindness. I fell asleep mid-thought and slept well into the morning.

That next morning I rode into Laramie, picked up the carders for the wool, and happily ordered the larger items through George Moss. Mid-April and still cool but a beautiful day nevertheless with that big, blue Wyoming sky, clouds skidding along the mountaintops to the west, and a bright sun looking deceptively warmer than it really was.

Pedaling toward home, I recognized John Thomas waiting for me where the road branched off to my cabin. Slouching nonchalantly in the saddle, he looked as if he hadn't a care in the world. As I pulled beside him on the bicycle, he looked down at me and gave that warm smile that lit up his face.

"I saw you coming. You were riding so fast on that contraption you were stirring up dust."

"I wish I could go that fast, but unfortunately I tend to poke on the way home. I have a lot more energy on the trip into town, but by the last stretch coming back I'm wishing for a magic carpet."

He got off his horse and we walked companionably toward my house, I pushing along the bicycle.

"You should try it, John Thomas. Have you ever ridden a bicycle?"

"If it doesn't have four legs, I don't think I could stay on it."

"Here, take a ride." I exchanged the bicycle for the reins of his horse.

"I'd never live it down," John told me, looking quickly around before positioning himself on the bicycle and pushing off, "if anyone found out about this." Until he found his balance, he teetered and wove precariously, but after the initial moments he looked as if he'd been born on a bicycle.

When he pulled up in front of me, I assured him, "Your secret's safe with me. You did fine. Next thing will be a horseless carriage." I took back the bicycle from him as he reached for the reins of his horse.

"Elmer Lovejoy built his own version of a horseless carriage ten years ago, but the machine didn't go over very well here. Scared the horses, made the beef tough, and curdled the milk, I'm told." His words made me laugh.

"I can tell you that San Francisco has its share of automobiles, but the beef was still tender and the milk sweet, so don't believe everything you hear. You aren't afraid to try new things, are you?"

I could tell by his expression that my question had made him think, and he didn't like the first answer he'd been about to give.

After a moment he replied, "Not afraid, but I don't always see the need for change."

I propped the bicycle against the side of the cabin and turned to face him. "Change and progress are what turn the world, so don't get left behind."

"You're sounding pretty cheerful since you're back from your trip," John Thomas observed. "Your venture must have worked out all right."

"It was a wonderful experience. I sold everything and then some. I couldn't keep the crews in cornbread, and they paid as much as two whole dollars for a pie. Imagine! I just came back from ordering—" I stopped abruptly because I had never told him my plans, and I wasn't sure I wanted to. Sometimes sharing the dream spoils the dream.

"Ordering—?" he prompted.

Somewhat reluctantly I explained my business plan, concluding with, "One of my projects this week is washing the wool. I've never done it, only seen it done, and I know it's heavy work, so I'm a little wary about it all, but Fergus said he'd help me. Between the two of us, we should be able to handle the job."

"Campbell will be moving his flocks north in a little while, won't he?" John asked casually.

"So he says. It'll sure be lonely around here without him, but he said he'll be back in the fall when it's breeding time, and that's just a few months away. Anyway, were you just stopping by for a visit, or was there something you wanted?" My question came out a little more blunt than I'd intended, but that only made him smile.

"Next Sunday is Easter. My mother sent me over with an invitation for Easter dinner unless you have other plans."

"No, I don't. That would be nice. Thank you and thank her. As long as it's not raining or snowing, I'll ride my bicycle over."

"I'd be happy to pick you up in the buggy."

"Oh, no, thank you," I assured him cheerfully. "That would be too much trouble. It's about as far to your place as it is to Laramie, so it won't be a hardship for me to ride over."

I knew he wanted to argue with me, but when he opened his mouth to do just that, I caught his eye and raised my eyebrows, daring him to tell me that he knew better.

We shared one of those moments when each person knows what the other is thinking, and then all he said was, "Some day you should learn to ride a horse."

"Your sister Becca gave me the same advice, but I think I'm too old to learn. And since it's a lot farther to the ground from your saddle than from the seat of my bicycle, I'll just stick with the bicycle."

He gave me a long, considering look. "You're a very stubborn woman, Miss Birdwell."

"I'll take that as a compliment although I don't consider myself stubborn. I think of it more as being determined. I know what's right for me and what I want. Then I make a plan and just like aiming for a target, I don't take my eyes off it."

John Thomas swung himself back into his saddle so that I had to look up at him as he spoke. "My family's full of strong-minded women, but you could hold your own with any of them."

"Now that's a real compliment,"—I shaded my eyes with my hand so I could get a look at his face—"knowing your sister and admiring your mother as I do, so thank you for that. Wyoming must be rubbing off on me."

He shook his head. "I don't think you should credit Wyoming. I think you brought your temperament with you when you came. I'll look forward to seeing you next Sunday."

In the days that followed I know I allowed his words to mean more to me than they should have. *I'll* look forward to seeing you, he had said, not *we'll*. As often as I chided myself for reading too much into his final comment, I couldn't help but feel pleased by the inference.

Chapter 7

Scouring wool was the worst chore I had ever attempted bar none. Worse than ironing, worse even than emptying the slops, and I speak from familiarity because I've done them all. I learned the hard way that sodden wool at least quadruples—if not more—in weight once it gets wet, a fact that forced me to start the task with smaller and smaller sections of wool each time just so I could handle them physically. Making the job worse, the wool needed several washes in very hot water before it was cleaned of all its oil and grime. Then it had to be carefully air-dried because if the wool got blown about at all, it became unmanageably fluffy, something else I learned the hard way. From beginning to end, my first exposure to scouring wool was a learning experience of what not to do, an experience that put me in a very bad temper.

True to his word, Fergus helped me whenever he could, but I knew he preferred to keep his distance. I snapped at him unfairly and too often. When the job was finished, I felt worn out in body and spirit.

"So you don't have an endless supply of energy?" Fergus asked as I sat on the ground with my back against the cabin wall. I was sitting squarely in the sun, eyes closed, as close to sleep as you can be and still be awake.

"I am done in, Fergus, just done in. Why didn't you tell me how hard a job it would be to wash that wool of yours?"

I opened my eyes, surprising an expression of such tenderness on his face that I felt immediately unsettled. In a moment the look had disappeared, but what I'd glimpsed troubled me. I thought of Fergus as a good friend, as good a friend as I had ever known, but nothing beyond that and I believed I had seen more than friendship in his eyes. Still, his unguarded expression had been as brief as a blink, and to consider it at all would only complicate my life, so I dismissed the moment from my conscious thought. No need spending time on complications that were speculative at best. I didn't have enough hours in the day as it was.

"I believe that's the first time I've ever heard you admit that something was hard for you."

"Lots of things are hard, Fergus, but what's the use of complaining about them?" I pushed myself up. "I'm going over to the Davises for dinner tomorrow, and I'm going to take a bath. Right now. I've already got the water heating on the stove."

Later I sat outside, indifferently carding wool, my hair loose and wild around my shoulders and drying in the almost-warm sunshine. Despite my intentions not to do so, I thought for a moment of that look on Fergus's face, of the depth of feeling I was almost sure I'd seen there, and I felt saddened. Perhaps I acted too free and easy with him, felt too comfortable around him, perhaps I'd led him to believe something that was not true nor ever could be. I hoped not. But then maybe I was just too imaginative, maybe the sun had struck that brown and bearded face in just the right way to shadow an expression that really hadn't been there at all. Since the latter explanation was what I preferred to be true, that's what I chose to believe.

Easter morning of 1905 dawned gray, blustery, and damp, not anything like spring. The weather was a disappointment but no longer a surprise. With my limited wardrobe, I had to wear the same dress I'd worn on my last visit to the Davises, but I had sewn on a new collar and bought new ribbons for my hair to try to give it a different look. Someday, I thought, I would have enough money saved to buy a new dress ready-made from the store or at least a bolt of new fabric, but until then I would have to keep updating what I had and pretending it didn't matter.

John Thomas was standing on the porch talking to his father when I came into view of the ranch house. He hurried down the steps and out to meet me, lifted the bicycle and carried it back to the porch for shelter.

"The clouds look like rain or even snow. You may need a ride home after all."

Remembering our earlier conversation, I remarked, "It's unbecoming to want to be right all the time, John Thomas, or to always have to have the last word." I heard him chuckle behind me as he followed me into the kitchen.

"I know, but it's so satisfying."

His reply made me turn to give him a disapproving look and then laugh in spite of myself.

"Well, at least you admit your flaws, which is more than most men do." I caught his father's eye and added, "Present company excluded, of course."

Lou Davis greeted me from the sink where she stood. "Forgive me for not being a very good hostess, but my hands are full right now, Hope. Come in where it's warm and relax. Yesterday spring was almost here, and today it feels like winter again."

Lou wore a smock over her church clothes, a locket gleaming golden at her throat, and had her hair pushed into a net at the back of her neck, with stray curls loose and falling all around her ears. Despite the streak of silver hair over her temple, I thought she looked youthful enough to be Becca's sister instead of her mother, eyes sparkling and cheeks flushed from the warmth of the kitchen and even more from happiness. Lou Davis seemed to carry a spark of joy inside her as tangible as a fire's burning ember.

"We're not the Ivinsons," she added, "with their central heating and electric lights, but you'll warm up if you sit in the kitchen for a while."

Because Becca and Ben were unable to join us that day, we were a smaller, cozier group of six: Lou and her husband, John Thomas and his younger brother, and their Uncle Billy. We ate in the formal dining room, expertly papered in beautiful blue and rose paisley with fine lace curtains on the windows, and we sat around a large, heavy mahogany table, but I thought Becca had been right. The kitchen was where a family best fit.

This visit was different from my first one in another way besides the room where we ate our meal. The first time, despite the warmth of welcome, I had been an outsider looking in on something that was new and strange to me. But in just a few weeks I had come to feel as if I belonged in the scene, comfortable enough with the people around me that they could have been family. A novel but glorious experience. What probably seemed typical and normal for them was a wondrously rare moment for me.

Later I asked John Thomas about the photographs on the sideboard in the hallway.

"My grandmother Rebecca Caldecott," he said of the fair-complexioned woman with heavy, dark hair, looking out from the photograph in the weighty gilt frame. The woman's dark eyes under elegant brows carried a serious expression with no hint of a smile. As closely as I examined the picture, I could find little of Lou's inherent joy in her mother's face.

"And this is my mother and her sister Lily when they were little girls."

I picked up that picture to study it more thoroughly. The two girls in the photograph looked very similar in appearance, but I recognized Lou standing behind the chair where her sister sat, the latter's posture making me think of a queen on her throne. Both girls wore immaculate white pinafores over high-necked dresses and had their hair tied back with big white bows. I thought Lou looked too serious for the occasion as if she felt the picture's success were her responsibility while her sister's half-smile belied the regal pose.

"She's a beautiful little girl," I said, pointing to Lily, "but she looks naughty."

Behind me Lou Davis said, "My sister was very naughty, full of mischief, and always in trouble. I was the serious one, but Lily could make anyone laugh if she chose. She always had a sparkle about her." Lou took the frame from me and stared at the photograph as if she'd never seen it before. Then with a small shake of her head, she handed it back to me. "Lily grew up to be an even more beautiful woman."

I looked at Lou wordlessly, knowing there was more to the story.

"She died many years ago, Hope, but I still miss her." I didn't know what to say to the sudden sadness I saw in her gray eyes. Her look reminded me of Fergus and his grief just below the surface, and I decided that perhaps it was not such a bad thing to be alone in the world with no one pulling at your heart, no sad memory in the making.

To cover the brief quiet moment, John Thomas pointed at another framed photograph of two young girls and said, "You'll recognize Becca here with my sister Katherine." Becca was a miniature Lou, but if Katherine resembled anyone, and from the picture I found any resemblance hard to pinpoint, it would have had to be her father. Katherine stood with her hands clasped behind her back, tall and slender and unsmiling, with dark, challenging eyes that looked straight into the camera as if she were daring the photographer to take her picture. I thought Katherine Davis a little intimidating even as a child, and when I said so, both John Thomas and Lou laughed.

"Katherine would like you to believe that, anyway," said Lou affectionately. "She's always embarrassed when someone glimpses her soft heart although I wouldn't want you to think she can't hold her own. John Thomas still carries a scar on his arm where Katherine stuck him with a fork for teasing her."

"I was just making a joke," he protested.

"Neither of you came off very well in that altercation and if I remember correctly, your father had to talk to you both." To me Lou explained, "I recall it was one of those "wait-until-your-father-comes-home" days. John needed only to look at the children a certain way for them to behave while I could scold until my face turned blue and not get the same effect. Poor John would come in at the end of his long day and find me waiting with a list of discussions I wanted him to have with the children. My recollection is that I was awfully short-tempered then, too, but we were always tired so maybe that accounted for it. Not that John ever complained, but I often wonder whether there weren't nights he'd rather have holed up in a line cabin somewhere instead of making his way home."

Not likely, I thought, remembering the way John Davis's gaze had followed his wife around the kitchen.

"Someday you'll find with your own family, Hope, that there's nothing quite like the disapproving look from a father to quiet children down."

I thought to myself that it was doubtful I would have a family, that it was not part of my future plans, and there was too much risk inherent with the idea to make it attractive, but I didn't say any of that. Instead, to change the subject, I picked up a picture of Lou and John Davis in a formal wedding pose. She, slightly smiling, sat on a bench, and her husband stood behind her, one hand holding his hat against his chest and the other resting protectively on his wife's shoulder. Lou had reached up to cover that hand with one of hers. In an unexpected way, Lou's posture with her arm across her heart gave the subtle impression that she was making a promise, a cross-my-heart kind of promise. I found the pose at once unusual and touching.

"We had already been married over a year when the photographer came through Laramie, and I had such an argument with the man about the pose," Lou said, as if reading my mind. "He was very set in his ways, said the man should sit and the woman stand, said that was how his wedding photographs always looked. Naturally I balked at having to do it like everyone else, and just to be different I sat and John stood, and then at the last minute I reached across and put my hand on his. But when Becca and Ben had their wedding photograph taken, they posed it the same way, so it appears we've started a tradition." She looked at John Thomas. "Of course, John Thomas can have his wedding picture taken any way he and his wife decide, but it would be nice if they continued the family tradition." He reddened a little, embarrassed, and his mother took pity on him with the invitation, "I was coming to tell you both that I set warm pie on the kitchen table and fresh coffee on the stove. You can help yourselves."

The sky began to spit a mixture of snow and rain just as I was ready to leave.

Lou peered out the kitchen window, then looked back at me to say, "Hope, I know you're quite capable of bicycling home even in inclement weather, but why don't you let John Thomas take you home in the buggy? He can drop off your bicycle tomorrow. The wind is picking up, and the rain could turn into snow before you reach the cabin."

I would have appeared bad-mannered had I argued with her sensible suggestion, and truth be told, I really didn't look forward to bicycling home with the wind and the rain in my face.

"Not much like spring," I observed to John Thomas, clutching my cape around my shoulders. "Does it ever come?"

"Spring has never come later than July." At my expression, he added, "I'm just kidding, Hope, don't look so horrified, although we did have our Independence Day parade spoiled by a freak snowstorm a few years ago. Another month and we'll warm up for sure. Can you wait that long?"

"I don't have a choice, do I? I'm just impatient because I have a lot planned for the summer. Is the cattle business run by the seasons?"

"Next week we start gathering the calves off the range for branding. At the end of summer, we'll have another round up and ship the mature head to market out of Rock River. We plant alfalfa and oats in the spring for feed and harvest in the fall when we put up the hay. All summer we're on the range, repairing the line cabins and the corrals and gathering stray horses. When it was just my father, Uncle Billy, and me, it seemed we were out on the range all the time. Now we've got ranch hands to help with a lot of the chores."

"You sound like you miss those earlier times." I thought I'd heard a certain wistfulness in John's tone.

"They were good times for me and I admit I sometimes miss those days, but I wouldn't go back. My parents bore the brunt of the work and they deserve to have it easier. When they moved here twenty-five years ago, Laramie was a lot different. No running water, no electric lights."

"Sort of like my place," I said, and he laughed.

"In a way, I guess. But until I came along it was only my father and mother and Uncle Billy out here, and Uncle Billy was just a boy. No neighbors to speak of and Laramie wasn't as civilized as it is today, just a rough town full of bad characters. My father wouldn't let my mother go into town without him, and he says they always walked down the middle of the street just to be safe. For a long time my father, Uncle Billy, and I did all the ranch work ourselves, and with my mother's head for business, we built it up to what it is today."

I was touched by the pride and affection in his voice when he spoke of his father.

After a pause he went on casually, "There's always a dance just before the spring round-up." I said nothing, waiting for him to continue. "They open city hall and set up the band there. It's quite an occasion. Everybody comes." Still I was quiet. John held the reins loosely and looked straight ahead as we moved along against the wind. "I wondered if you'd consider going to the dance with me. It's a week from Saturday."

Clamping down the sudden burst of happiness I felt, I answered cautiously, "I would consider it. I love to dance even though I'm not very good at it. I haven't had much practice."

"That would make two of us then."

I looked at his profile as he sat next to me. It seemed incredible that he wanted to take me to a dance, that this handsome young man from a good and loving family wanted to spend an evening with Bea Birdwell's bastard daughter. Incredible and wonderful.

"You don't have to spend time with me, John Thomas, just because you feel sorry for me or because your mother's taken me under her wing."

He pulled up abruptly in the middle of the drive, the cold rain now wet, fat, pelting snowflakes and the wind gusting enough to rock the buggy, and turned to face me.

"Sometimes you try a man, Hope Birdwell. Why would I feel sorry for you? You're more eager about life than anyone I know, and you're the prettiest girl I've ever seen. It's nice that my mother likes you, but that's got nothing to do with this conversation. I want to take you to a dance because I like spending time with you."

I found that sitting so close to him, caught up in the intense look from those gray eyes, made me a little breathless and caused a new, not exactly unpleasant, feeling at the very bottom of my stomach.

"I just wanted to be clear, John Thomas. I would much rather be by myself than have someone feel obligated to spend time with me,"—he started to interrupt but I kept talking—"but now that you've explained yourself, I'd be pleased to go to the dance with you."

He paused, as if my answer surprised him and said only, "Well, good. Good." He appeared to run completely out of words then and turned back to driving, both of us quiet the rest of the way to my front door.

"I'm always going to be plain spoken, John," I told him when we came to a stop in front of the cabin. "I don't have much experience in polite conversation, and I have even less patience with beating around the bush. I'm sorry if that's not very ladylike."

He came around to help me down from the buggy. The snow made the step slippery, and I lost my footing for a moment, falling against him and causing him to stumble backwards with a little grunt.

"Well, speaking of ladylike," I said and began to laugh at myself. "Apparently I'd better learn to walk before I dance so I don't embarrass either of us. Did I step on your toe just now? I promise not to do you any lasting damage when we're dancing."

John Thomas got the oddest look on his face at my words, staring at me as if some totally unexpected and incredible thought had suddenly crossed his mind. Then the expression vanished and he smiled, too.

"My toes are fine. You'd best go inside before you get any wetter."

Standing in my doorway, I watched him leave, then went inside to build a fire and pull a chair close to the hearth to try to get warm. I wasn't very fond of Wyoming weather, but I couldn't complain about anything else. I had made more friends here in a few weeks than I'd made in the first twenty years of my life. I had a home of my own and a little money in the bank and a plan for the future. And I was going to a dance with John Thomas Davis, a man that I'd been told every eligible girl in Laramie had angled for. Isn't life something? I thought.

"See, Mama," I said softly, "I told you. A woman can make it on her own," and then for no reason that I could name, I began to cry, the kindling crackling in the fireplace and me sitting there hugging my knees tight against my chest, gently crying and not knowing why. Fiddle tears, for sure.

Curly delivered the bicycle the nest morning. "Quite a contraption," he said with barely concealed scorn.

"I know you think that because it doesn't have legs it can't be worth much, but I'm a greenhorn so what can you expect?" I gave a demonstration ride around the yard. "You're welcome to try it, Curly." He gave a hoot.

"No, Ma'am. I'd look nothin' but ridiculous on it. By my way of thinkin', nothin' will ever replace a good horse. I'd like to see you out chasin' an ornery steer on that thing." The picture his words described made me laugh.

"You're right there, Curly, which is why I keep to the main roads. I wouldn't make a very good cowgirl."

He agreed with my observation more heartily than he needed to, but on his way out he added, "Not that you don't have the pluck for runnin' cattle, Ma'am, I'll say that," which was more of a compliment than I deserved or expected.

I spent the next two weeks getting the wool ready to spin and as soon as the ground dried, tilling up the area where I planned to have my garden. Turning up the heavy soil was slow, hard, and cumbersome work with only a hoe and a primitive hand tiller the Davises loaned me, but I wasn't going to spend any more money, even for tools that would have made my life easier.

I saw little of Fergus. It may have been my imagination, but I thought he was keeping his distance on purpose.

When I said something to that effect, he answered slowly, "It's time I was moving a little north, Hope. I admit I hate to leave you on your own, but I know you can take care of yourself, and I'm thinking young Davis will be keeping an eye on you as well."

"You'll be back in the fall, you said," I answered, ignoring his last comment, "and I can't imagine you'll be so far that I couldn't come and visit you if I had a notion to do that."

"You'd be hard-pressed to find me, Hope, but herders pass through Laramie all summer, and you can always send me word by them. We all usually cross paths at least once."

"You have to come back this way, Fergus, because I'm sure you'll want to drop off the lambs you promised me. I nurtured them like a mother, after all, and I have a fondness for them." He gave a snort.

"If I asked you to pick those bummers out of the flock right now, you know you couldn't do it."

"It's true that all sheep look pretty much the same from a distance, but that doesn't mean my babies won't recognize me as the woman who kept them alive. No doubt they'll follow at my heels out of affectionate gratitude."

He began a retort, caught my eye, saw that I was teasing, and gave a chuckle.

"You're a dreamer, lass. There's no dumber animal than a sheep. Not a one of them can remember from one day to the next to come in from the rain."

"That makes eating them a little easier, not that we're going to eat mine. I need them for nice warm vests and wooly blankets, so take good care of them for me." Then I finished more seriously, "I'll miss you, Fergus. It'll seem awful lonely without you."

"It's a lonely life for a lot of folks, Hope, but I don't think for you. You're not given to melancholy and you're not a moper."

I pictured myself weeping in front of the fire the other night and thought that was about as mopey as a person could get.

"I do my share of pining just like anybody else, only I keep it to myself. You won't go without saying good-bye, will you?"

"No, I'd not do that, lass. I'll be gone in a few days, but I promise to say good-bye before I leave."

I rode into Laramie the first week of May, certain that such a splendid day must mean that spring was finally here to stay. George Moss agreed.

"Usually we'd expect at least one more freeze, but this year if I were a betting man, I'd say not. You must be here for seeds and sets, Hope. You have the look of a woman eager to plant a garden." Between the two of us we decided what I should sow.

"Any word on my order yet?" I asked as I packed both my bicycle basket and my shoulder bag with goods.

"Patience, girl. It's only been two weeks, and I told you it could take as long as a month. I'll let you know as soon as everything arrives."

My attention was caught by a bolt of green silk on the store counter. Green wasn't quite the true color because it was more of a blue green, a color that made me briefly homesick for San Francisco Bay on a clear day. My hands, roughened by work and weather, caught on the fine, smooth fabric as I unconsciously stroked the material, and I knew I had to have it.

I did a quick mental calculation. There was no way I could afford enough for a whole dress, but I might be able to buy just enough for a shirtwaist. Then I could cut off the skirt from my plain gray dress and wear that with the blue green blouse to the dance. My mother had had a fine sense of fashion, wore clothes well, and enjoyed the look and feel of beautiful things. Until that moment, however, I had never appreciated that particular affinity of hers, not until I saw a bolt of blue green silk and wanted it more than anything, wanted it to set off my green eyes and my blonde hair so that John Thomas Davis would not regret he had asked Hope Birdwell to the spring roundup dance. Despite the practical—and now scolding—voice in my head, I left with not only a bundle of seed packets for planting but also a small parcel of blue green silk wrapped in brown paper.

The shirtwaist came together exactly as I envisioned, with a high crushed neck, full sleeves tapering to the wrist, and straight, severe bodice darts down to the waist. I was too full bosomed to wear a lot of ruffles and flounces, and this style would accentuate my small waist. There was even enough fabric left to use as a ribbon to tie back my hair. No use bemoaning the fact that my skirt was worn and a plain gray. I knew it wasn't the skirt that people would notice.

I've regretted a lot of things before and since, but I have never felt one moment of remorse for buying that silk. It was worth every hard-earned, well-squeezed cent when I stepped out my front door to greet John Thomas Davis that late Saturday afternoon and the setting sun caught the green of the blouse and turned it to the color of the ocean.

I saw a look of appreciation on John's face and something else besides, a brief, deep flare of emotion I couldn't name but that made me catch my breath when I saw it in his eyes.

Worth every penny and then some, I told myself inwardly, conscious of a bright, fragile, almost frightening happiness that threatened to make me uncharacteristically giddy. A voice inside my head was saying be careful over and over, but for just one night I decided to ignore caution. For just one night I would have a carefree and wonderful time.

"You look beautiful," John stated simply, handing me up into the buggy.

I was tempted to say something either flippant or self-deprecating but instead responded with a simple thank you.

"You look very nice yourself," I added.

He did look fine, almost formal, wearing a crisp white shirt and string tie, black coat and trousers, and a flat-crowned dark hat. Whether it was the clothes or just the way he carried himself, I commented that he particularly resembled his father that night.

"People have told me that before. I can't see it myself, but you couldn't give me a finer compliment if it's true. Do you favor your mother?"

I saw Mother from my child's memory, saw myself tracing the perfect arch of her brows with my finger, saw her porcelain complexion and rose bow mouth, sleek blonde hair and delicate cheek bones.

"Oh, no. She was beautiful." He looked like he wanted to interject a comment, but I continued, "Mother had beautiful skin, not brown and freckled like mine, and her hair was as smooth and soft as gold velvet. The only resemblance I can think of is the color of our eyes."

"She always considered me an odd girl, as if someone had switched me in place of her real daughter. As a child all I ever wanted to do was read and write and read some more, and those were pastimes that didn't interest her at all. She on the other hand had a great appreciation for the finer things in life, and those were things that didn't interest me. I don't know how it came about that we were mother and daughter, but like you, I was told often enough that I resembled her, so we must have been related."

I was embarrassed that I was talking so much and apologized.

"You don't ever have to apologize when you're with me, Hope, not for anything. Not ever."

"We'll see if you say that the first time I trip over your feet," I responded, making a joke to counter his serious tone.

"Not ever," he repeated, turning to look at me. "There's nothing you could do that you would ever have to apologize to me about."

I thought that he wouldn't have said that with such sincerity if he suspected my background, and I felt a quick dread that someday he would find out that I was the daughter of a whore who had been kept by a loafer in a crib on the notorious Morton Street. I couldn't bear the thought of the look in his eyes then, of the scorn and aversion that I might see there. It was easy to say, as I had told my mother, that this was a new century and no one would care about her line of work, but it was different now because I was afraid it would matter and people would care, that Lou Davis and Becca Wagner would care, worse, that John Thomas would care. I couldn't bear it if the warm admiration I had seen on his face earlier were replaced with distaste. But I was worrying for nothing, I told myself firmly. I was hundreds of miles away from my past, almost in a new world and certainly in a new life.

I never imagined so wonderful a time as I had that evening, with lively music and a constantly changing selection of dancing partners. Young men I had never met before flirted with me, and older men, who should have known better, did the same. But it was all in fun and I never felt uncomfortable or embarrassed by anyone's behavior. Even George Moss, older and shorter and stouter than I, grabbed me for a polka that left both of us winded.

When I told George that he was the best dancer there that evening he responded, "I'll take that as a rare compliment because you've taken a swing with everyone as far as I can tell. I can only say that homesteading must agree with you, Miss Birdwell. You're looking as fine and as pretty as a picture tonight."

"I credit fresh air," I said, still trying to catch my breath.

"Fresh Wyoming air. I can't believe I'm the only one it has that effect on." He started to reply, but John Thomas came up behind me and George gave him a rueful look.

"I'm too old for another round right now, John Thomas, so I'll hand her over to you with regret. Miss Birdwell, it was a real pleasure."

The next dance was a waltz, something pretty and slow.

"I can't keep up with you, Hope," John said, his mouth against my hair. For a moment I held myself away from him too stiffly but then, without conscious intention, I let the music take over, and before I knew it he was holding me so close that I could actually feel his heart beat against me.

How seductive this felt, I thought. How wonderfully relaxing and freeing to be held by someone and to be taken care of like this! How easy it would be to get used to the closeness and the warmth!

I smiled up at John Thomas. "I could say the same for you. Becca told me once that every eligible girl in Laramie has tried to catch your attention and it seems to me you danced with every one of those girls tonight."

"And why would my sister be saying something like that to you?" he asked, but his tone was intimate and his eyes smiling, so I didn't think I had said anything wrong.

"Well," I answered cautiously, "it just came up in the conversation one day."

"I would imagine it came up in a conversation about a red-haired woman from Denver, but I couldn't even hazard a guess about how the two of you ever got started on that topic in the first place. Becca has never let me forget that she was absolutely right, and I was simple and stupid."

"Not stupid." I stopped in the middle of the floor, nearly causing several couples to bump into us. "Maybe simple but not stupid, John. Don't ever say that about yourself. It's never stupid to care for people. You were young and that woman should never have taken advantage of your youth like that. She ought to have been ashamed of herself."

He gave me a curious look and pulled me back into his arms. "Anytime you want to spring to my defense, you go right ahead. It gives your eyes more sparkle than diamonds. But I *was* stupid, not to mention pig-headed, stubborn, and know-it-all. My family will be the first to agree that I get like that sometimes."

"Really? I hadn't noticed." I felt, more than heard, his low laughter.

"I deserve that, I guess, although I've tried to be on my best behavior around you tonight and not boss you around."

The music stopped, the orchestra took a break, and we walked toward the refreshment table, John forgetting to let go of my hand.

"You can boss me around all you want, John Thomas, I'm still going to do what I think is right, but I believe I prefer it when we agree on things."

"Which has happened when?"

I gave his question exaggerated thought before I replied, "You're right. No particular instance comes immediately to mind, but there's always a first time. I don't think we should give up expecting it to happen."

"I have no intention of giving up on anything about you."

He would have said more, I think, but we were interrupted by the sweet, melodious sound of a fiddle. The tone held more of the resonance of a concert hall violin, so lovely, so passionate and soaring above the noise of the crowd that everyone grew still.

"Listen. How beautiful! Who is it that's playing?"

"That's my Uncle Billy," John stated casually and then added, "From the look on your face, I guess I take his talents for granted. My mother says that even as a boy Uncle Billy had the gift of music, and as far back as I can remember he's played, sometimes for weddings and sometimes for funerals, but he's always played."

I stepped away to get a glimpse of the man playing the fiddle on the band platform, no vacant childlike expression on his face now, but eyes closed and lips smiling slightly. Intent on the instrument tucked under his chin, Uncle Billy had a dignity and poise that made him a different person entirely from the man who had sat in the rocking chair by the kitchen window smiling almost foolishly at nothing in particular.

I applauded with everyone else after he was done, but he was uninterested in the crowd and their response. Instead he scanned the gathering with increasing anxiety until he spotted Lou Davis. Then he gave her a big grin, obviously relieved and happy to find her, as if Lou's approval was all he wanted.

That was the first I had seen Lou all evening. She made her way through the crowd and upon reaching the platform, raised her head to say something to Uncle Billy that only he could hear. Whatever Lou said, her comment caused his grin to broaden. When he bent down, she stood on tiptoe to give him a light kiss on the cheek, turned away, and saw me across the room.

Lou Davis wore a full-skirted dress of soft raspberry rose with long, mutton sleeves, a white lace collar, and a sparkling brooch at her throat. The dress's design initially appeared so simple and unassuming that my mother would never have looked at it twice, but it was perfect on Lou Davis, as elegant and uncomplicated as she was. She mouthed a hello to me, waved briefly, and disappeared back into the crowd.

Just then a stranger came forward to ask me to dance, but before I could say anything, John Thomas said firmly, "This dance is already taken, Les, so go find another partner somewhere else. I think I saw Letty Meier by the punch bowl just waiting for you." John took me by the arm and led me back out onto the dance floor. "If I don't dance with you, Hope, I'll lose you again."

"It would take more than that to lose me, John Thomas," I said aloud without thinking, and then to cover the feelings I hoped he hadn't been able to hear in my tone, added, "I'm not going to take the chance of missing my ride home tonight."

I believe he had heard my murmured comment and I'm not sure he was fooled by my quick additional comment, so I was glad the band played a fast two-step, and both John and I needed to pay close attention to our feet. Otherwise, I think he'd have been able to read more in my face than I would have wished.

Because sometime during the evening, at some unnamed, unknown, and unexpected moment, I fell in love. One minute I was the same woman that had walked out of her doorway a few hours earlier and the next everything had changed.

I didn't know it could happen like that, that you could see a certain face for hours and feel only admiration and the next moment, without warning, discover that the same face caused your heart to race and a curious warmth to creep all the way up to the crown of your head. One moment you could view gray eyes with objectivity and the next find yourself lost in them, wanting nothing more than to see your own reflection in their depths.

The realization was a great surprise and even something of a disappointment, not immune after all but just like Pansy, just like my mother, susceptible to a compliment and a handsome face.

This won't do, I told myself sternly, and then, enveloped by John Thomas's scent and his arms, mentally added, Won't do tomorrow, anyway, but for tonight it will do just fine.

Riding home together in the moonlight of a cool, early-May night, it was as natural as could be to sit close with my hand tucked under his arm. I had the ridiculous, really shameful, inclination to rest my head on his shoulder, be lulled by his warmth and the steady sound of the horse's hooves against the packed road.

So this is what it's like to be in love, I thought with some wonder, this feeling of comfort and well-being and security. I had expected something more impassioned and less contented. I told myself I would approach my feelings more rationally later when I was out from under the concerted spell of the moonlight and this man but knew it was useless to try to distance myself at the moment.

Truth be told, I didn't even want to. I understood instinctively and in a curiously detached way that this evening had the potential to complicate my life and get in the way of my plans. Whether I would ultimately allow that to happen was not something I could consider objectively while I was so aware of John's warmth through his coat and shirt. Too many conflicting emotions swirled around inside me at the moment to be dispassionate about anything. I must have made some sound because he turned to look at me.

"Don't tell me that was a sigh and you're actually tired? If the orchestra hadn't packed up, you'd still be dancing."

"That was the most fun I've ever had in my life. I'd do it again tomorrow if I could, but I suppose you can have too much of a good thing."

"I'm not sure that's true, and I'd enjoy debating that with you sometime but not tonight. Spring round-up starts tomorrow and those are a couple of pretty grueling weeks, so I think I'll just relish the evening."

"Will you and your father both be gone?"

"Not exactly. Years ago the whole family went along on round-up. I can just barely remember Becca strapped onto my mother's back like a little papoose. After Katherine was born, my parents would load all us kids in the wagon and the family would keep up that way. Mother did all the cooking. She always said she had only one rule for her married life and that was that she wouldn't sleep apart from my father, so they did whatever it took to be together. By the time Gus was born, we had enough hired help, and my father was able to make it home at night."

"The people I worked for, the Gallaghers, were so different from your parents," I remarked thoughtfully. "I guess I thought that's how everybody lived."

"How was that?"

"Distant would be the best way to describe it. They never talked to each other, really talked, that I ever heard. Mr. Gallagher was always gone to his business or his club, and Mrs. Gallagher was involved in charity and church work. It was as if they lived in the same house but in entirely different worlds. Their big house was always quiet, not like your house, and they never—" I paused, thinking I had probably gone too far, but at John's prompting I finished, "—never touched each other or looked at each other with affection or shared a laugh or did any of the things your parents do. The only emotion I ever saw in the years I was there was when Mrs. Gallagher got the news that her husband was dead and that was just because I heard her crying in her room one night. I always thought, What was the use of being married if you never talked to each other? It didn't make sense to me."

"It doesn't make sense to me either, but I don't think my parents are typical when it comes to each other."

"No?"

"I've been around enough to realize that there's more between them than what a lot of people have. Laramie has its share of unhappy marriages and divorces. Wyoming can be hard on people, can make them hard, and sometimes I think that's what's normal, not the emotion my parents share."

We turned onto the rough drive that led up to my cabin. The moonlight was so bright it was as if someone had lit electric lights all along the way.

"John Thomas," I began, then interrupted my thought to ask, "How did you get two first names, anyway?"

"I'm named after my father and my father's younger brother Thomas, who died in the Civil War. *John Thomas* was my mother's idea, and my father says that he knew early on there were some things you didn't argue with her about, and my name was one of them. But I think the name pleased him, and he didn't spend much time protesting."

"I never could figure out what possessed my mother to name me Hope. I never knew her to be poetic."

"Maybe she had dreams you didn't know about."

That was an arresting thought. Mother had lived more in the present than anyone I'd known, never planning for the future or dwelling on the past, never reaching for a goal, always content with the pleasure of the moment. But had she had dreams, after all, that in my youthful self-centeredness I'd never recognized and certainly never asked about?

Lately thinking about her so saddened me that I purposefully pushed away any memories of her. I didn't have any more nights to spare crying in front of the fire.

"I'm sorry, Hope. Did I say something wrong? I didn't mean to say anything to hurt you." We pulled up in front of my cabin, and John turned in the seat to look at me. "You were so sad for a minute"—he put a palm to the side of my face—"and you have a face that was made for happiness."

For just a moment I wanted to close my eyes and curl into that touch, but the thought was so dangerously alluring that I pulled away instead.

"No, you didn't say anything wrong. It was just a momentary memory, nothing to apologize for."

He took his hand away as if my cheek had suddenly become a hot iron and climbed down from the seat to come around to my side.

I took John's extended hand and climbed down quickly, not giving him a chance to reach for me or try to swing me down. Then we just stood there, my hand still in his and the moonlight turning his black hair to silver. We were as motionless as a photograph. I started to say thank you for the evening when he leaned forward and kissed me gently, not touching me with anything but his lips. After a brief moment, he said my name in a husky voice, put both his arms around me, and kissed me again, not gently at all.

My only experiences with a man's touch had been unpleasant and unwelcome, so I was completely unprepared for the pleasure of that kiss, for the spark of response it kindled in me and the unplanned, instinctive movement of my own arms that went around his neck and pulled him down closer to me. Who would have thought that a man's lips could be that soft or that their touch could fill every part of a person's insides with a deliciously warm, almost burning, sensation? For a moment after that kiss he held me nestled in what seemed a perfect fit against his chest, the top of my head tucked comfortably under his chin. Then he put his hands on my shoulders and pushed me far enough away so he could look at my face.

He stumbled over my name, stopped and cleared his throat, then began again. "Stop looking like that, Hope."

His words flustered me. I thought perhaps I had acted in a way he considered improper, even shameful, although his tone didn't sound disapproving.

"Like what? I can't stop if you don't tell me what I'm doing wrong."

"Who said anything about wrong? It's those eyes of yours and that hair." His voice was rough. "There oughta be a law." I realized he intended a compliment.

"I could wear a hood over my head if that would help."

"God forbid. Your smile lights up everything within two miles, and I wouldn't want to be deprived of that." He disengaged himself from me, and I felt suddenly bereft and cold. "If you don't go in and I don't go home, I'll be in more trouble than I already am, but you made the man in the moon dance tonight." At my questioning look he added, "It's something my mother always said to us kids if she was planning something special or exciting for us. The man in the moon is dancing, she'd say, and we'd know to expect something wonderful."

He stood there mutely, just looking at me, and I felt suddenly shy.

"I had a splendid time tonight, John Thomas. It was kind of you to ask me to go with you when you could have had your pick of anyone."

He frowned.

"I don't like it when you talk like that, as if I'm doing you some kind of favor. Kindness had nothing to do with anything. The fact is I wouldn't have gone to the dance at all if I couldn't have gone with you. There's not another woman around who can match you in looks or spirit. I'm the one who should be thanking you, Hope, because I know there wasn't a single man there tonight, and some married ones if I read things right, who didn't envy me."

No one had ever paid me such a fulsome compliment and I was speechless.

"You're shivering," he went on. "You need to go in and I need to go home."

I thought if I were a different kind of woman, I'd reach up and pull him right back to me. I didn't think I could ever get enough of the feel and the smell of him, and I certainly didn't want to say good night, but I was still possessed of that small voice of caution and carefulness. John Thomas was right to pull back, and if he wasn't going to hold me, it definitely was too cold to stand outside any longer.

From the buggy seat he said, "I'll be gone the next few days, but if you need anything, Mother'll be home."

"I can't imagine what I'd need," I replied from the doorway, my common sense emerging now that he was at a distance, "but if I do, you can be sure that's where I'll head."

"All right then. Well, good night."

John Thomas still made no motion to move, simply sat there with the reins in his hands looking at me. Finally, with a visible shake of his shoulders and an audible deep breath, he straightened, gave a little wave, and started on his way home.

I stood in the doorway and watched him until the darkness swallowed him up and then continued to stand there, gazing at the spot where he'd disappeared, bemused and now concerned about this unforeseen turn of events.

This is not good, I told myself. The confusing emotions I felt whenever I was around that handsome young man were definitely going to get in my way. I had learned something about John Thomas Davis that night, but I had learned more about Hope Birdwell, and it was that self-knowledge I found most troubling.

I lit a small fire and crawled into bed, believing I wouldn't be able to sleep, my mind too busy with memories and questions. I hadn't thought myself capable of enjoying and responding to a man's touch. My only experiences had seemed forced and distasteful, and I assumed I had a cold nature. Now I knew differently. Not a cold nature at all but just the opposite, finding nothing repugnant or unpleasant in John's attentions.

If I were completely honest with myself, there had been a moment when I would have welcomed, and in fact had been tempted to initiate, an even more intimate and personal touch from him.

Not good, I thought again. I was more Bea Birdwell's daughter than I had supposed, surely more than I wished.

Isn't life full of surprises? I asked myself, not feeling delight at the question this time but a disquieting mix of annoyance and fear, before I fell deeply and innocently asleep.

Chapter 8

*I*n the morning I deliberately recalled the night before as if it were a bruise that I needed to poke gently to see if it still hurt. I tested a guarded mental picture of the expression in John Thomas Davis's gray eyes as he looked at me in the moonlight, cautiously revisited our kiss, closed my eyes and tried to feel the warmth of his hands, all to determine if my feelings remained sincerely engaged or I had merely succumbed to the heady mixture of novelty, moonlight, and excitement. Pulling my old work dress over my head, I didn't know if I felt gratified or disappointed to find a small but steady flame burning in my heart that had not been there yesterday morning.

"How could you let that happen, Hope Birdwell?" I scolded myself as I turned the corner of the cabin heading toward the stream to get fresh water. I ran into Fergus as I did so, who steadied me with a hand.

"You need to watch where you're going, Hope, instead of being so busy maintaining a conversation with yourself."

"But it's always such an intelligent and agreeable conversation, that I can't bring myself to give it up. Besides, you talk to yourself, too, Fergus. I've heard you."

"I'm talking to the sheep." His huffy response made me grin.

"Of course, you are, and I'm the Queen of England." I patted his arm. "Your secret's safe with me as long as you return the favor."

He fell into step beside me. "You're in fine fettle this morning. You must have enjoyed the dance."

"I had a wonderful time," I said, trying to keep any undue warmth out of my voice. Whatever I felt was my secret, and I wasn't sharing it with anyone, not even my Scot friend. "I danced every dance, and we didn't come home until the orchestra packed up first."

"I thought I heard the rattle of a buggy well after midnight."

"I don't think you could hear anything over the bleating, the coughs, and the wheezes of those animals of yours—of ours, I should say. But if we woke you up, I'm sorry."

"I was awake. Young Davis took good care of you, I'm thinking." More of a question than a statement and as intrusive as I had ever known Fergus to be. I didn't know how to take the remark.

"Yes, very good care," I replied coolly, then went on more briskly, "I'm making fresh coffee, Fergus. Are you interested in breakfast?"

He couldn't have missed the fact that I didn't want to talk about young John Davis with him.

"Nay, I think not. I was coming to tell you that I'll be off this morning."

"Off?" I repeated blankly. "You mean you're leaving now?"

"Aye. It's time. Probably past time. The woolies have eaten the grass down to the root all along the Wildflower and they need new pasture. You knew I planned to be on my way."

"I guess I did, but I fooled myself into believing it wouldn't really happen. Can't you leave tomorrow so I can fix you a few meals to take with you?"

"No need. I won't starve. I've lived off my own cooking for the last fifteen years and seem to have survived. Don't look like that, Hope. You'll be fine and I'll be back in the fall."

I sat the bucket on the ground and reached up to put my arms around him. He was taken off guard, surprised and holding himself rigid for a moment, and then he crushed me in a great hug.

"I'll miss you, Fergus, I will. Come back this way and don't forget about me."

He let me loose and flicked a finger against my cheek. "No chance of that happening, lass. You're not to worry now; I'll take good care of your lambs."

"It's not the lambs I'll be worrying about. You're the one who needs to take care."

Later in the day I stood at the back of the cabin looking down toward the creek, then followed the ascending line of hills up behind the stream until they disappeared into the next layer of shadows. The expanse of grasslands sat empty and quiet, no herder's wagon, no endless milling flocks of sheep, no dogs yipping at the creatures' heels, no great bear of a man striding in the middle of it all. I had told Fergus the truth. I really would miss him. I already did.

The weather held dry and warm all that week, and I did nothing but work the soil. I thought I had gained sufficient experience from working in the Gallaghers' gardens, but those well-bred plots were nothing like tough Wyoming earth. Digging through the sod and heavy dirt was a tedious, frustrating process, and only the mental picture of the green and generous results I anticipated from my labors kept me going.

I was lonely, too. The uniqueness of those first few honeymoon weeks on my own had worn off, and without the comforting sound of the sheep or a companionable cup of tea with Fergus, I felt isolated and vulnerable. Not so self-sufficient after all, I realized humbly, and not so different from everyone else, all of us sharing the common, human necessities of life.

Toward the end of that week, a wagon rumbled down the lane. The man driving and the woman next to him were so alike they had to be brother and sister, both fair with broad, ruddy faces and brown eyes.

"Klaus Haberdink," the driver said as introduction, reaching down to shake my hand. "This is my sister Elsa. George Moss said you were interested in chickens."

I went to peer into the back of the wagon. "Yes, a couple of laying hens. I have a yearning for fresh eggs."

Mr. Haberdink climbed down and lifted out the crate, stirring an outraged clucking.

"Pick what you want."

He quoted a price that seemed reasonable, and because I had been a city girl most of my life and thus wasn't as knowledgeable as I wished, I asked innocently, "Do they need a rooster?"

Elsa Haberdink, who had more bulk than her brother and so was making a slower dismount from the wagon, gave a boisterous whoop of laughter.

"Missy, every female needs a rooster at one time or another. You can't have reached the age you're at without knowing that." Her brother gave her a look of rebuke, but I laughed out loud.

"I believe you're right, but I was really talking about these hens."

I liked Elsa Haberdink. She reminded me of some of the good-natured women who had worked with my mother years ago, practical women with an earthy humor and a no-nonsense attitude about life.

After more discussion she and her brother ended up staying for tea, using the crate of chickens as a third chair.

"We heard there was some crazy young woman out here," commented Elsa. "We live north of you, north of the Davises, too, and we don't get into town very often, but I told Klaus we should stop just to see if what folks were saying was true." She looked me over in a thorough but good-natured manner. "You don't seem so crazy to me."

I was more surprised than annoyed that people didn't have better things to do with their time than talk about me.

"That probably depends on who you ask," I answered. "It's sure a lot harder than I thought it would be to get settled in, and I admit there are times I think I must be crazy to consider homesteading. But I'm not giving up just yet."

"Watch out for the coyotes now," advised her brother. "They can hear and smell them chickens for miles, and they'll be visiting, looking for supper before you know it. You should think about covering that shed door with wire and keeping them chickens in there out of harm's way."

After the Haberdinks left, I thought Klaus's suggestion had merit and made a mental measurement of the doorway. The thought of my defenseless hens ending up as some wild creature's supper didn't thrill me, but between some protective fencing and the rifle, which I was getting good at, I thought I could keep my chickens safe enough.

On my next trip into Laramie, I bought a small roll of wire fencing and hooked it to the handle bars. George Moss watched me from the doorway.

"You got that garden in now?"

"Almost, but I wish someone would have warned me what a job it would turn out to be."

"You wouldn't have believed it, and I don't think it would have mattered to you anyway. By the way, I hear everybody's back from roundup."

"Is that so?" I said coolly, thinking the teasing in his voice was a little impertinent.

George was uncowed by my chilly tone, however, and gave me a knowing half-smile before he went back inside. On the way home I decided there was more gossip going on around town than was healthy, and people ought to mind their own business. But I still felt like singing the whole trip home, and I suppose that wasn't entirely because it was such a pretty day.

Even now I think of those early weeks as the calm before the storm, a time overflowing with innocence and hope. I had the unfettered belief that all my plans would work out, that I could work hard and make a place for myself, that there was nothing that could possibly interfere with my dreams. The future would come together exactly as I pictured it, and why shouldn't it, after all? Hadn't I thought everything through? Didn't I have a plan?

Late in the afternoon I was clumsily nailing wire netting to the doorway of the shed, trying to figure out how to leave a flap open so I could still go in and out without compromising the hens' safety. Thinking the issue through too intently, I stopped paying attention to the task at hand and missed the nail entirely, hitting my thumb with enough force to bring tears to my eyes. I let loose with a word that ladies weren't supposed to know, let alone use, while I squeezed my thumb with the other hand to stop the throbbing.

"Now that," pronounced John Thomas, "was scandalous." I had been so focused that he'd come up behind me without me hearing his approach.

I felt a quick flare of happiness at the sight of him but responded mildly, "People who don't announce their arrival shouldn't complain about what they hear. Just like eavesdroppers, they have no one to blame but themselves if they overhear something objectionable."

"I'm shocked that a well-bred woman like you would know that kind of language," but he was grinning at me when he said that, and I don't think he was shocked at all.

"I never made any pretense to being well-bred, whatever that means. Maybe you have unrealistic expectations."

"Maybe I do. That remains to be seen," and I knew the comment held more meaning than its face value.

He had walked up behind me and was close enough for me to see the deep corals and pinks of the late afternoon sky reflected in his eyes. At that moment I knew there would never be another man to suit me except John Thomas Davis. There wasn't a thing about him that I didn't fine pleasing, but that was information I had to hold pretty close. It would never do for him to discover how I truly felt. What kind of power over me would such knowledge give him?

"Garden's in, I see."

I held out my hands, palms up. "Yes, and I have the blisters to prove it. I'd better see something growing there."

"Or else what?" He was laughing at me again.

"Or else Mother Nature is going to get an earful. How was your week?"

"All right. Long."

The silence that fell as we stood looking at each other wasn't awkward exactly, more like expectant, as if there were something essential that needed to be said, but we couldn't find the right words to say it. The extended pause became too much for John Thomas.

"I just came by to see how you were doing," speaking the innocuous sentence simply to fill the lengthening quiet.

"I'm doing fine, thank you."

Another pause.

"Campbell must have moved on. I don't hear any sheep."

"Yes, Fergus left a few days ago. I didn't expect to be so lonely without him. You can really get used to having someone around."

"I know."

Because I thought he was going to say more, things I didn't want to hear just then, I hurried the conversation along.

"I haven't heard if my order's in from Chicago yet. Would you mind checking with George Moss the next time you're in Laramie to see if the loom's arrived?"

"I'd be happy to, and I can drop it off when it comes. You'd be hard pressed to fit a loom in your basket and bicycle it home."

"I could put it on wheels and pull it home behind me, I suppose, but your bringing it by would be easier for me."

"I'm happy to help. And it will give me an excuse to stop by and see you again." I looked for evidence of teasing in his gray eyes but found none.

"If you needed an excuse, which you don't. I hope you know by now there's not a person in your family who's not welcome here. If I lived to be a hundred, I could never repay everything you and your family have done for me."

The little furrow between his brows that signified his annoyance or displeasure deepened noticeably at my words.

"No one expects repayment, Hope. That's not how it works around here. And I wasn't speaking on behalf of my whole family."

"I know you weren't," I responded simply, "but I was."

He gave me a quick, searching glance and backed up. "I'm expected home, so I'd better get moving."

"Greet your mother for me."

He swung himself into the saddle. "I will. Have you had time for any rifle practice?"

"Yes. You'd be surprised and proud of my progress. I hit the can the other day dead on."

"Why would that surprise me? As far as I can tell, you usually do exactly what you set your mind on doing. If you're not careful, I'll have you riding a horse next."

I looked doubtfully at the huge animal on which he so casually sat.

"If that ever happens, John Thomas, I guarantee you the best pie you've ever eaten."

"Miss Birdwell, you don't realize what a betting man I am. That's a challenge I can't refuse."

Watching him go, I hadn't imagined that a person could have the contradictory feelings I was experiencing. How was it possible to feel relief that he was gone, his departure a welcome reprieve from the almost painful feelings of attraction and pleasure I felt in his presence and yet still want to run after him down the lane, calling his name and begging him not to leave? If that was what love was all about, I was pretty sure I didn't like it, except for those times when I liked it a lot.

John delivered the loom and the spinning wheel at the end of the next week. During the intervening days I had time to give myself an on-going and exhaustive lecture about my goals for the immediate future, none of which included any kind of involvement with any man anywhere. That wasn't in the plan or on the schedule, I told myself sternly, so you need to get over it.

John Thomas and Curly unloaded the loom and the wheel and set them up in the back room of the cabin.

"Gonna get hot back here in the summer," Curly observed.

"I suppose I could put the loom up on the roof," I remarked brusquely, "which you'll notice is the only space I have left in this place, but since I don't like heights, I believe I'm better off with it back here."

Then I felt bad that I'd spoken sharply and added, "The spaces between the boards still let a good breeze through, so I don't think it will be all that bad." I walked outside with them. "I've said thank you to you folks more than I should be allowed to, but I do appreciate your help. I couldn't have done all this by myself. The man in the moon is dancing at my house now."

John smiled at the reference and said, "You'll be busy for a while then."

"I have plenty to do to fill the summer," I answered happily. "George Moss has already said he'll look at the cloth I weave, and if he thinks it has merit, he'll buy from me to resell in his store. I can never be as good as the woman who taught me, but I have a steady hand on the loom and a good eye for design, so I don't think he'll be disappointed. At the end of summer, people will be ready to think about staying warm this winter, and I'm hoping they'd rather buy from a hometown girl than the Sears catalog." I stopped abruptly, then added, "I guess with only a few months residence, I can't really call myself a hometown girl, can I? But I feel like one. I feel like I've lived here forever."

I knew John wanted to say something, but fortunately with Curly present, he thought better of it. I say *fortunately* because I had resolved to keep as much physical and emotional distance as I could between me and that tall, black-haired young man sitting next to Curly on the wagon seat. It seemed to me that if John Thomas didn't talk to me and didn't touch me, I'd be just fine.

"If you need anything, just let us know," was all John Thomas ended up saying.

Later, looking around at the newly planted garden, the impromptu chicken coop, and the carded wool ready to be spun, I thought that all I needed now was time.

Not long after her son's visit, Lou Davis rode over to bring me a gift.

"I heard you were putting in your garden, and I wanted to bring you these." She handed me a small envelope with the name of the contents written on the outside.

"Sunflower seeds?"

"I'm letting you in on one of our family traditions," she said, smiling. "I plant a stand of sunflowers every spring to the amusement of my neighbors and my family. I've had my share of tragedy with those seeds over the years, but by now folks know that they tromp through my sunflower garden at their own peril, and my children are careful not to let the chickens anywhere near the seeds. Years ago there was one especially painful episode you'll have to ask John Thomas about sometime."

"But why sunflowers?"

"Kansas was my home for my first twenty-five years, Hope. It's where my parents and my sister are buried, and it will always be special to me. I don't imagine you've ever been to Kansas, but if you went in the summer, you'd see sunflowers everywhere. They're hearty and strong, and I've known them to survive drought and locust and tornado and anything else you can think of. There's nothing like coming up over a ridge, thinking you'll see nothing but more empty horizon, more flat and dusty fields on the other side, and finding a stand of sunflowers instead, their big yellow faces following the sun." I thought I detected a hint of longing in her tone.

"Are you still homesick for Kansas?"

"Homesick." Lou repeated the word slowly and thoughtfully as if she'd never heard it before. "It's a funny word, isn't it? Sick of home. Sick for home." After the smallest pause she answered my question. "No. I couldn't get homesick for Kansas when I'm home right now. This is my home right here."

"But I can tell from the tone of your voice that you loved Kansas. Was it hard to leave?" Her eyes widened in honest surprise.

"Oh, no. John was headed for Wyoming, and I wasn't about to let him go anyplace without me. I had a happy childhood in a wonderful place called Blessing, Kansas, and it's true I loved it there, but when I met John, I found out I had been all wrong about what home was."

"I don't know what you mean."

"I know you don't, not yet anyway. You must think I'm talking in riddles, but someday I guarantee you'll know exactly what I'm talking about. Someday you'll understand what it means to be home."

I looked over at my small, snug, weathered cabin. "I think I understand *home* now."

She shook her head in disagreement but responded kindly, "No, you don't, but it took me twenty-five years to figure it out, so you're still way ahead of where I was at your age. Anyway, plant the seeds in a nice sunny spot and water them when you think of it. Then in the fall you can harvest the seeds and plant them again next summer."

I liked her assumption that I would still be here next year at this time, that I could make it through the summer and survive the dire Wyoming winter everyone warned me about.

Except for his eyes, I had never thought John Thomas bore much resemblance to his mother. The chestnut curls showing under her hat blazed red in the sunlight, looking nothing like John's raven black hair, and she was slimmer and certainly more graceful than he, but there was something in the way she sat in the saddle so confidently—a "straight-up" rider I'd heard it described—that made me think of him. Then again maybe everything made me think of him, and wasn't that a sobering thought?

"Fergus must be gone, Hope." Lou's voice held a question.

"Yes, for a couple of weeks now. It's lonelier than I expected it to be without him, not that I don't have enough to keep myself busy."

"It's easy to get used to having someone around, I know. Do you need anything?"

I need to stop mooning over your son, I thought to myself, but only said, "Not unless you can get me a few more hours in the day. Otherwise, I'm fine."

As if in response to my joking request to Lou, the days grew longer and lighter as June approached. I was soon caught up in the rhythm of the loom, the soft swish of the shuttle, and the steady hard click of the pedals.

Mrs. Paine, the Gallaghers' housekeeper, had taught me the art of weaving. She, always formal and circumspect in appearance and dress, had pulled me aside one day to ask if I would be interested in learning to weave, her manner somehow furtive as if the idea of lessons was unsuitable to her station or a waste of time that should be spent on something more worthwhile. Yet a loom was set up in the storage rooms behind the kitchen for all to see and its presence was hardly a secret to anyone in the house. I sometimes thought the housekeeper acted that way because she enjoyed weaving a great deal and thus somehow assumed it must be wrong.

Whatever her motivation, Mrs. Paine was very skilled at the activity, fast and instinctively creative with design and color. I soon realized I didn't possess her level of inventiveness, but I learned to work equally as fast with a technique almost as good, and I know she was pleased with my progress. I never saw her happier than when she was weaving, both she and the shuttle humming along.

Like The Professor she was a patient, good teacher, and I think she developed a fondness for me during the course of those lessons. The shared craft seemed to turn us into conspirators, spinning our own thread and weaving our own material there in the back room, partners in a secret vocation. Now the recollection seems slightly peculiar, but at the time I was young and anxious to learn as much as possible as quickly as possible, so I didn't give the odd circumstances a second thought. I have added Mrs. Paine to my mental list of people whose lives have intersected mine in a seemingly random manner and yet have ended up affecting my future in a direct and significant way.

Like riding a bicycle, weaving is a skill that, once learned, is easily recalled, so it didn't take me long to regain pleasure in the sound and the feel of the process. When I finished my first project, a rag rug for my floor, I spread it out in the yard and sat back on my heels to admire it. Practicality aside, I was proud of the effort and the finished product. It wasn't the most beautiful floor covering I'd ever seen, how could it be, made as it was from old worn scraps of clothes that even rough sheepherders couldn't wear any more? But the rug was tightly woven, substantial, and precisely edged. Mrs. Paine would have been proud of a finished product that would last through many Wyoming winters.

The day stands out as one of double accomplishment. Well before sunrise I was awakened by my hens' loud, panicked squawking coming from the shed next door. I knew their racket had to be caused by the presence of some wild and uninvited menace and grabbing the rifle I stormed outside to discover a gray-brown, mangy, doglike animal with a sharp snout and full tail intently scrabbling to get around or under the wire that covered the shed's doorway.

We could see each other clearly in the moonlight, and as I approached, the beast turned to look at me, curling back its upper lip and showing very pointed teeth.

"I wouldn't plan on chicken dinner anytime soon," I said to the creature grimly and without a thought, almost as if I didn't know I was doing it, I raised the rifle to my shoulder. The coyote backed up in a slow and slinking manner and turned to run. I hesitated for a moment. I had never killed anything, not even a chicken for chicken dinner, but these were my hens, and I wasn't about to share them. I pulled the trigger and, over the sound of the rifle, I heard the creature give a sharp yelp and saw it drop.

I was still a city girl at heart, I guess, because I felt sad about that killing. Dead, the coyote only looked like a scraggly, skinny, hungry dog that had come looking for a quick supper. I crouched next to it and apologized out loud.

"I'm sorry, but my hens are off limits. You should have stuck with rabbits."

I left the carcass there to bury in the morning, and walking back to the cabin, felt a strange mixture of exhilaration and regret. I knew I could do whatever I had to do to survive, do it by instinct, and not tremble a bit. At the same time, I wished everything could simply coexist. With so much death in the world, so much loss and grief, I wasn't proud that I had contributed to it, even a little bit.

But that was a foolish, citified, and too sensitive way of thinking, I told myself as I stopped to gaze up at the night sky, probably the result of the moonlight making everything seem a little dreamlike and mysterious. This was the real world after all, with nothing mysterious about the wide open spaces of Wyoming. I had no one to depend on but myself and I couldn't afford to be fanciful.

In the morning the dead animal looked even more pitiful to me, and I dragged it by its tail farther away from the house to bury it, interrupted in the middle of the chore by John Thomas.

"I wondered where you were," he said, walking down the small decline behind the cabin.

When he saw what I was doing, he volunteered, "Here, let me do that" and reached for the shovel. My brief hesitation caused the frustration I heard in his tone. "It's just a neighborly offer, Hope. I'm not saying you wouldn't do a fine job on your own without my help."

I handed him the shovel with a smile. "I'm sorry, John. I know you think I always have to have my own way, but I'm just used to taking care of myself. I didn't mean to be rude. I'd appreciate it if you would dig for a while because my hands haven't recovered from putting in the garden."

John was surprised by my conciliatory tone and words and met my smile with a full one of his own.

"That's all right. I grew up in a house of women a lot like you, so I'm used to being taken to task for saying the wrong thing."

I became too interested in the way the muscles along his shoulders and back pulled against his shirt while he dug, and when he said something to me, I had to ask him to repeat his words.

"I asked how many tries it took before you hit him."

"Just one, sad to say for the coyote, because he must have seen from my expression that I was going to teach him a serious lesson about bothering people's chickens. He took off like his tail was on fire."

"Good aim."

"Good teacher."

We shared that same smiling moment we had experienced once before, each in tune with the other's thoughts. Then John Thomas took the back of the shovel and pounded down the mounded dirt.

"The Cattlemen's Association still pays for coyote pelts. Some people make a living off of killing the critters." We walked companionably up the hill toward my cabin.

"I wouldn't want to make my living by killing anything on a regular basis," I said. "I haven't got the stomach for it."

"I poked my head inside looking for you and saw your new rug. Did you make that?"

"I did. I was awfully tired of a dirt floor."

"I could build you a wooden floor easily enough," he offered eagerly, "and I'd be happy to see if there isn't a way to rig running water from the creek to inside the cabin for you."

His was a tempting offer for a lot of reasons. Not having to trek down to the Wildflower for water every morning, noon, and evening would be wonderful. Having John Thomas around on a regular basis would be even more wonderful.

Wonderful but not wise, so I stopped abruptly and said, much too coolly and dismissively, "I could never accept that from you. It wouldn't be right. Maybe next year at this time I'll have the wherewithal to hire the work done." I could tell from his expression that my words had hurt and angered him.

"You're a stubborn woman, stubborn to a fault. Don't you realize that a person can be too proud? Why do you think you have to do everything by yourself all the time?"

"Because I am by myself," I retorted angrily. "You conveniently forget that not everyone has access to the kind of family and resources that you have. I want to be independent, and I won't allow myself to be obligated. I may be stubborn but you're presumptuous. When did I ask for your opinion, and what gives you the right to be critical of me?"

"I wasn't being critical. I was only making an observation."

"What nonsense! Of course you were criticizing me. How else would you interpret the word stubborn? It's hardly the kind of compliment ladies swoon to receive."

My latent temper, usually well controlled and private, made me raise my voice. I stepped closer and tapped a forefinger against his chest.

"You know what annoys me the most about you, John Thomas Davis? Let me tell you. It's when you get that patronizing tone in your voice that says you know better than anybody else, especially me, and my womanly opinion counts for nothing. That really bothers me."

"And you know what—?" he started to say in a similar temper, glaring back at me. Then his expression changed, and without warning he put both hands on my shoulders, pulled me so close I could hardly breathe, and kissed me. Passionately.

After a while he continued softly, "You know what bothers me about you, Miss Birdwell? Everything. Every little thing, every freckle, that hair that it's all I can do to keep my hands out of, those green eyes, that mouth that I see in my dreams. Everything."

I raised my face to his. "Those are much nicer compliments than being called stubborn. Being critical of a woman's temperament is not particularly endearing, however true it might be. I would think some other woman might have pointed that out to you by now."

"Are you reminding me of my youthful follies?"

"Never. Unlike some people I know, I try not to dwell on the faults and imperfections of my friends."

He said in a murmur, his mouth hovering right over mine, "Friend is the nicest thing you've ever called me. It's a place to start, anyway."

The next kiss turned into something a little too intense for me, a flash of shared emotion that made me push away, both hands on his chest, and say shakily, "It's broad daylight, John Thomas, and you should probably go. I think this is most likely a mistake."

He released me instantly, stepped back, and said in a hoarse voice, "I'm sorry. I overstepped, but I'd never call it a mistake. At least it didn't feel like a mistake to me."

"I have a plan for my life that's important to me, John, a dream that I've had inside my head since I was a child. Kissing you is very agreeable, but it's not part of that plan."

"It could be."

I looked at him standing there, tall and lean and brown, serious now but capable of a warm smile that started somewhere deep within and eventually lit up his whole face. I could still taste him. You could change your dream, I thought to myself. You could include this man in the dream and see what happens.

But following on the heels of that tantalizing idea came the sobering thought of everything he didn't know about me and even more compelling, the memory of what it meant to be dependent on the whim of men. I came to my senses with a start and quickly backed away.

"No. Not now it couldn't."

"Because you have something to prove," John prodded gently.

"Yes, I guess you could put it like that, but that's not how I think of it. I can't explain it in a way that would make sense to you because your life hasn't been what mine was. But I need to be able to take care of myself and make it on my own. I don't have time for distractions."

"Is that what I am?"

I gave him a long, sober look before replying, "Oh, yes, John Thomas. You are certainly that."

"How about a distraction just once in a while?"

To my relief the serious tone was gone and he was teasing. I thought he had purposefully lightened the conversation for my benefit, and I appreciated the respite.

"I don't think it works like that," I said, responding as lightly.

"I almost forgot that I came over here for a purpose." He paused for a minute, and I could tell he was reliving the reason for his forgetfulness.

"And what would that purpose be?" I prompted.

John Thomas took a deep breath, exhaled audibly and slowly, then said, "My sister Katherine is home for a break from her schooling, and we're having a small barbecue Saturday noon to celebrate her homecoming. My mother," he emphasized the two words, "thought you might like to join us."

I looked at him doubtfully, thinking that being anywhere in the man's general proximity was temptingly unwise and just too unsettling. Apparently reading my mind, he laid his hand over his heart as if taking an oath.

"I promise I'll be on my best behavior, Hope. I apologize for today. I was out of line and it won't happen again. Please come."

"I'll bicycle over if the weather is good," I agreed finally by way of compromise, and he didn't even argue.

Later, working at the loom, I made several mistakes in the fabric and more than once had to pick apart and reweave what I was working, a rarity for me.

"This is what comes of distractions," I told myself aloud, peeved at the time wasted in rework, "and this is why I can't afford them."

I knew I had to make and sell enough woolen items this summer in order to earn enough money to survive the winter. I knew I had to nurture and tend the garden, so I could put up enough food to live on through the winter when I was told I would be snowed in without the possibility of escape. If I wasn't successful in either of those endeavors, I didn't know whether I could hold out another year with much of my cash gone, invested in the house, the garden, and the loom.

I couldn't tolerate the thought of failure, couldn't bear the idea of leaving this place, of having to go back into service, of never again knowing the intoxicating independence, the heady freedom of movement and thought that I possessed on my own land in the middle of the austere Wyoming grasslands. I couldn't risk losing everything, which was why I wouldn't allow any distractions, especially distractions as agreeable as a man's breath on my cheek or his hands in my hair. Maybe I'd have time for those diversions one day, but for the time being, they would have to wait.

Chapter 9

John Thomas had not been quite accurate in his description of the celebratory barbecue to which I'd been invited. Men were stationed at several fire pits, slowly turning large haunches of beef on spits. An equal number of tables spread across the yard, all covered with pots and bowls that gave off the most delectable aromas. And people were everywhere, filling every corner of the yard and crowding the porch.

When John Thomas came over to greet me, I told him, "If this is your idea of small, John, I'd hate to think what a large gathering would look like! Half the town must be here!"

John was on good behavior from the start, walking a careful distance away from me, his tone and manner friendly and nothing more. I felt contradictory relief and disappointment.

"That's the way it always happens with my family. One thing leads to another. The celebration started out small, but my mother kept mentioning Katherine's homecoming to people, and, of course, they all said they'd like to see her. Mother's known for setting a generous table, so I've already told my sister she shouldn't think all these people came because of her."

"Where is Katherine?"

But I wouldn't have had to ask the question. Despite the fact that she'd grown up considerably, I recognized John Thomas's younger sister from the childhood picture he'd shown me Easter Sunday and had already picked her out before he pointed. Katherine had the Davis look about her, not so much in physical appearance but in the way she carried herself, erect and confident, like both her parents, like her siblings, too.

Coming up behind us, Lou Davis rested an arm over my shoulders as she greeted, "I'm so glad you could join us, Hope. How's the garden coming?"

"Nothing green yet but I have every confidence. And I planted the sunflowers on the southwest corner of the house, so they'll get plenty of sun." John Thomas raised his eyebrows at my words.

"Those seeds have always been like gold in our house, so if Mother's shared them with you, Hope, you're the recipient of a high honor." He gave his mother a surprised and inquiring look, but she only laughed.

"I told Hope to ask you about the time you mixed my seeds with the chicken feed, John Thomas."

"The wrath of God had nothing on my mother when her sunflowers were threatened. I had to examine every inch of the chicken yard on my hands and knees, then go through the bag of feed with a spoon and hand pick out every sunflower seed. It took me a full day. My favorite time of the year and the first day of spring roundup, too. Everyone but me was gone for the entire day, even my sisters. I was about ten, so being stuck at home while my father and the hands were working out on the range was the worst punishment imaginable. Home by myself sorting through chicken feed!"

His mother didn't show a flicker of remorse at the recollection, her tone cool and unsympathetic.

"Even then, the punishment didn't begin to fit the seriousness of the crime. I had told you very clearly and on more than one occasion to leave those seeds alone. You may have noticed, Hope, that my son sometimes has a habit of doing what he wants first without considering the consequences and then apologizing later, expecting the words will make everything right as rain again."

"Yes," I responded cheerfully, "I have noticed that," and purposefully didn't look at John Thomas when I spoke.

"Come and meet Katherine," Lou invited, drawing me away from John Thomas. "I believe you have quite a lot in common with my daughter."

I didn't think so and couldn't imagine why Lou would, either. I had never gone to school, and Katherine was studying to be a doctor. That difference alone seemed insurmountable.

Close up, Katherine Davis at first seemed as daunting as I had thought, something cool and regal about her, a touch of dignified reserve, definitely her father's daughter. She had thick honey-colored hair that looked too heavy for her slender neck, hazel eyes flecked with gold, a thin face with high cheekbones, a firm chin, a straight aristocratic nose, and—an unexpectedly sensual feature in her otherwise elegant face—her mother's wide and generous mouth. From what I knew of the family, this daughter had to be younger than I, not even twenty yet, but she looked far more poised and composed than her years.

When I put out my hand to Katherine, she took it in a firm grip and gave me a searching look, then smiled. With that smile I recognized a closer resemblance to her family, especially to her father and brother, as its slow warmth eventually reached her eyes and burnished the gold flecks there. Besides her mouth, Katherine also had her mother's frank, friendly manners.

"Once I saw you come in on the bicycle, I knew who you were, Miss Birdwell. May I call you Hope? Mother has written so admiringly of you." At those words, Lou Davis drifted away leaving me alone with Katherine.

"You have it backwards, I'm afraid. Your mother's the admirable one. She's been kinder to me than anyone else in my entire life. Sometimes I feel like she's adopted me into your family."

"Do you?" Katherine gave me a look tinged with some amusement. "Be careful. Mother can't help herself, but I hope you aren't haunted by unexpected feelings of debt and obligation that independent people sometimes feel as a result of Mother's generosity."

I was surprised Katherine had so quickly identified feelings I did indeed struggle with and tried to agree with her without sounding ungrateful to her family. "Haunted is much too strong a term, but I do wonder how I'll ever repay her."

"I understand exactly. If you let it, kindness can be more of a burden than meanness. I know my parents would do anything for me and I love them for it, but I have to make it on my own. That's so important to me."

She spoke with a vehemence that identified her as a kindred spirit, and I realized that Lou Davis had been right about Katherine and me sharing a common bond that had nothing to do with education or upbringing.

I wanted to talk with Katherine further, but behind her a man said her name. Over her shoulder I saw a depth of emotion in the man's brown eyes that I well understood, but as Katherine turned to face the speaker, I watched the flare of passion disappear behind a bland friendliness as she greeted him by name.

"Who's Sam?" I asked John Thomas later.

"Sam Kincaid?"

"He's about your age but broader and taller than you, with dark eyes and hair, a mustache, and a rough face. The face of someone who's spent a lot of time outside."

"That's Sam Kincaid. He's been our foreman for a few years now, and he's a good friend, too. Why do you ask?"

"He was talking to Katherine, and I just wondered."

John Thomas gave me a quick look, and I realized he was a little jealous, that he thought I was interested in Sam Kincaid. How blind men are sometimes! Anyone with half a brain could see that Sam Kincaid didn't have eyes for anyone but Katherine, but it wasn't my place to say that. I had my own troubling issues of the heart without butting into someone else's.

I knew a number of people at the barbecue, people I had met in and around town, including Becca and Ben Wagner, George Moss, and Amos, the man from the title office who was the first person I'd met on my arrival in Laramie. The Haberdinks were there, and the young couple who ran the Second Street Bakery and Café, and the editor of the newspaper. Walking through the crowd and having people recognize me, call my name, ask how I was doing, and act as if I were an old friend gave me, for the first time in my life, a sense of belonging, a sense of home.

Later, over the laughter and conversation, I heard Uncle Billy's fiddle playing, its unmistakable sound racing along with joy, and realized he was sharing his happiness at Katherine's homecoming. I thought, but not in an envious or resentful way, how wonderful it must be to be so loved and so welcomed that parties were thrown and music played in your honor.

From where I stood I saw Katherine raise her head as she heard the music, say a quick word to the person she was with, and walk off briskly in the direction of that happy sound. From the small smile she wore, I knew she recognized the music as the gift it was intended to be and was on her way to thank the giver.

When it was time to leave, I sought out Lou and her husband, who sat shoulder to shoulder on the front porch steps. As I came around the corner, I saw John lift Lou's hand and kiss the palm, a small, intimate gesture that affected me deeply. Despite the silver hair, he so resembled his son that I had a sudden picture of myself sitting just so with John Thomas, the two of us growing older together just as his parents were.

How had Lou Davis left behind everything dear and familiar to follow this man and still managed to retain her free and sovereign spirit? Clearly she cared for her husband, but she gave no sense of being dependent on him. You couldn't know her for five minutes without realizing she was a person in her own right, a unique identity and a force to be reckoned with. Yet to my mind Lou had put herself at serious risk when she left her childhood home in Kansas to travel with her husband to Wyoming. What had she desired from life and had her expectations changed after her marriage? How had she walked the line between independence and vulnerability? How did she continue to stay true to herself and her own heartfelt needs yet find such transparent happiness sitting on the porch next to the father of her children, a man she plainly loved and respected and who openly cherished her in return? How had she—how had they?—got to the place they were now without experiencing the corrosive influence of secret regrets and lost dreams?

For years I had believed there was only enough room in a person's heart for one set of dreams. I thought marriage would have to be 'either-or,' an arrangement where one person's hopes and aspirations dominated at the expense of the other's, and that understanding of marriage kept me confused about the pleasure and the risk of loving someone. Yet something in that private moment between John and Lou Davis presented the unexpected but hopeful notion that it might be possible to love without regret and give without losing.

From the beginning, I realized that John Davis was a reserved man, not given to public demonstrations of affection, but if he realized I had seen his small intimacy, the knowledge didn't seem to bother him. In fact, he continued to sit holding his wife's hand as I said goodbye. I was surprised when he asked about the coyote, turning his remarkably clear blue eyes on me as he spoke.

"John Thomas said you only needed one shot," he remarked. "You must have steady nerves and a good eye."

"I startled the poor creature and it froze. I just took advantage of the moment."

At my words, John Davis, Senior, turned to give his wife a smile before replying to me, "Then you've learned the secret of success, Hope. It took me a lot of years to figure out that it's always about taking advantage of the moment."

"I have been told that's the secret of success in life," I agreed and noticed his grip tighten on Lou's hand.

"You've been told right. If you don't take advantage of the moment, you could lose out on everything."

I couldn't decide if John Davis was reflecting on his past or commenting about my future. Maybe both. I knew John Thomas was close to his father and respected his opinion and so might have shared something of what had passed between us. I suppose that thought should have bothered or embarrassed me, but it didn't. The older John Davis didn't need words to inspire trust and display integrity. I thought he was the kind of man who would innately do the right thing, whether that meant maintaining a confidence or being faithful to his wife. There was no way he would have shown up looking for consolation at The Sanctuary. Clearly, everything he wanted or needed was sitting next to him on the front porch.

I had already started pedaling down the Davises' drive toward the road that led home when I heard someone call my name. I stopped with one foot on the ground, my skirt bunched up, balancing the bicycle against my other leg. John Thomas sprinted up behind me, using pretty good form for a man who seemed to spend more time on horseback than on foot.

"You were leaving without saying goodbye." I detected surprise in his voice and disappointment.

I said flatly, "I told your parents goodbye because you'll recall that it was your mother who invited me, and I told Katherine I was happy to meet her because she was the guest of honor. I went looking for you but you were occupied with a pretty, brown-haired girl, and I didn't want to interrupt you."

"I've known Sarah Cassidy since we were both kids. We went to school together." I held up a hand.

"John Thomas, that's really more than I need or want to know. I was just explaining why I didn't say goodbye to you." He narrowed his eyes, a sign that he was going to say something he would later regret.

"At least Sarah Cassidy doesn't consider me a distraction."

"No? Then she can't know you very well, after all." I pushed off on the bicycle.

"Will you wait a minute?" He grabbed hold of the back of the bicycle, nearly causing me to lose my balance, and came around in front of me as I righted myself. "Just wait a minute. I only wanted to tell you that I was glad you came. That's all." His suddenly humble tone disarmed me, and I smiled in spite of myself.

"Me, too. I had a good time. I always do when I'm with your family. I really liked Katherine. I didn't think we'd have anything in common, but we had a lot more than I expected. I wish I'd been around to know her sooner."

"I wish you'd been around a lot sooner, too, but that doesn't have anything to do with Katherine. Don't give me that look. I said I'd be on good behavior, and I was, wasn't I?"

"Yes." I tried to sound as if I didn't regret his efforts.

"But I will say this, Hope Birdwell: No man in his right mind would choose brown hair once he saw how the sun turned yours to pure gold."

"I see you've taken my advice and practiced up on compliments." I was determined to keep the conversation light.

"I mean every word I say and you know it, don't you? Don't you?" He spoke in a low voice and glared at me.

I answered honestly, "I believe you're as truthful a man as your father. I don't see how you could be anything else, growing up like you did in that house with those parents."

"It matters a lot to you where and how a person grew up, doesn't it?"

"It's more important than I can explain or that you could understand, John Thomas."

"I could try."

Looking at him standing there, a good man, open-hearted and nothing hidden, nothing cluttering his conscience, I thought there was no way I could tell him that it was important to me because of who I was, what I lacked, and what I had missed out on for nearly all my life. So I only shook my head.

"It's getting late and I have to be going, John." If he stood there watching me pedal off, I wouldn't know because I didn't look back.

In June the garden began to grow, although Wyoming was nowhere as hospitable to gardeners as California had been. I had spring peas crawling across a handmade trellis, the beginnings of healthy pickle vines, peppers, frail tomato plants I doubted would survive, carrots, onions, corn, squash, and small hills of potatoes. I trudged back and forth from the Wildflower with countless buckets of water and got down on my hands and knees to remove any weed that dared intrude into my space.

"My space," I repeated jealously to each plant as I weeded and watered, "and don't you forget it. You're here by invitation only. This is my home and you will do your part to keep me here."

Toward the end of June, I packed several samples of my woven wool into the basket on my bicycle and took them into Laramie for George Moss's inspection and, I hoped, his approval. I was more than a little nervous. I'd peddle door to door myself if I had to, but it would be so much better and easier if George would buy the cloth from me and then resell it from his store shelves. He was methodical in his examination, picking up each piece of fabric to finger it, hold it up to the light, even rub it against the back of his hand.

"Hope," George said, finally, "I didn't know what to expect from you. I was worried I'd have to tell you no thanks and watch your face lose its glow, but I'm happy to say that this is exceptional cloth, as good as I could find anywhere around Laramie and better than what I could order from the catalog. It's almost hard to believe you made this."

"Well, I did," I retorted indignantly. "I'm responsible for all the carding, the spinning, and the dyeing that went into the fabric you're holding. I brought some of the items I made from my wool, too. I'm a good seamstress and I work hard."

"There's no need to carry on, young lady. I don't doubt what you're telling me. I like what I see and I believe we can do business." I know my eyes lit up.

"Mr. Moss, you couldn't have said anything more welcome. I'm so happy I could hug you. Thank you."

With a clerk in charge of the counter, the store owner and I went into the back room where we worked out the details of our business arrangement. George bought everything I brought in to show him that day and not just out of pity so I wouldn't have to carry it all home again, either, because he asked for more by the end of August.

"Whatever you get done by then, I'll buy, and we'll see how it sells. If people take an interest, I might be willing to contract for more." He ran his hand over a man's vest I had laid out. "How did you get this so soft?"

"It's all in the technique," I said, rising.

He smiled at me. "I'm not trying to steal your trade secrets, Hope. It was just an innocent question."

"I have to guard my livelihood, Mr. Moss. You're looking at the source of my survival for this winter and the next year, if not for my whole life." He walked me to the front door.

"When you're twenty, your whole life seems like a very long time, Hope, but I'd guess that you'll get other opportunities besides weaving and sewing."

"Maybe, but I don't have a crystal ball, so I can only plan one year at a time. Thank you."

I pedaled down the street to the newspaper office, stopping there as I usually did on my way out of town to pick up some reading material to take back with me. About the only thing I missed from San Francisco was being able to keep up with the news on a regular basis. By the time I got the newspaper its news was already dated, but old news was better than nothing, and after every trip into Laramie, I was able to cram several weeks' worth of events and announcements into the next few days.

The newspaper office had been an unlucky stop for me once before, and it proved to be even worse that day. I came out the front door with my hands full and tripped over someone's foot. Stumbling against the porch railing, I caught myself and turned to apologize for being clumsy, not realizing until I looked up that the outstretched foot had been staged and purposeful.

"Well, well, well. It sure has been a long time since I've seen that pretty face."

My stomach turned in such a way that I thought I'd be sick on the spot. There in front of me, swaggering and sinister, with bold eyes and a nasty smile stood Ivan Fletcher. That he should be standing on a Laramie boardwalk was so unbelievable that I was speechless.

"How about a kiss for an old friend?"

I backed away from him too hastily, almost losing my balance again as I stepped down from the boardwalk onto the ground.

"Go away," I whispered fiercely, "and leave me alone." I packed the newspapers into the basket with hands that shook and climbed onto the bicycle.

Fletcher lounged against the porch support, looking me up and down in a way that was insulting and frightening, letting his gaze linger purposefully so that I would understand exactly what he was thinking.

"I'll tell you, Hope, I wouldn't have thought you could get any prettier, but all this mountain air must agree with you. You've filled out real nice. Real nice. I kinda forgot your attractions."

I tried to catch my breath so my voice would sound steady before meeting his look full on. I had done nothing to be ashamed of, and I hated the way he made me feel, dirty and guilty as if I had.

"I don't know you and I have no intention of talking to you again. I have friends here now and if you bother me, I'll tell them. They'll take care of you."

"I heard you made friends here. Real important friends."

He straightened up, his hands still in his pockets, and sauntered down the steps to stand within an arm's length of me.

"I heard that people think a lot of you and that you've even got a beau, but I'm betting nobody knows you like I know you 'cause nobody knew your mama like I did." Something in my face must have changed because Fletcher smiled. "I bet your mama's line of work would come as a surprise to those important friends of yours, don't you think? People are the same in Wyoming as they are anywhere else, and they couldn't help but wonder if the mother was a whore, did the daughter follow in her footsteps? I know people, girlie, and believe me, your friends would look at you a lot different then, speculating about your talents and the men picturing things that would make you blush. The fine folks of Laramie might decide a woman like you's got no place in their town. They're trying awful hard to be civilized, I hear."

I stood there, mesmerized in some awful, inexplicable way by his drawling monologue until I finally pushed myself away from the porch, refusing to listen any longer.

Behind me I heard him add, "I'm not done talking to you, not by a long shot. There's an outstanding debt on your mama's account that I expect you to pay off. I wouldn't sleep too sound if I were you 'cause when you least expect me, there I'll be."

I don't remember making that ride home. I think I passed people, and I hope I greeted them in a way that wasn't suspicious, but I couldn't say for sure. I was cowed in spirit and shaken to my very core. When I got home I went into the cabin and latched the door behind me to sit on the edge of the bed with my hands pressed between my knees, trying to keep myself from trembling even more violently than I already was. What had just occurred was beyond belief. The surge of happiness and hope—yes, and pride, too—that I'd felt after talking to George Moss had vanished as if the meeting had never happened. My only memory of that visit to town was of a thin, leering, mustached face.

Many weeks ago I had crouched next to a broken chair in the very room in which I sat trembling and said to Fergus, "I don't want anything to spoil this for me." Now I despaired that what I had feared then was destined to happen, that all my plans, my home, my new friends, my hope for a bright and happy future would surely be spoiled and ruined, and for the life of me I could not think of a way out.

Unlike some problems, this one did not look better in the morning. I slept poorly for several nights, Ivan Fletcher the last thing on my mind before sleep and my first thought every morning, his menace intruding into my dreams.

For the first few days after meeting him, nothing could remove his face from in front of me. I took to carrying the rifle with me when I went outside and locking the door whenever I was working at the loom in the back room. Inside me churned a queer mixture of terror and fury that sometimes made me feel I would explode. I recognized the feeling as the same frustrated outrage I had felt at fourteen, trapped and manhandled by a stranger who saw me as some kind of helpless victim put on the earth solely for his pleasure. How dare Ivan Fletcher find me here and ruin everything! And why, oh why, hadn't I told the truth from the beginning when the topic of my background and parentage had first come up?! If I had done so, Fletcher would hold no power over me, and my freedom and independence wouldn't be at risk. I tried to think of how I could still bring up the subject.

"I'd like to tell you about my mother," I would practice out loud, picturing Lou Davis with her clear eyes standing before me, and then no further words would come. I didn't know how to proceed, how to tell the story of Bea Birdwell's life and my tagalong childhood without making it sound sordid and tawdry and pathetic. I tried to imagine telling John Thomas, too, but thought that would be even harder for me. I didn't want John's pity and I dreaded his disdain. If Fletcher began to talk about me around town, the Wagners would surely hear the rumors and George Moss and the banker and the newspaperman and that nice couple from the café, and I believed Fletcher was right. Respectable people would look at me differently after that and my life, my carefully constructed life in Wyoming, would never be the same again. How could it?

The next week the inevitable happened. With a full bucket of water in each hand, I trudged up from the Wildflower, coming around the corner of the cabin toward the garden. I heard something, maybe the snort of a horse or jangle of its bridle, and knew instantly that Fletcher was there. Anyone else would have called out and announced himself.

I dropped both buckets, the water sloshing out and drenching my skirt, and turned to go in the opposite direction, around the back of the cabin to the other side so I could somehow sneak through the front door and get to the rifle I had foolishly left propped against the wall next to the loom. I never wanted anything as much as I wanted that weapon in my hands, but I didn't move quickly enough. Fletcher came around the corner behind me and moved forward fast, grabbing my upper arm, jerking me around to face him, and dragging me toward him.

"I told you that when you least expect it, there I'll be."

I willed myself to pretend that his touch and his proximity didn't terrify me and stood very still, saying with a bravado that fooled neither of us, "You're trespassing. I'd be in my legal rights to shoot you."

"You hear that, Tony? I believe she's threatening me."

I looked over Fletcher's shoulder to see the ranch hand Tony mounted and watching from a distance behind us.

"That figures," I said, unable to keep the disgust from my voice. "If ever there were two who crawled out from under the same rock, it's the two of you."

"You have a nasty way about you and a sharp tongue." Fletcher tightened his grip on my arm. "I could take a lot of pleasure in teaching you better manners."

"You should understand what it's like here before you threaten me," I told him. "If you lay a hand on me, it won't matter who my mother was. There are people here who would find you and hang you as soon as look at you. This isn't a place you'd understand. They treat women different than how you're used to treating them. You ask Tony if I'm not right. He knows what I'm talking about. So it would be in your best interests not even to think about hurting me." Fletcher let me go.

"Maybe. But maybe teaching you a lesson would be worth the risk and I'll just take my chances. We'll just take our chances 'cause Tony might want in on the fun, too."

"Tony got beaten bloody the last time he came here uninvited. Unless he's a complete fool just longing for the feel of a rope around his neck, he should keep his distance, just like you should." I moved to step around Fletcher but he stepped in front of me.

"So you don't care if I drop a word in someone's ear about your mama and it don't matter if I start talking out loud about what I know, huh?"

"I didn't say that," I admitted unwillingly, shamed that I couldn't tell him to say what he wanted and go to the devil.

"It's what I thought, then. You're on to something here, looking to get connected to a family I'm told owns a lot of the county. Who'd have thought that the little housemaid who could hardly say boo might actually have the chance to marry into money? You won't want to mess that up, at least until the vows are said."

"You're a fool. Don't you see that the moment you open your mouth, you'll lose any power you think you have over me?"

"So what's it worth to you to keep me quiet?"

I thought quickly. "I'm not saying that anything you know could be used against me, but I like peace and quiet and I'm willing to pay for it. I have a little money saved up and I might be getting more later in the summer, so keeping out of my life could be worth your while."

After giving me a long, thoughtful look, Fletcher replied, "You might have something there, girlie. I had to leave San Francisco in a hurry because of a little trouble over one of my girls, and I didn't have time to bring a lot with me."

"What kind of trouble?" I had to ask but perversely knew I didn't want to know the details.

Fletcher reached down to his boot and pulled out a knife, short-handled to fit his grip perfectly with a long, straight, wicked blade.

"One of the tarts thought she could cheat me."

He rested the edge of the blade lightly against my cheek so I could feel its sharp, cold steel on my skin. I stood motionless, knowing that if I moved the blade would cut.

"I couldn't let that happen. If one does it, they all think they can get away with it. Those girls are my livelihood. I own them, so I had to teach her a lesson none of them would ever forget. Even in the dark, no man would look at her now."

He shifted the weapon so that the point of the knife pressed gently into my cheek and with two fingers from the other hand traced a line across my forehead, down my cheek, and under my mouth, saying as he did so, "I cut her here. And here. And here. Woman squealed like a stuck pig the whole time."

I exhaled slowly and carefully, then spoke. "So you had to leave on the run with the law after you?"

"Who thought anybody cared about what happened to a slant-eyed whore? You trip over them along the waterfront, and nobody gives a damn what happens to them."

"But somebody cared about this one."

He took the knife away but slid his hand around my neck, pressing me back against the rough wood of the cabin.

"San Francisco turned too respectable and got civilized and there's a couple of nosey women there who won't mind their own business. That's why I think I may set up shop here, right here in Laramie, Wyoming. I know you'd like that." He brought his face so close to mine I could smell his stale breath. "It didn't take me long to find out where you went. All I had to do was describe your hair and your eyes, and the man at the train window remembered you right off, so I said to myself, Someday I'll go where my little Hope went. Her mama owed me money, and I'll need to get that debt paid."

Fletcher still held the knife in one hand so all I could do was stand stiffly as if at attention, pulled back away from him as far as I could get, staring at him, wishing him dead. His dark eyes met my look with a knowing, cocky smirk.

"Oh, you'd like to kill me, wouldn't you?"

"Maybe I will some day," I said evenly. "Maybe when you least expect it, there I'll be." My words made him laugh.

"I'm setting up a stable over the Gaslight Saloon, gonna wire some of my girls and tell them to meet me here. None of them's like you, though. The way you look and the way you talk would be a real draw. I could make it worth your while."

"I'd throw myself in front of a train before I'd willingly be in the same room as you. It's bad enough I have to breathe the same air." He released me abruptly.

"Big talk now, but when it's winter and you don't have a cent because you've given it all to me to keep me quiet, we'll see how you talk. There's no telling what you might be willing to do when you're cold and hungry. It sure changed your mama's opinion of me. Now you go bring me that money you were talking about."

I slid past him, went inside, came out with the bag that held what I had recently received from George Moss, and tossed it to Fletcher's waiting hands.

Tony, who had been able to see but not hear all that had transpired, still sat on his horse. He didn't meet my eyes and I thought he seemed uncomfortable.

As I passed him I said, "You've made a deal with the devil, Tony. You had better watch your back with him around." Fletcher, counting the money, looked up.

"No, no. Tony and me are friends. We have you in common. All it took was for me to describe the girl I was looking for, and he knew exactly who it was. Ain't that right, Tony? Uppity woman, he said, that uppity woman who thinks she's better than the rest of us. I knew we were talking about one and the same." Fletcher climbed up onto the seat of the wagon he'd driven out. "This is our little secret, Hope, yours and mine. As long as you keep me happy, I'll let you keep that precious peace and quiet you like so much. Now you may think you can go crying to your cowboy and he'll protect you, but he don't know the first thing about a man like me. My guess is he plays by the rules, and that's always a big mistake when you're dealing with me. Unless they're my rules." He laughed. "You know I could hurt him, Hope, hurt him real bad, so let's keep our little business arrangement between the two of us. That way nobody gets hurt and everything can keep going just the way it is. Isn't that what you want?"

"Yes."

"Good. You'd best get to work before I come back and you're not able to give me what I want." He jangled the coins in the bag he held. "You wouldn't like what might happen. I get real upset when someone don't follow through on what they say, and you have such a pretty face, that would be a shame, a pure shame."

After he left I wanted to wash myself all over, top to bottom, just to rid myself of the smell and the feel of him. Ivan Fletcher was a bad man, as wicked as they came, and I had no doubt I was in real trouble.

I said the words out loud again: "I'd like to tell you about my mother—" and stopped again. Telling the truth seemed the only way out for me, but I still couldn't figure out how to do it. If I wasn't careful, I thought it could get too late for the truth. Maybe it already was.

Chapter 10

Outwardly in the days that followed nothing changed. When I wasn't working in the garden, I was adding to the pile of woven fabric I was preparing for George Moss. In the mirror's reflection I looked the same, too, although, despite my broad-brimmed hat, the sun had turned my hair a shade more golden and my skin too brown to be fashionable.

But inside me everything had changed. Every click of the loom, every stitch I took, every soft and beautiful thing I made was going to Ivan Fletcher, and that knowledge stripped the work of joy. The only item I resolutely kept separate was the wool bed cover I was working on for the Davises, my thank you for all their kindness. When finished, the blanket would be beautiful, dyed in the warm colors of a Wyoming sunset with a woven edge of deep purple that reminded me of the shadows the mountains threw at dusk. No one should have that blanket but Lou Davis, not George Moss and certainly not Ivan Fletcher.

My nerves seemed always on edge. Every noise I heard made me jump, every sound, even from a distance, made me touch my rifle for reassurance and poor comfort. I had no appetite and I slept fitfully, sometimes even rising in the night to check that the lock on the door was firmly fastened.

Worse than living in fear, however, was the consuming, corrosive anger and hatred that ate away at me constantly. All I could think of was Ivan Fletcher, loathing him and wishing him obliterated from the earth, picturing him dead and loving the picture. The unhappy woman I had become was not who I wanted to be, and hers was not the life I desired, but I was trapped in a muddle of my own making and could not see a way of escape.

One morning I went in search of a rabbit for supper. Because the rifle had taken on great importance to me, I practiced daily and so was able to bring home my own game more often than not. In earlier times I would have been happily pleased with myself, self-sufficient to a fault, but I couldn't find that same satisfaction any more. How could I consider myself self-sufficient when I couldn't protect my home and my livelihood, when I allowed myself to be at the mercy of such a despicable man?

That particular morning, however, I hadn't been successful and I plodded home, planning another meal of cornbread and honey. My garden produce was still not quite ripe enough to enjoy, but thankfully I could count on fresh eggs to make a hearty supper. My chickens certainly earned their keep, and at one time I had considered adding a couple more fowl to my little coop, but not any more. I no longer had any money to spare.

I walked toward my front door when I heard someone say my name and saw a man step out from inside the cabin. Without conscious thought I stopped abruptly and raised the rifle to my shoulder but then realized John Thomas stood in front of me. He was obviously as startled by me as I had been by him, but when his glance moved to my face, I saw the expression in his eyes change.

We hadn't seen each other in quite a while and I think he had been about to make a joking remark, perhaps tease me about my hunting prowess or about coming home empty-handed, but instead he asked, "What is it?" Just like that. When had it happened that he could read inside me without my saying a word?

"I'm sorry," I said, quickly lowering the rifle. "You startled me."

"I could tell that. What's wrong?"

"Nothing. Nothing's wrong. I was deep in thought and you startled me, is all." I leaned the rifle against the side of the cabin as he stepped farther outside into the morning sun.

"I was looking for you." He indicated the inside of the cabin. "I didn't mean to intrude. The door was open, and I thought you might be working in the back room and hadn't heard my knock."

"It's all right, John. You just startled me, is all," I repeated for the third time. He came forward and put a hand under my chin, lifting my face up into the sunshine and giving me a searching look.

"What's wrong, Hope?"

I backed up quickly, not wanting to be so close to him because at that moment there was nothing I wanted so much as to be held by him, to feel all that muscle and that strength under my hands and inhale deeply of the smell that came with him, the smell of leather and horses and the land itself. I had no doubt that such a combined assault on my senses would act as an aphrodisiac, and I couldn't afford that weakness.

I dropped my eyes a moment, marshaled my emotions, then looked up and said calmly, "Really, John Thomas, there's nothing wrong. I was thinking about the rabbit that got away and just didn't expect to see anybody here. There's nothing wrong with your family, is there?"

He hadn't missed my quick step away from him and was frowning, the small crease that appeared between his eyebrows when he was troubled or frustrated very prominent.

"No. We're all fine."

"And Katherine's back at school by now, isn't she? Your mother told me you'd be putting her on the train. Was that last week?"

"Yes, it was last week." He continued to stand there as I babbled on, watching me closely, frowning and clearly bothered by something in my voice or behavior.

"I'm sort of in the middle of something that I need to get back to, John Thomas. It was nice to see you again."

He took off his hat and held it in one hand, ignoring my broad hint for him to leave, acting instead as if he intended to stay a while, and in order to keep my resolve I knew that would never do. I took another purposeful step away from him, trying to give the impression that I couldn't stand another moment of being away from my chores.

"I don't like this, Hope. I wish you'd tell me whatever it is that's bothering you. Maybe I could help."

"Nothing's bothering me. I'd tell you if there were," I replied, adding to the towering stack of falsehoods I was piling up between us. Pretty soon I wouldn't be able to see over it, the heap of lies would be so high.

But looking at him standing there with that serious, almost disapproving look on his face, I knew that if John Thomas Davis ever found out how Ivan Fletcher treated me or touched me or talked to me, he would feel obligated to defend me as passionately as he kissed me. Ivan Fletcher was right about John, that he was a man honor bound by a code that I didn't completely understand to do the right thing at whatever personal cost to himself. John was impulsive besides, and the methodical and calculating Fletcher would have a greater advantage because of that. Life wasn't like fiction, where good eventually and invariably prevailed and by the end of the story evil was victoriously vanquished. If that were the case, women wouldn't have to sell themselves to put a roof over their heads, and children would never go homeless and hungry. Life was a place, as my mother had told me years ago, where "people are unkind and men are not to be trusted." Except for this man, I thought, except for this man I will love until the day I die, God help me. At my words, John shook his head in disbelief

"I could just keep standing here until you talk to me." The defiant helplessness of his words combined with the stubborn set to his face made me laugh, despite the despair I felt at his presence.

"I am talking to you, John, but you're not listening, which is exactly like a man. You can stand there as long as you like, but I imagine it will get boring for you after a while because I'll be working in the back room. It'll be just you and the chickens." He put on his hat, not returning the humor.

"I got one smile so I ought to be satisfied, but I still don't like this." After another intent look at my face, he added, "I almost forgot the reason I rode over. I was coming to talk to you about Independence Day."

"Is it that time already?"

"Next week."

"I guess I lost track of time."

"The Fourth of July is a big celebration around here, a tradition as far back as I can remember. The day's special to my parents for more than patriotic reasons, something about when they were courting, I think. We shut the ranch down for the day, go to town for the parade, host a pig roast, and have a big baseball game all afternoon, which is a sight to see with all those cowboys off their horses. The day ends with a big dance in town. It's probably the day everyone looks forward to the most all year. I thought you might like to come with me."

My darling, I thought, I'd like nothing better than to spend the whole day with you, and the whole night, too, if you'd have me, but aloud I said, "I don't think I can afford the day off. I have too much to do, and it's July already. Something tells me winter will come early to Wyoming, so thank you, John, but I can't."

"It's just one day. I'll come over early in the morning and water the garden for you while you get in some weaving, and I promise to bring you home at a reasonable hour, so you won't be tired the next day."

"I can't, John Thomas," I repeated firmly.

He didn't answer or argue, only stood there watching me, puzzled and worried, trying to figure me out.

Finally he spoke quietly. "You know I'd do anything for you, Hope. Do you believe that?"

"Yes."

"And if something's wrong or someone's bothering you, if you're worried or frightened about anything, you only have to tell me. You're just one person and sometimes one person isn't enough. I could help you. You could let me help you for a change, dammit."

The peevish profanity of his last sentence spoiled the speech a little, but I knew he was sincere and his offer was more tempting than he realized.

"You mind your language and don't start with me, John Thomas. I don't need or want your help. I just want you to go away and leave me alone." I could tell I'd hurt him as soon as the words left my lips.

He turned away from me but then turned back long enough to say, "You, Hope Birdwell, are a liar. Don't take up poker and expect to win because I don't believe you. No woman who kisses me like you do really means what you just said." I felt myself blushing but attempted a steady tone.

"I happen to enjoy kissing on general principles, so don't let that go to your head. Even you can be wrong sometimes."

"That I can, but not when it comes to you."

Watching him leave, I reflected that I could bear whatever came my way except something terrible happening to John Thomas Davis. After only four months, it was as if he had always been a part of my life, as if I'd been born loving him and would take that love to my grave. The thought of graves made me shudder. I had to make sure John didn't go to his grave prematurely out of some misguided chivalry. I knew with a dismal sinking of my heart that what I feared had occurred, and it was too late for the truth to make a difference. If John ever found out about Ivan Fletcher, there would be hell to pay and it would be all my fault.

Independence Day came and went like any other day, and I tried not to picture what I was missing. If the thought of dancing with John Thomas crossed my mind, I refused to let it linger. If even for a moment I began to recall how it felt to sit very close to him in the moonlight, I pinched myself hard, a trick I had learned years ago from Pansy, who used the tactic to stay awake in church. I worked ferociously all day, started early and finished late, needing a lantern on both ends of the day. I had to leave the door open for light and so kept the rifle close at hand as I worked. I would not be made vulnerable by surprise again.

The garden's first offering was sweet, fresh peas. I ate them for every meal, even breakfast, and still had enough to put up in old canning jars I'd borrowed from Lou Davis.

The weak tomato plants gave me only a few mediocre red globes, but I could pull fresh young tender carrots from the ground and watch squash begin to take shape from robust blossoms.

For a while my life felt almost as it had at the beginning. I would forget and think about next year, think that I had never been happier than living like this until I remembered the nasty, sneering face of Ivan Fletcher and the chill of his blade against my face. Then everything inside me would stop, my heart cease beating, my breath catch in my throat, and I would be overwhelmed with apprehension and resentment and dread. Life could never be what it had been last March, and I would never feel that optimistic rush of pure joy and adventure again. Everything had changed.

Becca Wagner visited one afternoon. She had the same easy assurance on horseback that I'd noticed in her brother and her mother, but while Becca rode astride as Lou did, she wore a split skirt, not men's pants.

"I don't think Ben would really mind if I followed my mother's example, but some of our parishioners would. It's the twentieth century, but they can't seem to leave the last century behind. So my concession to my husband is this split skirt. It's still not the same because trousers are so much more freeing with none of the bother of a skirt, but at least I don't have to ride sidesaddle. Ben would never ask that of me because he knows I just couldn't. It's an awkward and unnatural way to ride."

"Did your father ever mind that your mother was sort of a—" I paused, trying to find the right word to fit Lou Davis.

"Rebel? Radical? Revolutionary?" Becca laughed. "No, my father delights in my mother's independence, always has as far back as I can remember. He never made a business decision without Mother's counsel and approval and never traveled without her."

"That my father relied so much on Mother's judgment bothered some people terribly. As if it were any of their concern! Sometimes the unkind remarks folks made about apron strings or about Mother wearing the pants in the family just infuriated me! I know my parents must have heard the comments, too, but people's talk never seemed to affect either of them. My mother couldn't hold a grudge if she had to, and as long as she's happy, so is my papa."

Becca sat across from me at the table, sipping tea from an old metal coffee cup with the same grace she would have used with fine china. Changing the subject, she observed, "I haven't seen you in weeks, Hope. It seems you used to come into town a lot more."

"I have a lot to do now."

Becca looked at the jars of canned peas and the stack of fabric in the corner.

"I can tell that. You're such a hard worker, Hope, and you never complain. I really admire that about you."

I refused to let her kind words bring tears to my eyes. No more fiddle tears for me. She reached across the table and took one of my rough, brown hands in both of hers.

"We missed you on the Fourth of July. You always bring such elegance with you wherever you go, always so poised and strong and confident. You often make me feel scatter-brained and spoiled. I could never have made a go of this place like you have."

I know my jaw dropped. Was that really how Becca saw me, or was she just being kind? Elegant, strong, confident, and poised? How could she find any of that in me, tanned brown from the sun, my hands worn and rough, wearing the same clothes over and over until they had all faded to the same bland color.

"I'm not like that at all," I replied finally. "I'm common." My comment made her smile.

"Next to my mother and my sister, you're the most uncommon woman I've ever met. All of us feel that way. John Thomas can't say enough nice things about you." I pulled my hand away from her, and she said hastily, "I'm sorry, Hope. I didn't mean to say the wrong thing. I was just making conversation." She changed the subject once more. "Since I haven't talked to you recently, you don't know about the problem at the church."

"What problem?"

"The church roof has developed several leaks, which, of course, isn't a problem when it's not raining, but even if it doesn't rain one more time this side of winter, we can expect a big mess with the winter snows if we don't do something about the problem now. The west side, where the winter sun has a tendency to linger, is like a sieve. So we're sponsoring a box supper to raise funds, and I thought you might like to come."

When I asked what a box supper was she explained, "All the ladies pack a basket or a box with a good-sized meal for two. Then the men bid on each one and the successful bidder shares the contents with the lady who packed the supper. Every husband knows very well that he'd better bid high on his wife's box or he'll never hear the end of it so we usually do pretty well, and all the proceeds go to the church. Ben's always a little uneasy with the idea, but then he is from Philadelphia and he can get stuck on what's proper and what's not. We've always had fun with boxed supper socials here, and everyone's good-natured about them. I know you'd enjoy yourself, Hope, and because it's in the evening, you could still get your work done during the day."

At first I was sure her brother had encouraged Becca to make the trip to my cabin carrying a personal invitation to the church social. But on second thought, maybe he hadn't, maybe this was just Becca's thoughtful way, and I didn't see what harm there could be in attending, whatever her motive.

It was a public church function and to my thinking the last place Ivan Fletcher would dare show his face. Lots of people would be there and I could see John Thomas from a distance without worrying that I would betray myself as I might if I were alone with him. Besides, the festivities presented a worthy cause and a way to pay back a community that had been good to me. Becca seemed honestly pleased when I said I'd come.

"That's wonderful! I'm so glad! I'll pick you up in the buggy around five this Saturday."

"You don't have to do that. I can bicycle in."

"I know you could, but it will be late when we're done, and I'd feel better knowing you got home safely. There's a new element in town that has me worried, a bad element. Ben's noticed it, too. Laramie's always had its unsavory sections of crime and prostitution, especially along Grand Street, but we've noticed an increase in violence over a broader section of town, and the city fathers will have to deal with the problem sooner rather than later. It's better if someone brings you home rather than you being on the road by yourself that late. Plenty of people go home your way. In fact, my parents would be happy to oblige, so I'm sure it won't be any problem for you to hitch a ride at the end of the evening."

Anticipating the box supper made me more cheerful than I'd been in a month. The afternoon of the event I filled my basket with fresh bread, the last of a slab of cured ham, fresh green beans and tomatoes in a dressing that was my own recipe, hard-boiled eggs, and my specialty mock apple pie. I just hoped it wasn't the lone basket that no one bid on. That would be embarrassing.

Then I took a warm bath, put on my green silk blouse, pushed all my hair on top of my head with pins that might stay in all night if I were careful, and waited for Becca Wagner.

"How pretty you look!" she exclaimed when she pulled up in front of the cabin, but she was the one who was pretty, dressed in a scoop-necked, lilac-colored dress that turned her dark blue eyes to purple, her glorious chestnut hair soft and loose around her shoulders. Riding into Laramie with her, I thought that if I had a sister, I would have wanted her to be just like Becca Wagner, as warm as summer, open, affectionate, and straightforward, nothing pretentious or superior about her despite her beauty. She chattered cheerfully the whole trip and by the time we got to the church, I was feeling happy and almost myself.

Becca put me to work decorating the tables and the podium that were set up outside in the church yard. By suppertime people had begun to arrive, and the head table became heaped with boxes and baskets. Many of them were tied with large, colorful bows and ribbons that I realized were code, a way of identifying the suppers to ensure the bidder picked the right one.

After a while I retreated to a corner, enjoying the laughter and the talk that swirled around me. It reminded me of the dance last May or of Katherine's homecoming party, where I had felt comfortable and welcomed, where I had known a sense of belonging that was new and astonishing to me. In a way, celebrating a homecoming of my own. For only a moment I allowed myself to feel grieved and saddened, knowing the welcome wouldn't last, knowing something terrible must inevitably happen and I would no longer be accepted here. But tonight I was determined not to think into the future. Tonight I would quietly revel in the closest thing to family and home I might ever know. Tonight, I thought, I am making a memory and everything will be all right.

Lou Davis came up to me, surprising me with a kiss on the cheek that displayed real affection.

"I'm so glad to see you, Hope! I've missed you. You've been working so hard. Tonight will be an enjoyable break for you, and it's certainly for a good cause. Last fall John and some of our men put a new roof on the parsonage, and if it had been up to my husband, they'd have gone ahead and done the church then, too. There's never been anything he wouldn't do for Becca, being in her pocket since the day she was born," —Lou spoke fondly, loving them both— "but I drew the line at our repairing the church roof. I said we would help, but making sure our house of worship is fit for the Almighty is everyone's responsibility, not just ours because our daughter happens to be married to the minister. You'll see the result of that decision tonight. Poor John will pay too much for my modest supper as if there were anything new in the basket that he hadn't tasted many times over the last twenty-five years, and, very good man that he is, he'll eat every bite and say it's delicious. And the real wonder is that he'll mean every word."

Lou gave a quiet laugh as she concluded, expecting me to see the humor, but instead I commented quietly, "It's because he loves you."

She looked at me sharply, seeming as startled by my sober tone as by the remark, and then smiled directly into my eyes.

"Yes, he does, Hope, he does, and isn't it remarkable after all these years that he still carries a flame for me? I've never truly understood why, but I've stopped wondering about it, and instead I just thank God every day that I wake up next to John Davis. I never expected my life to turn out the way it did. Never. My sister Lily was the beauty and the charmer of the family, not me. Young men fought over her. I was a dull young woman with ink on her fingers and dust in her hair, who kept the books and would rather read than dance."

"And look at you now."

She did look, literally shifting her stance so she could scan the gathering of people, never losing her warm smile. I watched Lou study the crowd until her gaze came to rest on her husband, who stood across the yard in conversation with a woman. John Davis, Senior, lifted his head as if he were somehow aware of his wife's wordless attention, then turned briefly and caught her eye for just a moment before Lou faced me again.

"Yes, Hope, look at me now. Isn't it just something?" she asked with exactly the same amazed tone I had felt the night of the spring dance, as if it were beyond belief that such good fortune should have come her way.

I was surprised and humbled by my own innocent self-absorption in thinking I was the only person, man or woman, to have such feelings.

"Now I have to go rescue my husband from Fern Bledsoe. She's cornered him, and I know she's complaining about something or other, she always does, and John cannot abide a complaining woman. He's always polite about it, though, I'll say that for him. My husband has the patience in the family. That sterling quality bypassed me entirely. Have a good time, Hope, and leave your cares behind for a little while."

Easy for her to say, I thought, watching her go up and place her hand on John Davis's arm, then turn to smile and speak to the lanky woman who had been monopolizing the conversation with him. I had to admire how smoothly Lou accomplished her purpose, detaching her husband from the woman in an easy, flowing manner and walking off with him, her hand tucked under his arm. She turned very briefly, gave me a quick wink, and then grinned in so mischievous a way that I was still smiling at the memory after they were out of sight.

I hadn't seen John Thomas all evening and couldn't decide whether I was happy or disappointed about his absence. Maybe he really had been hurt by my asking him to leave me alone the other day. If he had, it was all for the good. He could go find the brown-haired girl, and they could live happily ever after. I knew that's what I should want, but as long as I didn't have to admit it out loud to anyone, that wasn't what my heart wanted at all. I wanted to be so familiar with John Thomas Davis that he would recognize everything I cooked and still say it was delicious whenever he ate it and mean the words with all his heart every time he said them. I wanted to be able to read his mind across a room and finish his sentences for him. I wanted to go to sleep very close to him every night and wake up even closer every morning. I wanted to be able to love him without secrets and fears, just love him, day in and day out, good days and bad, but I didn't see how that could ever happen.

When it came time to bid on my packed basket, George Moss started the bidding off, giving me a smile. Well, I thought with relief, at least my offering won't sit in humiliating solitude without anyone choosing it, and I smiled my thanks back at him. Then someone else bid. I looked up, knowing it was John

Thomas's voice and hoping my face didn't radiate the happiness I felt. He didn't even look at me, just stood nonchalantly looking at the man who was doing duty as auctioneer. George gave one more bid followed by a good-natured shrug when John Thomas topped him. The auctioneer paused for a minute and I thought the bidding was all over when a new voice spoke out of the darkness. I knew instantly who it was.

Turning, desperately hoping that I was wrong, I saw Ivan Fletcher standing in the shadows at the back of the crowd. How dare he come here and intrude on this gathering! My hands clenched into fists and I stared at him, furious, willing him to read the loathing on my face. Go away. I sent the message loud and clear with every line on my face and pose of my body. Go away.

Fletcher caught my eye and knew exactly what I was feeling, relished it, I could tell, enjoyed my discomfiture and fed off my fear. My only protection was to try to get hold of my emotions and pretend a disinterest I was far from feeling.

After a brief, curious quiet, John Thomas bid again, followed by Ivan Fletcher almost immediately bidding higher. John looked at me only once, a steady, searching look, and all I could do was silently tell him that it wasn't my wish that this should happen, that this stranger was not my choice. It was important to me that he understand this, and I think he did because he turned his attention back to Fletcher and didn't take his eyes from him during the rest of the bidding. Slowly people stopped talking, aware of a tension that hadn't been present earlier, as the bidding went higher still.

"Fifty dollars," said John Thomas so easily a person might think that kind of money grew on trees, and Ivan Fletcher folded. He turned both palms up and shrugged, turned to me with his nasty smile and a small salute and faded into the darkness. The crowd gave a collective exhale and the moment passed, everyone's attention now on the next boxed supper up for bid.

I had been transfixed throughout the exchange, one hand pressed against the base of my throat, hardly breathing. I saw John Davis, Senior step up and say something to John Thomas, who nodded soberly before he picked up my basket and came toward me.

"I think the front church steps are available," he said. "I'm hungry." John didn't smile but I didn't think he was angry, either. Taking my hand, he led me to the steps at the front of the church. The mellow glow of the streetlights gave his face a golden cast; I suppose it did the same for me.

After we sat down side-by-side, John Thomas asked, "Did I make a mistake just now? I didn't think you wanted to spend time with that man."

"No, you didn't make a mistake."

"Do you want to tell me about it?"

"No. No, I don't." I uncovered the basket, made a sandwich, and handed it to him without saying more.

"All right, then," he said, and we sat there without speaking until John thought to ask, "Aren't you having anything?"

"I'm not hungry," I told him but thought, Except for you, except for the sight and sound and touch of you. I'm starved for that.

I wrapped my arms around my knees and sat looking out into the quiet street, the sounds of talk and laughter distantly behind us. After a while I felt his hand on the back of my neck, the gentlest, the briefest of touches. I shivered.

"Please don't do that," I said and shook off his hand because his touch was painful in a way I couldn't talk about.

John obeyed immediately, placing a palm on each knee as if he didn't know what else to do with his hands.

"I don't know who that man was, but I'll find out. I think my father knows something about him."

"Please leave it alone, John Thomas. It's nothing for you to be involved in. It's not your business."

"Anybody who can make you look like you did tonight, who can put a look on your face that I never want to see there again, is my business. I've made it my business."

"You don't have a right to do that."

"I gave myself that right a few weeks ago."

"Why?"

"Do you really not know why?"

He turned his head toward me, and despite myself I met his look, saw the tenderness and the fire there, saw myself reflected in the depths of that look, got lost in it, started to drown, and had to come up for air just to keep from dying in that look. I shook my head like some poor dumb creature.

"No," I said, but I didn't really mean that. In a deep and secret part of me I had known for a long time.

"I'll tell you then. I love you. I think I've loved you forever, even before I ever met you, as crazy as that sounds. I feel like I've been marking time, just waiting for you to come along in my life because when you did, it felt exactly right. I don't know any other way to explain it. From the first moment I saw you I knew you were exactly right for me."

"And it isn't because you look like you do, although I'm a man and that sure got my attention the first time I saw you. It's what's in here." He laid his hand over my heart, searing through the fabric of my blouse so that I thought later I would find his handprint indelibly burned into my skin. "It's that heart of yours, your strength and your spirit that I can't live without. When I'm with you, I feel like I can do anything, be anything. You make me a better man. I believe God made us to be together, Hope. We fit. I don't know how else to say it."

He paused, searching for the words to explain more clearly what he wanted to say, but after a moment his face reflected defeat.

"I don't know how else to say it," he repeated. "I don't have the words. Except I love you, Hope Birdwell. Love you more than life." John spoke the words like a sigh, so quietly and humbly that I thought my heart would break. I didn't know how to respond. If things had been different, I'd have acted differently. I'd have turned and brought his head down to mine and, church steps or not, I would have kissed him longer and harder than he'd ever been kissed in his life. I would have said, 'Let's go get Ben Wagner so he can marry us right now, or I'll turn into the kind of woman your mother wouldn't approve of.' I'd have given him whatever he wanted as long as he wanted it.

But I couldn't say or do any of those things. Not now. Because nothing must happen to John Thomas Davis, not one raven-black hair of his head be harmed, and if I unburdened my emotions to him, I realized there was a very real chance something terrible could happen to him. Because I was a woman, I understood in a way John never could the kind of man Ivan Fletcher was, a man who carried a knife in his boot, a man who lived off the degradation of women, who nursed a grudge for the sheer satisfaction of enacting a vicious revenge, who took pleasure from others' pain and would enjoy hurting John Thomas because he knew doing so would hurt me, too. I stood up abruptly.

"Please don't say those things to me. Please don't. I want to go home."

John stood, too, saying my name softly, and I put a hand up to his mouth.

"Please, John Thomas, don't say anything more. I mean it. I don't want to hear it."

He captured my hand with his and held it against his lips, deliberately kissing the tip of each finger, lingering over each one as if he could taste it.

"Please," I said again, but the word came out a whisper, and I don't think I was asking him to stop. "I need to find Becca so I can go home." My voice cracked on the last word.

This is what Lou Davis meant, I thought, that home is more than a building or a plot of land. Home is where love lives. A tree would be home for me as long as this man was perched there beside me. I pulled my hand away and turned toward the back of the church where there were lights and music.

"I want to go home, John."

From behind me, John Thomas said, "I'll take you home."

"No, I don't think that would be wise."

He grasped me determinedly by the arm and turned me back to face him.

"I'll take you home, Hope. I've never pressed my attentions where they weren't wanted, and you can trust me not to do that now. We don't have to talk, but I'll take you home."

I bent to gather up the basket and the remains from supper, saying as I did so, "All right, but I want to leave now."

"Wait here."

I stood on the church steps until he pulled up with the buggy, the July night suddenly feeling like January as soon as he'd gone. We shared a miserable trip back to my cabin, neither of us speaking a word the entire way. I wanted so badly to say what I'd been practicing. 'I want to tell you about my mother,' I'd say, and then tell him everything I should have told him from the start. But I knew it was too late for that confession now.

Because I had allowed Ivan Fletcher to become my partner in a lie, I had given him power over me, and he savored that power, would use it to challenge John Thomas and goad him into an altercation, would delight in the chance to hurt him.

Fletcher was a street fighter, the kind who attacked from behind, who hid in alleys, who lived by no one's rules but his own. What if John Thomas were hurt because Ivan Fletcher hated me or desired me or whatever it was he felt for me? I couldn't take that risk.

When we reached the cabin, I said, "Thank you," and when he would have come around to help me, I added, "Don't trouble yourself to get down. I don't need your help."

I climbed down from the seat gracelessly and went inside without a backward glance, where I lit a lamp and waited to hear him leave. That didn't happen right away. He must have sat there for several minutes, but it might only have seemed that long because the silence was so excruciating. Finally I heard the sounds of the buggy, the creak of the wheels, and the horse snorting as he pulled away.

"I can't bear this," I said out loud, to no one in particular, to God maybe, or to my mother, wherever she might be. I didn't see a way out unless I did something, unless I figured out a way to kill Ivan Fletcher before he hurt anyone else. I wasn't shocked by the thought. I had killed a coyote for threatening my hens. Fletcher was more of a brute than that mangy coyote and John Thomas was dearer to me than any chickens, so what was the difference?

I wondered if I could really do it, get that malicious face in my sights and pull the trigger as if I were looking at just another coyote. I remembered how Fletcher had enjoyed telling me what he'd done to that poor woman, the sensual pleasure he'd felt moving his fingers down my face as he described the experience, and I thought that not all animals had four legs. In the middle of that murderous speculation, I fell asleep.

In the morning my thoughts of the night before seemed like insanity. Of course I couldn't purposefully kill anyone, couldn't plan it out, coolly align the shot, and pull the trigger. What had I been thinking? That would be just plain wrong, uncivilized, in direct opposition to everything Ben Wagner preached from his pulpit, a vendetta mentality that belonged in the last century, not in these enlightened times.

If I were threatened and had to protect myself or someone else, I believed I could do it in a moment and never feel a regret, but I could never plan it out, lie in wait, and kill from hiding. To do so would make me worse than Ivan Fletcher because I knew right from wrong and I was sure he didn't understand that distinction at all. Something was lacking in the man. Conscience or heart or whatever you call it, he didn't possess it. Perhaps he never had. But I had both conscience and heart whether I wanted them or not.

The next week I took another stack of goods to the store in Laramie. George Moss looked at everything and paid me willingly, once more admiring the yards of woolen fabric, lightweight but tightly woven in muted colors that would appeal to anyone. Besides the fabric, I included some of the items I had knitted or sewn: sweaters and vests and scarves. He liked it all.

"I don't know how you have time to do all this. Doesn't seem there could be enough hours in the day." He glanced at me, then gave me a second, sharper look. "You're looking a little peaked, Hope, not your usual perky self. Are you sure you're all right out there?" I just nodded in response.

I rode home with thunderclouds gathering on all sides and the air heavy and humid, a summer storm not far off. By the time I pulled the bicycle into the shed, the sky was black, lightning flashed everywhere, and the steady, ominous roll of thunder moved across the flatlands. I stood in the doorway watching and hearing the display all around me, the wind whipping my skirts about and the rain bouncing off the doorposts and splashing against my face. Glorious. You could track the storm as it moved across the sky, the mounds of gray clouds along the horizon the exact color of John Thomas's eyes.

I would have to stop thinking about him, I thought, stop recalling moments between the two of us because doing so was a useless and painful pastime.

As the storm subsided, I stepped out into the fresh, cool air. The garden had flooded, but I couldn't be unhappy about that because the rain offered at least a full day, if not two, free from lugging water up from the creek. The horizon was clear again, the black clouds already gone, sunshine and serenity restored. That storm had been the fastest, fiercest one I'd ever experienced. Grand and frightening, like this land, threatening and testing me to see if I were strong enough to survive. There was a time I would have taken the challenge in stride and responded with one of my own, but I wasn't so confident any more.

In the distance I saw a rider approaching, cantering up through the mud faster than seemed safe. John Thomas pulled up a little ways from the cabin and made no move to dismount. He didn't even greet me.

"Are you safe?" he asked. I must have given him a puzzled look because he explained his presence by saying, "Our summer thunderstorms can be pretty upsetting if you're not used to them. I was out so I thought I'd check to be sure you weren't too alarmed."

"Alarmed? Why would a storm alarm me? It was a magnificent show. Was that a typical summer storm for Wyoming?" It seemed funny to be talking to him from a distance, as if we were strangers. An unwilling smile crossed his face.

"I don't know what I was thinking to imagine you might be a little unsettled by all that racket. Did you even notice it was storming?"

"Of course, I noticed. You don't have to talk to me as if I'm blind or deaf or have a problem paying attention. I just didn't find anything to be afraid about. It was only a storm, after all." The banter seemed briefly like old times, teasing and sparring with each other, friends again.

"Are you afraid of anything, Hope?" he asked. When I didn't answer, he spoke tersely. "Sorry I meddled. I didn't mean to take up your time. I'm leaving."

After he was gone, I contemplated his question. Was I afraid of anything? I remembered the days when I had feared nothing, when I was certain I could do whatever I set my mind to if I just worked long enough and hard enough and didn't let anything or anyone get in my way. That girl who had stepped off the train, wearing her city shoes and carrying all her worldly goods in one satchel, had been fearless. But afraid now? Oh my, yes. How ironic that when I had nothing, I was carefree and unafraid with the sky the limit and my dreams as good as accomplished. Now that I had people and things I cared about, I was close to being terrified, which wasn't how I had expected it to be.

I feared Ivan Fletcher and what he could do to me or to people I cared about. I feared losing this place, feared not making it through the winter, feared going back to service and losing my freedom. Worst of all, I was afraid I had so completely messed up my life that nothing could possibly make it right again.

Chapter 11

$\mathcal{N}$ot long after the storm I sat down at the table for a quick lunch of bread and fresh vegetables from the garden. Lou Davis's blanket lay folded on the bed, almost done. From where I sat I could see the threads of purple and red and orange I had woven through the whole piece. I could also see the end of my wool supply, which caused me some despair. If I'd been able to hold onto the money from the sale of my goods to George Moss, I would have had just enough to provide for myself through the coming winter. In the spring, besides any wool my own sheep might have provided, I would have gone with Fergus to the shearing again, this time better prepared and with that standing offer from Pershing Filbert of five dollars a day and a bundle of his best wool.

Now, however, all my enthusiasm for my carefully crafted plans had vanished. I could only sit there, resting my forehead in my hands, as close to despair as I had ever been. What would any of this matter if I had to keep filling the bottomless pockets of Ivan Fletcher? How maddening that he should benefit from my dreams and my work and my plans!

As if thinking of the man made him materialize, a shadow fell on the table through the open door and Fletcher stood there, grinning at me.

"Didn't hear us coming, I'll bet." He stepped just inside. "We came the back way, off the main road. A little muddy but no use announcing our visit."

He stepped to the table where I sat and straddled the chair across from me. Behind him Tony hovered in the doorway, keeping an eye outside and nervously stepping back and forth across the threshold as he did so.

"I'll get the money," I said, pushing my chair back, but Fletcher reached across the table and put his hand on mine. "There's no hurry. No hurry at all. We can just talk a while."

"Tony looks like he's in a hurry."

"Tony's a little uneasy. He gets that way. He's worried someone'll take offense to our little visits here."

"Then he's got more sense than you." I tried to pull my hand away, but Fletcher gripped it harder until I told him, "You're hurting me."

"Am I?" He tried to bring my hand up to his mouth.

"Stop it." I yanked free and pushed away from the table.

"Didn't seem to bother you with young Davis the other night. I believe you couldn't have slipped a piece of paper between you, you were that close." My shock must have showed on my face because Fletcher's mouth widened into an even broader grin. "You should never think I don't know where you are and what you're doing and who you're doing it with. You're my investment. You owe me." I stood up.

"Because you're a coward, you've lived off women your whole life. You aren't smart enough to have the slightest idea how a real man treats a woman and you never will. There's no way you could ever understand a man like John Davis, no way at all. I'll get your money and you can get off my land."

Fletcher stood up, too, the arrogant smile fading from his eyes, replaced with something vicious and stone cold.

"You think I'm scared of his reputation? You think I can't hold my own against a man like John Rock Davis?"

"John Rock Davis?" I repeated blankly.

"The old man, the father. I've heard of him, heard my share of stories, but that was thirty years ago. He's slowed down and he don't have the same reflexes. Old Davis pays Tony a visit and thinks that'll scare me like it did Tony here." Fletcher gave a derisive snort. "Thinks an old man's reputation is gonna scare me." He stepped around the table toward me. "You didn't know what kind of family you was getting mixed up in, did you?"

Everything he said was news to me and at the moment not very meaningful news, but the name John Rock Davis must have carried weight with Tony if not with Fletcher. That would explain why they'd come up the back way and why Tony acted so fidgety.

"I don't think that's your business," I told him. I took the little pouch of coins from its place in the sugar jar and handed it to him. "Here. It's all I've got right now. I'll have more in about a month or so, and then I won't have any more after that. Not until spring." Fletcher shifted the pouch from hand to hand, looking at me with narrowed eyes.

"Then what will we do?"

I didn't answer. I knew that once Fletcher saw any sign of fear in me, like all bullies, he'd torment me more, so I was not about to reveal the despair I had felt earlier. I'd had a lifetime of hiding my emotions, and all that practice would have to hold me in good stead now.

Fletcher took a step toward the door as if he were leaving and then suddenly, swiftly turned back, reached for me, twisted one of my arms behind my back, and pulled me toward him. When he put his mouth over mine in a vile, thrusting kiss, I raised my free hand and hit him hard along the side of his head by his ear, a jarring enough blow to cause his head to jerk back and away from me. At first the unexpected force caused him to loosen his hold and I pulled away, hoping to slip out of his grip and reach my rifle, but I was caught in an awkward posture and lost my footing.

Fletcher recovered quickly and caught me by the front of my blouse. The worn material ripped right down the middle. The man looked ferocious, lips drawn back from his teeth animal-like and eyes sparking black with fury.

"You did that once before and I let you go, but no woman raises her hand to me twice."

He gave me a shove, causing me to fall backwards, lose my balance completely, and slide into a sitting position on the floor with my legs straight out and my back against the wall. In a second he was kneeling in front of me, straddling my outstretched legs, the sharp point of his knife right at the base of my throat.

I knew he could kill me and no one would stop him, that he was enraged enough to do it, that he need only give one quick thrust, and that wicked blade would push through my throat and pin me to the wall. At that moment Ivan Fletcher held all the power and knew I realized it, too. That sense of control fueled some twisted part inside him. He could kill me or scar me or abuse me any way he chose, and we both knew I was not strong enough to protect myself.

The knowledge of his power terrified and infuriated me. I recognized the familiar helpless, outraged feeling I had experienced before, but I was older now and I had learned some things. I might not be as physically strong as he was, but I was smarter and I had my own strength and my own kind of control—inside, where he couldn't get to it. Shaking, panting, sick with terror and fury, I still knew that I must keep a part of me inviolate, whatever he did. The deliberate determination to endure gave me the only strength I had access to at the time.

"If you move, if you even twitch, I'll kill you," he said and I knew he would. The certainty was written across his face, in the snarl of his mouth and the cold fury of his eyes. I sat very still, his weight on my legs, and the knife itself becoming a creature with life and breath all its own, like a coiled and menacing snake, its tongue flicking against my throat. Fletcher didn't seem to be breathing at all, but I could hear my own shallow, quick breaths. They were the only sounds in the room.

"You could ask me real nice not to hurt you and maybe I wouldn't. But you'd have to ask it real, real nice."

He's going to hurt me anyway, I thought. It wouldn't matter what I said or did, he was just playing a game with me, so I only watched his face, not speaking.

Next to us, Tony spoke. "You'd better not. What if—"

"You shut up." Fletcher spoke to him without taking his eyes away from me. "If you don't have the stomach for this, go outside and make sure I'm not interrupted."

If I could have, I'd have tried to make eye contact with Tony, tried to ask him wordlessly for help, but he was to my side and from the way he left, closing the door quickly behind him, he was as frightened of Ivan Fletcher as I was.

"You act so proud, like you're too good for the likes of me, just like your mama did, both of you with your noses in the air as if I'm garbage with a bad smell. You're the daughter of a woman who loaned herself out to any man with four bits to spare. They didn't take the time to take off their boots and you're no better than she was. You know it and I know it, even though you act like you wouldn't be caught dead with me. Well, I could change that. You know that, don't you?" When I didn't answer, he pressed the knifepoint more firmly against my throat, enough to cause a little puncture so that I felt a small warm drop of blood trickle down my chest. "Don't you?"

"Yes." My mouth was so dry that the word jerked out of my throat unwillingly, as if someone else had spoken.

"We need to understand each other." He spread open my torn blouse and stared at me a moment, deep in thought and not really seeing me, then reached to push down my chemise, exposing my left breast. The cool, flat blade of his knife rested against my skin lightly as he knelt there, still thinking.

In spite of the summer's warmth, my whole body had begun to shake, my breaths shaky, too, watching his face, steeling myself when I saw his lips turn up in a brief, self-satisfied smile. He met my look completely, wanting me to know he planned something horrible and there was not a thing I could do to stop him, a man exultant with power and a terrible anticipation. Then he turned the knife so that the blade's razor sharp edge balanced against my breast.

"Ready?" he said, his smile widening, and drew the blade down.

That moment still reappears with all its bloody clarity in my dreams. When I least expect it, when my life is calm and untroubled, when I have not given a thought to Ivan Fletcher, I can still be caught unawares by the memory, by the terror of that moment. As if I am only an impersonal spectator to a horrific scene, I hear my hoarse, rapid breaths turn to whimpers I cannot hold back. I watch him at his task as intent as any artist, observe the deliberate slice of the knife and the sudden red, beaded line that followed as the razor-sharp blade split my tender skin. I see once more the look of perverted, sensual pleasure on his face when he sat back on his heels to examine his handiwork.

"Not your face—this time." Fletcher put the knife under my chin and lifted my face to his. "Your whole life you'll carry my mark, and you'll remember never to raise your hand to me again, won't you?"

I sat incapable of movement or speech, his weight heavy on my legs and the warm blood from the wound beginning to soak more rapidly through my undergarment, then onto my stomach and pooling at the waistband of my skirt.

"I'm talking to you. You'll remember to treat me with respect now, won't you?" he asked, pressing the knife into the soft skin of my neck.

"Yes." I would have said or done anything to get him away from me.

"Yes, sir, to you, girlie. Say it."

I licked my lips before I spoke, feeling suddenly faint and ill. "Yes, sir."

The cabin door opened forcefully and Tony stuck his head in far enough to cry in a panic, "Someone's coming. I can see a wagon."

Fletcher stood over me, then bent to sheathe the knife once again in his boot. He said nothing more, only smiled at me before he left.

I remained mute and motionless, my blood continuing to seep from short, deep slashes that formed the unmistakable shape of an F on my breast, a mark, his mark, I knew I would carry all my life, whether the wound left a scar or not.

As soon as I heard their wagon pull away, I pushed myself upright, stumbling a little from light-headedness, bunched up a rag, and held it against the wound, trying to staunch the bleeding. I felt dazed and sick, unable to think clearly enough to know what to do or how to act, hanging on to my self-control by the thinnest of threads. I heard the sound of a wagon, and then Lou Davis called my name from the open doorway.

"Hope, did I just—?"

She stopped, suddenly immobilized by a sight that must have shocked her when I raised my eyes from the wound to meet her gaze. Blood continued to soak through the cloth I held and run down my chest. I couldn't speak and I wasn't weeping, but she saw something in my face that broke her brief stillness and caused her to come forward and put her arms around my shoulders. I tried to pull away.

"You'll stain your clothes," I explained calmly, but Lou put her own hand over the cloth between us and drew me close.

"I thought I saw riders. Who did this?"

She held me quietly, long enough for my heartbeat to slow and my breathing to calm. Then we sat on the edge of the little bed, so she could peel away the cloth and look at the injury. I hadn't answered her question and she didn't ask it again. Instead, she stood and reached under her skirt to rip off a broad section from the bottom of her petticoat, then tore that part into several pieces, dipped one of the smaller strips in the bucket of water, and rubbed it against the bar of lye soap by the basin.

"I'm afraid this will hurt, but we should clean the wound before we go for the doctor."

"No doctor, Lou."

"Hope, I should take you into Laramie to see the doctor right now. I think this could take some stitches. Otherwise, it may not stop bleeding."

"No doctor," I repeated.

Despite the heat of the day, I was still shivering, and Lou found an old shirt to put around my shoulders as she worked. At her ministrations, the wound, which had seemed numb at first, began to hurt, aching like a bone-deep bruise. When Lou dabbed the soap lightly against my gashed skin, I cried out from shock and pain.

"I'm so sorry, Hope. I don't mean to hurt you." She didn't look at me when she spoke but continued to work calmly and quickly, washing and rinsing the wound.

"You've done this before," I commented, speaking more to distract myself from the pain than from any real interest in the subject.

Recognizing my need and my intention, Lou made casual conversation for my benefit as she worked.

"More times than I care to remember. Broken bones, gunshot wounds, and an assortment of cuts and punctures. We weren't always fortunate to have a doctor close by. Years ago Laramie seemed to go through a lot of them. Either they were incompetent or they didn't like the isolation. I'm sure that's what got Katherine thinking about the medical profession."

When Lou was done, she folded what was left of my ripped blouse into a compact pad, put it over the cuts, and wrapped more petticoat strip around my shoulders as a bandage to keep the pad in place. Then she helped me out of my bloody chemise and I gingerly slipped my arms into the shirt I had been wearing draped over my shoulders.

"I'll bring more cloths from home. I have gauze and tape there, too, and I can make a thicker pad for the wound and a better bandage to keep it in place. If I hurry, I can be back in an hour."

I was lying on the bed by then and reached for her hand. "Please don't go, Lou. Not just yet." I started to tell her I'd appreciate some company, but before I could finish the sentence, I began to cry, surprising us both. I've always been careful with tears, considering them a time-consuming indulgence and an embarrassment, but once started, I couldn't stop crying, my sobs so harsh and gasping I didn't think it possible they were coming from me.

Lou sat at the edge of the bed, holding my hand in one of hers and stroking my hair with the other, tenderly saying the common phrases people always repeat at such times.

"Everything will be all right. Hush now. Don't cry. It will be all right." If she'd been my real mother, Lou Davis couldn't have been gentler or more sincerely concerned about me.

After a while, after I was calmer, she stated kindly and without any reproach in her tone, "I know this was an intentional wound, Hope. I can tell it's in the form of an F, but I don't know why someone would do that to you or what that letter means. Is there anything else that happened that you want to tell me about?"

I took a series of ragged breaths and sat up, carefully swinging my legs over the edge of the bed.

"No. Not what you think. Not that." I stood up, one hand around her arm, and we went to sit at the table. "I'm sorry. I'll be all right now."

"We need to report this to the authorities."

"No." My tone was as firm as hers.

"Hope—"

"Lou, you must not tell anyone about this. It needs to be our secret. Promise me."

"I can't do that."

I met her look across the table and said urgently, "Please, Lou. Think what would happen if John Thomas found out about this. He'd feel obliged to do something himself, you know he would, and you don't know the man who did this. I do. He could hurt John Thomas badly. He's capable of killing him, and he'd want to because he knows that hurting John Thomas would hurt me."

"How do you know this man?"

"I knew him in San Francisco, not a long time and not well, but he bothered me there. When I left, I thought I was leaving him behind, but he found me here."

"Was he the man at the social?"

"Yes." I stretched my good arm across the table to grasp her hand. "Listen, Lou, you don't understand this man, but I do. He's not like an ordinary man. It's like he's missing something inside. He enjoys hurting people. You know if John Thomas found out he'd go after him. You know that. And it isn't that John's not brave enough or smart or strong enough. It's just that he doesn't understand about men like Ivan Fletcher, how dirty they are, how they fight, how they treat women, how they like to hurt and kill."

"Fletcher," Lou repeated, making the connection with the incision on my breast, disgust on her face and in her eyes. Then she added, "Maybe you're underestimating my son, Hope."

"No, I don't think so. John Thomas is so—so passionate." I searched for the right word and wasn't self-conscious when I said it. "He thinks with his heart, which is a wonderful thing most of the time."

"Except for those red-haired actresses." I gave her a weak smile.

"Yes, there is that. But he's stubborn, too, and now that he thinks he cares for me, he'd go out as Lochinvar to do battle, to defend and protect me." I paused, then added simply, "I never meant for John Thomas to care for me, Lou. That was never part of my plan. All I wanted was a home of my own and a place to settle and belong. It just happened."

"My dear, the day John and I rode home after dropping you off, that very first day, I told him we had just met the perfect girl for John Thomas. Do you think it was an accident that I volunteered my son's services to help you get settled in? I threw you two together any time I could. From the very first day, I knew it was an inevitable match, and I couldn't be happier to be right."

"Don't be kind to me. I don't deserve it."

"What happened here is not your fault," she stated firmly, then added less firmly, "and we should tell the authorities."

"No. Why endanger John Thomas? He doesn't have to know."

"But what if this Fletcher comes back? You can't take that risk and I can't take that risk for you."

"He won't come back," I lied. "He said he wouldn't. He wanted to humble me and he did and he's done now. He said it was enough to know I'd carry his mark on me for the rest of my life. He won't be back. Please, Lou. We mustn't tell anyone." She disengaged her hand from mine and stood, not angry but very firm.

"I have never been able to keep a secret from my husband from the day I met him, and now it's too late to even try. He knows every expression of my face and inflection of my voice better than he knows his own. He'll know something's wrong."

"But you don't have to tell him what."

"I don't have to tell him anything, and I won't for a while. John will respect my privacy, but he'll worry and I don't like that. I won't lie to my husband, Hope. The thing that troubles me is that you're right about John Thomas. He's so in love with you he can't think straight. Like his father he's a very good man with a strong sense of what's right, and he carries a scorn for bullies that he inherited from me. Unfortunately, he also has his parents' worst qualities: my outraged impulsiveness and John's cold inflexibility. I need to think about this."

Lou came around behind me and leaned down with her cheek against my hair.

"My poor girl. If I were a man, I'd take care of the problem myself, and no one but the two of us would need to know. Unfortunately, women understand the kind of man you're describing all too well. I wish I could do that for you." Then she straightened and advised briskly, "You shouldn't use your left arm for a while or the wound could split open and start bleeding again. The bleeding appears to have stopped now, but if it does start up again, press a thick pad of cloth against the wound and lie down. I'll come back first thing tomorrow with gauze and salve and rewrap the bandage. I'm worried about infection, too, so we have to keep it clean. Will you be all right?"

"Yes."

Her tone softened. "You try to sleep, Hope. I've piled the old rags in a corner to take back with me tomorrow. By the time I get home, everyone will be there, and I'd rather not have to explain anything to them right now. There's a jar of fresh water on the table for you, and I'll check on your hens before I leave so you can just rest. I hate leaving you alone, but if I don't get back, someone will come looking for me, and I know you don't want that. Lock the door after I've gone."

I could see Lou didn't feel right about leaving and wanted to stay, but finally she reached for the door, saying as much for her assurance as mine, "Those are nasty cuts but they'll heal. Everything will be all right."

I didn't believe her, and my doubts must have shown on my face so clearly that she could only shake her head as rebuttal and leave.

I had a hard night and wished more than once that I wasn't alone. The solitude I had once treasured had become threatening and lonely. I wanted someone to talk to and knew just the person I would have preferred, but he was off somewhere else, probably enjoying the company of that girl with brown hair without a thought for me because I had told him to leave me alone. And so, John being John, he would do as I asked.

So in love with you he can't think straight, Lou Davis had told me, but what should have been comforting only made matters worse. I knew John Thomas better than I knew myself, and if one breath of today's brutal assault drifted his way, he would take matters into his own hands. What I found so endearing about him also caused me the most unease: his ability to love passionately and feel deeply, his stubborn streak, an ability to hold on and keep holding on against all odds. That incredible faithfulness I recognized as an inheritance from his father. John Thomas might accuse me of transparency, but he was the one who could be read like a book. With him there would never be any holding back. In both love and war he would always give one hundred percent, and how could I fault him for that? He just needed to be protected. His mother understood that as well as I, and I would have to trust her good judgment.

I slept a little toward morning, but the incisions throbbed and kept me from finding any lasting rest. My emotions didn't want to let me rest, either. When I closed my eyes, I could sense Ivan Fletcher in the room, feel him kneeling against me, see the concentrated pleasure in his eyes as he carved his letter on me, now and then glancing up at my face to be sure I was terrified, waiting for me to cry out or beg, hoping I would, then looking down to cut a little more, slow and methodical and evil. Making a point. Teaching me a lesson. Showing me who was boss.

I had locked the door and then used my hip to nudge the table against it, but I could not get warm, despite the nearly suffocating confines of a windowless cabin at the end of a summer day. Waves of chills made my teeth chatter and my hands shake. For a while I had expected Fletcher to kill me, so I supposed I should be glad I felt so miserable. It proved I was alive. Some small comfort at the time.

Lou Davis returned just after daybreak, riding this time and with a rifle I'd never seen her carry before thrust into the sheath on her saddle. I had already brewed coffee and had just come in from gathering breakfast eggs, clutching two in my right hand because my left side was much too tender to endure any movement or pressure. I held my left arm across my chest and tried to keep it very still, which made all my movements clumsy.

Lou unloaded gauze and bandages, salve and soap from her saddlebags.

"How are you this morning?" When she looked at me more carefully, she added, "Don't answer. I can see how you are, not that I wouldn't be feeling the same."

She moistened then carefully peeled off the bandage, exposing the raw, red F, crusty with dried blood and oozing something yellow and unpleasant. The sound she made was wordless and quickly stifled before she got down to business, washing the wound again, dabbing it with the lye soap, finally applying salve to the cuts with gentle, competent hands. I admired her a great deal and wished I could be as calm and kind and strong as she. At the time I felt the exact opposite in all respects.

After she put on a fresh bandage, she washed her hands, gathered up the used rags, and thrust them into her saddlebags.

She finished without speaking and when she was done said, "I'll take the trash home with me and burn it. No use heating up your kitchen, and if we bury it, the coyotes will have everything dug up before our backs are turned."

"Are you angry with me?"

Lou sat down abruptly and repeated, "Angry with you?"

I felt like a child again, guilty of some wrongdoing of which only my mother was aware, punished with her silence that was all the more painful because I didn't know what I'd done and so was incapable of regaining her good will. My conscience felt even worse with Lou Davis because I knew I'd been dishonest with her, knew that because of me someone she loved had been placed in danger. Hardly how I wanted to treat a woman who had been kinder to me in the few months I'd known her than anyone else had ever been in all twenty years of my existence.

"You seem angry with me." I continued, almost in a whisper. "I'm sorry this happened, Lou. I'm sorry you and your family are involved. I wish you could go away and pretend you didn't know about it. I never intended to cause anyone any trouble."

"Hope, if I seem angry, it isn't at you." I heard John Thomas in her words. "I can't imagine what you could ever do that would make me angry. I'm furious at the man who did this. I can't see those slashes without thinking how frightened you must have been and how monstrous an attack it was. I can't deny I'm angry but not with you."

We sat for a moment in companionable silence until I asked hesitantly, "Did you tell anyone?" At my question, her face, her wonderful face with its glow of warmth and generosity, dimmed.

"John noticed something was wrong right away. I knew he would. For better or worse, he's read my mind from the first moment I met him. In our family it's hard to keep a secret. I suppose we're closer than most because we live so isolated. If one person is bothered about something, everyone knows it, and sooner rather than later. Last night John and Gus, Billy, John Thomas, and I sat down for supper and I thought I was acting perfectly normal. Feeling pretty proud of myself, too." She smiled faintly. "Then I looked up and all of them were staring at me as if a third eye had popped out of my forehead." I laughed a little at the way she said it, but it was clear she was troubled.

"Later John suggested we go for a walk, and I knew what was coming. When he asked what was wrong, I couldn't say 'nothing' because that would have been a lie, and I won't lie to him. Years and years ago, before we were married even, we made a deal to tell the other person the truth, even if the truth hurt, so I just told him I needed to think about something for a while."

I hated that I should be the one to cause that troubled look on her face.

"My husband won't ask again, at least for a while, because he trusts me to talk to him when I'm ready, but I don't like keeping anything from him. Secrets build walls, Hope, and I can't live that way. I may eventually tell him everything and let him use his best judgment on what to tell John Thomas. The trouble is, I'm not sure exactly how John will react. He can be quite fierce sometimes. Implacable. Even frightening."

"John Rock Davis," I said, repeating the name Ivan Fletcher had used.

Lou raised both eyebrows in questioning surprise. "Where in the world did you hear that? Yes, John Rock Davis, a man of some reputation many years ago, before he became my husband and turned into a family man."

"Did you reform him?"

"Oh, no!" Her words an immediate and startled response, as if the idea shocked her. Then she continued more emphatically, "Oh, no, Hope. John didn't need me to show him how to be a good man or how to do the right thing. He knew that long before he met me. I've never believed you can reform a man from the outside. Change has to come from what he carries inside, from the choices he makes in life and the conscience he bears, and John was true in that respect long before we met. I just settled him, is all, gave him somewhere to belong, gave him someone to come home to. He'd never known that before in his whole life, and it made all the difference."

Lou looked her age that day, looked as if she had slept as poorly as I, her face too pale, the fine creases around her eyes very noticeable, her lips almost colorless, and a hard vertical line between her brows, like John Thomas's when he was thinking hard about something. Finally, she sighed.

"Speaking of home, I wish you could come home with me for a while, but I know you wouldn't come. Would you?" She looked at me hopefully and gave a small shrug when I shook my head. "Then I'll come by in the morning again. If the wound looks any redder, I may have to insist on taking you to the doctor." Her tone brooked no argument and I didn't try.

"I'm sure it will feel better tomorrow. Do you think it will scar?" The thought of bearing an unmistakably shaped scar was enough to make me ill, forced to see that mark every day for the rest of my life. I remembered Fletcher's promise of a return visit and wondered how long the rest of my life would be.

The look of outrage and anger crossed Lou's face again. Absentmindedly her hand went to her own hairline, to the place where I had once observed a long white scar. The scar didn't show at the moment because her hair was down, but I could tell she had briefly recalled it. Finally she gently responded to the fear and revulsion in my tone.

"I think it will fade, Hope. Everything fades with time. We'll have to wait and see."

After she left, I found I could sew with my right hand if I sat at the table holding the fabric down with my left elbow as I did so. The process was slow going, but it kept me busy for the day, kept thoughts and worries at bay. My breast felt hot to the touch, tender and puffy, and by the end of the day the cabin had collected enough heat to drive me outside.

I sat in a chair with my back against the wall, the rifle close by my right hand, and looked out at my land. A few mule deer drifted toward the creek where earlier I'd caught a glimpse of some pronghorns. I could hear the meadowlarks calling to each other, their clear, flutelike tones creating a concert just for me. Sunset colors crept down the distant mountains and turned the trees and grasses to orange, set the whole scene softly, gently aflame.

"I don't want to live anywhere but here," I said aloud. I knew I fit here, belonged in this wonderful, frightening, unsympathetic, demanding, embracing place. Around me I could feel the land settling in satisfied fulfillment as if it, too, in the same way John Thomas had talked about earlier, had been waiting years for me to appear, as if it recognized that we were meant to be together. Almost like a lover. I had known from the moment I stepped off the train that I could match the land in temperament, and it never would have conquered me. People, though—people were another story all together.

In the middle of the night, I was awakened by a familiar sound it took me only a moment to identify. Rising and throwing a shawl around my shoulders, I went outside, the bleating of sheep incessant and everywhere, the welcome sound of bagpipes dinning the night air. Holding my hand against my chest to keep the bandage in place, I felt like weeping from relief and happiness. Then I began to walk faster.

"Oh, Fergus!" I cried before I even reached him. "You're back! I thought you wouldn't be here until fall." I caught his white grin in the moonlight.

"I'm just passing through, lass, but I couldn't resist a serenade." He put both arms around me in a hug that caused me to gasp at the pain from the pressure on my breast.

"What's that?" he asked, concerned.

"I hurt my shoulder," I explained, "and it's still a little tender, but never mind that. I'm so glad to see you! How long can you stay?"

"A little while. I'm following the Wildflower east a ways, so I thought I should stop and see how it fared with my partner."

"I'm busy. The garden's overflowing. Do you like sweet corn? It's the best I've ever tasted. And Mr. Moss has agreed to buy all the wool I can weave to resell in his store. I made a cap for you, Fergus, not that you'll need it just yet. And I shot a coyote that was after my hens, one shot is all and dead center." I took a breath and he interrupted with a laugh.

"Save something for the morning, Hope. I'll do the breakfast cooking this time."

"And I'll bring the coffee." Then I put my good arm around him again and hugged him once more. "Oh, Fergus, I'm so glad to see you." The words came out sounding more plaintive than I'd intended, and he held me away from him to study my face in the moonlight.

"I don't like the sound of that."

"I have just been awakened from a deep sleep by the unmelodic droning of the pipes, so don't read anything into my tone. You'll see in the morning that I'm fine. And I don't have to ask how you are. You look your usual bearlike and healthy self."

I walked back to the cabin feeling that a burden had been lifted from my shoulders, conscious of a great relief that Fergus was nearby and surprised by how much I had truly missed him. For the first time in a number of weeks, I slept well and awoke refreshed and almost happy.

Chapter 12

"So," I said at breakfast, fresh eggs and homemade bread and a slice of cured bacon on each of our plates, "how long will you stay?"

As promised, Fergus had a plate of hot food waiting for me in the morning, and we sat companionably at a small makeshift table by the bank of the Wildflower. He shook his head regretfully.

"I'm moving on tomorrow, lass. There's not enough grass grown back for the woolies to feed here yet. They ate it down to the root, and we have to give the land a chance to recover."

I made a small sound of protest, which caused him to continue, "It's gratifying to be so welcomed, Hope, and I'll be close enough that you can walk over and visit whenever you have a moment. Just over that hill to the south is new grass, so we'll settle there for a few days. We'll just keep moving in that general direction for a while, then come back this way in early fall until we have to move farther west as winter closes in."

"Are you taking care of my lambies?"

"Absolutely. See for yourself." Then he grinned, daring me to pick my bummers out of the flock and knowing full well I couldn't have done it if my life depended on it.

"You've made your point," I said, making an unladylike face at him. "They all look alike to me, all long black faces and white woolly bodies. I'm at your mercy."

"Now that's something I never thought to hear you say. Your lambies aren't lambies anymore, but they're pining for you just the same, and I'll drop them off on my way back if you want. Otherwise, I can just keep them with mine over the winter. I promise to treat them like gold."

"I admit I was looking forward to having something other than my hens to talk to through the long winter, but it makes sense for you to keep them if you're willing to do that."

"That's what friends and partners are for," he responded easily, and at his tone knew I had the old Fergus back, all the moody melancholy gone. "Now what did you do to your shoulder? Seems to be causing you some pain."

Lou Davis's arrival on the horizon saved me from a lie, which was a good thing. I had enough lies to keep track of as it was. Lou walked down the ridge from the cabin and over to where Fergus and I sat.

"Hello, Mr. Campbell. It's early in the season for you to be here, but I know Hope is happy to see you, whatever the reason." Fergus stood at Lou's arrival.

"I'm just passing along the Wildflower, Miz Davis, but thought I'd catch a moment here before moving on."

We chatted for a while and then Lou said, "Hope, I've brought something for you." As we walked up the ridge together, she added, "I'd feel better if he were staying longer and closer."

"I agree, but I'll take the company for as long as I can get it."

"How are you feeling?"

"I'm sore but I'll be fine." I couldn't tell her that I was more heartsick, worried, and deeply ashamed than physically hurt.

Lou had a cool, calming touch that felt good to my skin. "Maybe it's a little better, but it's still too warm and red for my peace of mind," she observed, resting her cool fingers on my skin and scowling at the wound as if it were being difficult on purpose just to annoy her. "I'll give it one more day before I insist on the doctor." Her tone did not invite argument, and I recalled John Thomas's words from my first morning in Wyoming: *Don't argue with my mother when she sets her mind on something.* I saw what he meant.

As she rewrapped the bandage, Lou told me, "John and I talked this morning. We woke up and he asked again and it seemed the right time to tell him."

"How much did you tell him?"

"Everything important but not all the specifics. I said a man was bothering you and although I didn't mention any names, I think John knew who I was talking about. He got quiet first, not always a good sign, and then told me about a conversation he'd had with Tony who used to work for us. Is Tony involved in this somehow?" I didn't answer and she went on. "I said you wanted to keep it quiet. We talked about John Thomas and the right thing to do. My husband still doesn't know the worst, but he's not easily fooled, and he knows there are details I'm not sharing. Thank the good Lord I married a patient man, who trusts my judgment, so we decided to keep what we know to ourselves for the time being."

She looked relieved, the small worry lines around her eyes gone and some of her natural good spirits restored.

"You do seem calmed," I commented.

Lou was packing things up to take back with her and stopped her activity to give a thoughtful reply that shared some of her past.

"That's true. I hadn't thought about it like that, but I feel calmed, relieved, and unburdened. John's always had that effect on me. It's one of the reasons I love him, I suppose. I trust my husband's judgment without reservation because unlike me, he doesn't allow emotion to make his decisions for him. He's much better at thinking things through than I am. I have the lamentable habit of opening my mouth when I shouldn't, and I've suffered the consequences because of it."

"In our early years together we had considerable adjusting to do, both of us so different in a lot of ways, and we had our share of disagreements and stubborn moments that stretched out too quiet for too long. But thank God we always ended up talking things through, and, of course, it helped that deep down each of us wanted to make the other happy. Still do, for that matter."

"When it came to making a life together in Wyoming, we had each other and no one else for miles. We were blessed that trusting came easy to both of us. The times I felt distanced from John were few and far between but they were always unsettling, as if my world was off balance. Something not right and I honestly couldn't think about anything else until the problem was resolved. I surely don't have his patience or his restraint."

She paused and smiled in memory. "But despite our differences, I felt a kinship with him from the first moment I saw him, and I believe he felt the same."

"Someday will you tell me the story about how you two met?"

"Someday. Our story had its own drama."

She looked back from the doorway where she stood trousered and slim, her hair pushed up into a high crowned hat that clearly exposed the scar along the side of her face. From a distance she could have been mistaken for a boy.

"Terrible and violent things happened then, too, but we weren't beaten by them. I have a feeling it will be the same for you, Hope."

I appreciated her confidence but didn't share it. At that moment I couldn't see a way out unless I left Laramie, and I wasn't yet ready to take such a drastic action. I could go back to San Francisco, I supposed, find Pansy, and stay with her until I found employment again. I thought Mrs. Gallagher might even give me a reference, but the idea was still too painful to consider, too final. That alternative was a last resort, and I believed there had to be other options if I could just collect my scattered thoughts and stop dwelling on the terrible thing that had happened three days ago.

I spent that evening talking to Fergus, enjoying his company and thinking how very comforting it was to have him nearby.

"Tell me where you've been," I asked, sitting on the wagon tongue as he built a small fire. No matter how hot the days got, the evenings cooled down so that a little warmth always felt good.

"No place exciting, and my view of those bobbed tails is always the same." Then he proceeded to tell stories as only he could, making the ordinary an adventure and investing everything with humor, his Scottish accent strong and pronounced.

I felt very contented in Fergus's presence and once in a while, across the fire, thought I saw a softness in his face that hadn't been there before.

After a companionable pause, I asked hesitantly, "Fergus, would you ever marry again?" His head came up sharply at that.

"Why would you ask that?"

"I just wondered. It's been only you and the sheep for such a while, I don't think there's room for a woman in your life."

"There's always room for the right woman."

I'd had plenty of opportunity to watch him with the sheep, observe how he handled the new mothers and their spindly-legged offspring, and I knew him to be a kind man with gentle hands. Life with Fergus might not be so bad. Not the same as being with John Thomas, of course, but I had come to realize that nothing could ever match what I felt for him. A woman couldn't have more than one great passion in her life. To expect more seemed greedy. When it came to John Thomas, I had been unwise to let my imagination and my emotions run away with me, and doing so had ended up causing nothing but trouble. If I could distance myself physically and emotionally from John Thomas, I believed he would eventually lose interest in me, and Fletcher would no longer pose a threat either to him or me. For some reason, thinking about sharing the details of my mother's profession or my strange childhood with Fergus didn't cause me a moment's uneasiness, and if I had no settled home, if I moved around with Fergus, Fletcher wouldn't even be able to find me.

"You're awful quiet, Hope."

"I'm tired, is all."

"I wonder if that is all. It appears to me that a little of your shining light has dimmed. There's worry in your eyes that was never there before. Have you had a falling out with young Davis?"

A falling out, I thought wistfully. How I wish that's all it was, a disagreement, a spat, something light and inconsequential where the making up would be sweet and loving and well worth the brief flare of a quarrel.

"No. There was never anything there to fall out from. I'm fine. That's your Scot's imagination working too hard."

"You never told me how you hurt your shoulder."

"No," I agreed, "I never did," and then fell quiet. "Have you found her yet, Fergus?"

"Who?"

"The right woman. You said there would always be room for the right woman, and I wondered if you were still looking for her."

"I had her once, lass. Seems to me that asking for the same blessing twice in a lifetime when some people don't even get it once is asking too much. I couldn't ask the Almighty for more than He already gave me."

"I understand about asking for too much. I think it's safer to ask for the barest minimum, and then if something more happens, consider it a wonderful surprise. Otherwise, life can be too disappointing and hurtful to bear."

"Would you like to tell me what's happened these weeks I've been gone? You aren't the same girl I left."

"I'd like to tell you, Fergus, but I can't. And I fear you're right. That other girl, the one who was here when you left, has gone into hiding for a while."

Then, because I felt safer here than I had in a long time, warm and cared for and surrounded by the familiar, I shamelessly asked, "Fergus, could I spend the night with you? Could I stay with you? I don't know much about life, but I can learn and you're a good man. I know you'd never do anything to hurt me." I stumbled over the last words, not exactly sure how to say what I meant, but from Fergus's expression, he understood what I asked. He became motionless for a moment, then got up abruptly from his seat on the ground and came over to where I sat.

"You don't understand what you're asking," he said, as harshly as he'd ever spoken to me. He crouched down in front of me. "I don't know what to make of you right now, Hope."

"I don't want to go back up to that dark cabin and lie there by myself. I want to stay with someone."

"And I'm the closest, not to mention the only, human around at the moment. Is that it?"

"I didn't mean it like that." He stood up and moved away, as I continued earnestly, "I'll stay as long as you want me to stay, Fergus, and you won't have to keep me around if you get tired of me or if you find you can't care for me, I wouldn't hold it against you or pretend it was anything but my idea."

With his great height, broad shoulders, and beard, he stood like a Colossus in front of me.

"You're talking nonsense, girl. Are you feverish? What man in his right mind would get tired of you? I stopped looking for the right woman when I lost my Lorna, but if I was still looking, I could stop right here and right now with you."

"Then may I stay, Fergus?"

He said very softly, "You don't love me, Hope."

I didn't dishonor him by trying to dissemble. "Why does that matter? We're friends, aren't we? Why would we need anything more? When did love become so important? I like you and I trust you, and I think you feel the same about me. A lot of couples go through life together without even that much between them. Maybe you could learn to love me, if it's that important to you, and if there's something I could do to make that happen, you'd only have to ask once. I work hard and I don't eat much, Fergus. I promise you wouldn't regret it."

"You don't know what you're saying, lass. For a man who's been alone as long as I have, even one night with you would be like something out of a dream, but sooner or later we'd both regret it. There would never be a time you weren't wishing I was someone else. I don't need to learn to love you, Hope, I already do, but you'll never feel the same way about me with another man living in your heart. I'd always know he was there and that's not good for a man's self respect. It's no way for either of us to live and we'd both end up miserable. I thought at one time it might have worked, wanted it to and dwelled on it too much, but I can tell the moment has passed, and it's too late to try. It wouldn't work." He held out his hand to help me rise. "But you can sleep here tonight if that would make you feel better."

The inside of Fergus's wagon smelled like him, the musky smell of sheep and soil, smoke and pipe tobacco, the smell of a man who worked with animals and the elements, and I was comforted by its familiarity.

He pulled a cover over me and up to my chin, then pushed back my hair, his fingers lingering lightly against my cheek. After a moment he lit his pipe and sat on a stool next to the bunk.

"I'll sit here until you're asleep if that's what you want."

I lay slightly on my right side, holding my left arm against my chest, and turned my face toward him.

"Yes, that's what I want. You're a good man, Fergus Campbell."

"Aye, that I am. Every once in a while so blasted good, it flies in the face of reason." His tone made me laugh as he had intended, and I fell asleep to the rustling, muted sounds of the sheep outside and the rich smell of Fergus's pipe next to my bed.

I slept so soundly and dreamlessly that when I awoke in the very early morning, it took me a while to remember where I was. Fergus's empty chair jogged my memory and I stood up, rearranged my hair, and straightened my clothes, the now-familiar ache settling into my left side. I thought that even after the wound healed and even if the scar faded, I would always feel the same telltale ache there.

When I went down the steps, I couldn't see Fergus anywhere. It was the time just before daybreak, no longer fully dark with a hint of morning behind the clouds. A beautiful, wild time, when the grasslands began to sing a welcome to the rising sun and light slowly crept across the foothills, shadow after shadow disappearing in the morning's approach. My favorite time.

I walked up the ridge to my home and tried to recall the reason I had been so frightened of it last night. Now the building was the same familiar, weathered, and slightly lopsided structure it had always been. I was able to think of it objectively—my house, my home—determined not to be driven away.

I felt nearly myself again, the deep and despairing fear that had seemed to paralyze my mind and emotions slowly turning into a memory. Ivan Fletcher's face was distant and unclear, replaced by this beautiful morning, by the knowledge that there were very good people in the world and that some of them called me friend. I couldn't leave this place. Somehow I would make things right.

I wondered if I would feel ashamed of my behavior last night or mortified at having my brazen offer turned down, but I didn't. In fact, when Fergus came to say goodbye later in the morning, it seemed the night before never happened.

"I'm just south over the next ridge," Fergus reminded me. "Not far away at all. If you need me, follow the creek and you'll find me."

"Hear you first, more likely," I replied, smiling. "Those woolies make quite a racket for being dumb animals." Then I added seriously, "Thank you, Fergus."

"Aye," was all he answered, and we've never spoken of that night since.

That morning held Lou Davis's last visit for a while. "I'm relieved to say that I think it looks worse than it is now. Healing acts that way sometimes."

She examined the wound critically before she smoothed salve over the cuts, their puckered edges still crusty but holding together and the yellow ooze that had alarmed both of us completely gone.

"You'll need to use this ointment to keep your skin soft so the cuts don't tear open and remember to watch how you use your left arm. John or I will come by every day to check on you. You don't have to say anything, just give a wave and we'll know you're all right."

"You don't have to go to any bother."

"I know, but wanting to do something and having to do it are two different things."

I slipped my arm back into my blouse and slowly buttoned it, finally able to move my left side without feeling the same level of tight soreness I had known for the past several days. Lou set some newspapers down on the table.

"John Thomas brought these home yesterday. There's a troubling story on the top page."

Without a word I reached for the paper lying before me. The front page editor's column said that Tony Rubio—funny but I'd never thought of him having a last name—had been found face down in an alley with his throat slit. I put one hand over my mouth as I read the article, suddenly sick to my stomach, vividly recalling the sensation of cold, razor-sharp steel pressed against my skin. Had Tony felt a slight puncture first, as I had, then panicked, knowing what was going to happen but powerless to prevent it? I hadn't liked the man, but he shouldn't have died that way. Tony must have had some kind of falling out with his malignant associate because I was certain Ivan Fletcher was responsible for the murder.

The editor cited this "murderous act" as proof that Laramie had become the residence of a certain "bad element." As a community proud of its civilized growth, four banks and a theater, electricity, a tree-lined main street, and a beautiful new hotel, such a "barbarous act" stood in the way of progress and could not be ignored. The authorities, the editor said, must act quickly to find the culprits and use the "full force of civilized law" against them. I certainly agreed with the sentiments, but Ivan Fletcher was a man for whom civilized law held no fear. Too slippery and arrogant, a man who thought himself invincible and beyond the law.

"Tony Rubio used to work for us. I know he bothered you a while back, and I know John had a private conversation with him, but I don't understand how this fits with what happened to you. I believe, though, that two knifings in one week's time are more than coincidence."

"Yes, they are," was all I said.

I recalled Tony's jumpiness when he had last been in my cabin, the way he paced and nervously stepped in and out of the doorway. That kind of behavior would not endear him to Fletcher, who would read it as weakness or fear. Perhaps Fletcher had grown tired of Tony and his behavior, had decided he was untrustworthy or had simply found him annoying. That's all it would have taken to sign Tony's death certificate. Perhaps my knowledge of Fletcher's culpability would give me leverage when he next appeared in my doorway. I didn't volunteer any more information, and Lou wouldn't pry.

"You need to keep your rifle handy, Hope. John won't let me leave unless I carry mine with me now. It's a throwback to twenty-five years ago and I don't like it." Lou stopped on her way out. "Lately my son has been as unsettled as I've ever seen him. He told me you didn't want him around, and now I understand better why that was. But expect a visit. He won't be able to stay away much longer."

That afternoon, in almost immediate fulfillment of Lou's prophecy, I watched John Thomas approach the cabin. The big bay he rode was easily identifiable as was the tall, easy way he rode him. Someday I would have to see what it felt like to be that high off the ground on such a large animal, but I wasn't in any hurry for the sensation. At the thought, I realized dispassionately that "someday" might never come for me, and that knowledge brought with it a surprised self-revelation. I had spent most of my life living in the future and waiting for tomorrow. Maybe I had missed something because of that. In some respects, I had always faulted my mother for living solely in the present and drifting through life without goal or plan, but maybe I needed to learn how to spend more time in the moment at hand.

When, still mounted, he opened his mouth to speak, I invited, "You can get down, John. Otherwise, I'll get a crick in my neck from looking up at you."

I was relieved to be rested and in control of my emotions, knowing I would be able to enjoy his presence and perhaps even reclaim the camaraderie we had known weeks ago.

"I haven't seen you in a while," he said, "so I thought I'd check to be sure you were doing all right. I saw Campbell moving south."

"Yes, Fergus stopped by last night. I was pleased to have his company."

"Your garden looks good. How's the weaving coming?" He was searching for safe conversation and I took pity on him.

"Fine. I haven't done much the last few days so I really have to get busy. It's August already. When should I expect the first snowfall?"

"August," he answered seriously and then laughed at my expression. "No, not August, but winter's made its presence known in September before, so I'm only exaggerating a little bit."

"I've made something for your parents," I volunteered. "Wait here. I'll show you." I brought out the blanket, its rich warm colors vivid in the sunshine. "Will they like it, do you think?" He traced the design with his fingers and looked up, admiring.

"It's beautiful. I don't know how you go about making something like this, but my mother especially will appreciate it. It's got the sunset colors she loves."

"I'm glad," I said happily, reaching out both arms without thinking to take back the wool from him. I experienced a sudden and intense pain on my left side that made me inhale abruptly, wince, and drop the blanket. John Thomas caught it before it hit the ground.

"What's the matter? Did you hurt yourself?" I accepted the blanket from him more carefully this time.

"A small accident," I admitted easily, "but I'll be fine. I feel a little pang now and then, is all."

"What happened?"

"I was clumsy and twisted my shoulder. It's nothing."

The furrow between his brows deepened as he stared at me. I looked back innocently.

"Don't start, John Thomas. I'm not in the mood to be dictated to on such a pretty day. Your mother was here this morning, looked at my shoulder, and pronounced me fit and healthy, so don't play the doctor with me. That's Katherine's role."

After a moment he smiled, but I thought the smile didn't quite reach his eyes.

"I wouldn't dream of dictating to you."

"Then your memory's somewhat flawed, but I've decided to turn over a new leaf and am determined not to argue with you."

"Ha."

"It's unbecoming of you to sound so skeptical."

"Can a leopard change its spots?"

"Can a man be more annoying?"

We both laughed at the same time.

My darling, I thought, you are more dear to me than diamonds, but aloud I confessed, "Obviously my new leaf is already wearing thin, so you'd better let me get back to work."

He was very careful to keep the conversation light. "If you need anything, you know where to find me. Find us, I mean."

"Yes, I do, but I believe I'm settled for a while. Do I remember right that your parents' wedding anniversary is in August?"

"Around the end of the month sometime. You'd have to ask Becca for the exact date, but being the oldest, I know it will be their twenty-fifth this year."

"I'll have to figure out a way to put a big bow on this blanket and give it to them then. Are you planning a party?"

"Would you come if we were?"

"I believe I would. I'm awfully fond of your mother."

"Then we're definitely planning a party. Well, that's not exactly accurate. As usual, Becca will do all the planning, and I'll do all the work."

"I like that arrangement. It has the ring of progress to it."

"That depends on the perspective."

"Nonsense. It's a universal improvement and exactly what I'd expect from a suffrage state like Wyoming."

"Thirty years ago there were at least fifty men out here for every woman. They'd have painted the state pink if that would have brought in the females."

"Are you telling me you don't agree with women having the vote and sitting on juries?"

"I wouldn't dare disagree with those sentiments. If my mother didn't disown me, my sisters would kill me." He mounted his horse and looked down to laugh at me.

"Don't scowl at me like that, Hope. It scares me. You know I was teasing. Did you know that when Wyoming was offered statehood, we were told it would only happen if we'd forego our women having the vote?"

"No, I didn't know that history."

"I was a boy, but I remember my father talking to my mother about it over supper. It made an impression on me that he felt so strongly about it, that they both did. Wyoming replied that we'd bring our women into the union with us as full citizens or we wouldn't come at all. You'll notice we've been a state for over fifteen years now, and our women not only vote but even get elected to office. We take all that seriously. If it were up to us, women would be voting in national elections, too."

"That accounts for how strong-minded your mother and your sisters are."

"It doesn't account for you, though." But he was too serious when he said that, and I wouldn't be led into dangerous territory.

"I have work to do even if you don't. Good-bye, John," I told him, turning away, but I was smiling as I went inside. For better or worse, whatever happened, I did love that man.

Another day and I felt almost back to normal, my injury still tender but clearly healing and a plan slowly forming at the back of my mind. Fletcher would be back, not just for the money but even more because he had enjoyed tormenting me too much not to return to do it again. I would have no more money to give him until the end of the month and maybe not even then because the physical discomfort in my arm had kept me from weaving for several days and I had fallen behind. I didn't think any excuse would matter to him. If I understood Ivan Fletcher, and I believed I did, his killing of Tony Rubio, undetected as far as he knew, would make him bolder and more arrogant. He would return sooner rather than later, and I must be ready for him.

It was mid-morning later in the week, and I was in the back room working at the loom when I heard him. I couldn't have said what I heard or how I knew, but my hands trembled and my heart moved up into my throat and I just knew. Fletcher came through the main room to stand in the doorway of my workroom, and if he was surprised that I was waiting for him, he didn't show it.

He took one step inside the room and I, holding the rifle steady and aimed at his chest, said, "I wouldn't come any closer if I were you."

He lounged against the doorframe, no fear on his face, only that baiting smile that haunted my dreams.

"Or what will happen, girlie? What should I be afraid of?"

"I will take great pleasure in putting a hole in your chest."

"You think you got the nerve for it?"

"I think if I do, no one will ask any questions. I'll tell them you're the person who killed Tony Rubio, and I'll show them the knife to prove it. I'll say that Tony told you I was out here all alone, and you came out to do me harm. I'll say I had to kill you, and it will be self-defense, plain and simple. No one will ask any questions."

"You've thought it all out, haven't you?" If there was fear in the room, it didn't come from Ivan Fletcher. He acted amused and cocky, almost admiring. "That's if you've got the nerve to pull the trigger." He straightened up, looking around the room. "It'll make an awful mess in here if you do pull the trigger, us being as close as we are. I'll spatter all over the walls and you'll get blood on that pretty thing you're working on there."

"You shouldn't have killed Tony. That got too many people's attention."

"He was becoming a nuisance, whining about the Davises, afraid someone would find out that I'd cut you. I told him you wouldn't be saying anything and to leave it alone, but he wouldn't listen, and you know how mad it makes me when someone don't listen to me." He took one step toward me.

"Don't come any closer," I warned and cocked the gun.

"You know what I think, girlie? I think you don't have the nerve to pull that trigger. I don't believe for a second you can do that. There's no killer in you. You're as weak and scared as your mama was. You're a pitiful woman just like her, full of fine talk and promises but with no guts to follow through."

"What if you're wrong? Are you willing to stake your life on it?"

"You know," he drawled thoughtfully, "I believe I am," and lunged toward me. And because I hesitated for a split second, wavered in my concentration, listened to his hypnotizing voice, and in the end doubted my ability to follow through with what I had been planning for days, I missed. Not by much, but I missed.

Fletcher had just enough time to knock the rifle barrel up and away from him. The noise was deafening in the little room and my shot tore uselessly into the roof. Particles of the ceiling, like early snow, floated down on both of us.

Without a word, he wrested the rifle out of my grip and placed it gently against the wall. Then he took both my hands in his and yanked me out of that room, yanked me hard through the next room and out into the yard. I felt the wound, just now healing, split open and begin to soak through my shirt.

"The thing is," he said, continuing our conversation as if it had not been interrupted by my trying to kill him, "I like you. I do. And I think you could get to like me. We could do business together if you'd get off your high horse."

"You're a crazy man!" I cried, so confounded by his thick-headedness that I wasn't even afraid. "I am not going to do business with you, and I don't care what you say about me or who you tell. Don't you see? That just doesn't matter any more." As I said the words, speaking slowly and distinctly hoping to get through to him, I realized they were true. The lies were over; the fear was gone. I felt buoyant with relief. "I am not going to let you torment me. The game is over, and you didn't win."

"So you don't care if you lose your chance to marry into money?"

"You are such a fool," I replied scornfully. "Such a stupid fool. I don't need anybody's money. That was never important."

He looked around the yard. "But this is important, isn't it?"

"What?" Fletcher's soft tone, suddenly and ominously sympathetic, confused me. I couldn't make sense of him.

"This place, this old run down place, your little home here. That's what's important to you." He was right and he knew it and he saw it in my face.

"What will you do when it's winter and you got no place to stay and all those fine friends of yours don't want anything to do with you? You know what you'll do, girlie? You'll come begging to me, asking me to take care of you. You'll say, Please Ivan, take me in, I'll do anything you say, just take me in. That's what your mama said, and you're her daughter more than you know." Fletcher went under the overhang of the lean-to and picked up a shovel I had there, then without a word stepped back inside the cabin. I ran after him, not sure what he was planning but sure I wouldn't like it.

Inside he was swinging the shovel around the room, knocking things off my makeshift shelves and breaking the preserving jars so that vegetables spilled onto the colorful rag rug on the floor. He upended the table and lifted both chairs, smashing them into pieces against the wall, then grabbed what books he could find and with two hands ripped them apart, scattering pages around the room. He was powered by a malicious rage that was more terrifying because it was devoid of the heat of hate or anger or lust, a rage as cold as ice, as cold as death. There wasn't a thing I could do to stop him.

"You're a crazy man!" I exclaimed again amid the chaos. "What is this getting you?"

He didn't answer. By then I don't think he even remembered I was there. He found the kerosene and began to sprinkle it on everything, on the loom in the back room, on the bed and the Davis's anniversary blanket folded neatly at its foot, on anything he could reach, discovering the pile of woven cloth I had ready to take to George Moss and dousing that, too.

I reached the box of matches ahead of him, intent on dumping them all in the standing bucket of water before he could get to them. Seeing what I planned, he pulled me back by my left arm so that my right hand came up instinctively to protect the bleeding incision, and he was able to snatch the box of matches out of my hand before I could drop it into the bucket.

"You can stay in here if you want," he remarked from the doorway, "but it's gonna get hot pretty fast," and he tossed a lit match into the room, then a second and a third, casually flicking the matches against his thumbnail and shooting them into the cabin with enjoyment, smiling with pleasure at each arcing flame. A blaze flared up beside me, and then another, but it was hardly the inferno I think he anticipated. Items caught on fire leisurely, one by one, one thing sometimes igniting something else, and not everything burned. The wool merely smoldered and through the door into the back room I saw that the loom seemed only to singe and not flame at all. Still, it was a terrible sight to see.

Smoke began to waft out the door and into the yard where Fletcher was kicking through the garden, stomping on what plants he could, knocking over the cornstalks, snapping off the sunflowers that had begun to bloom, a man possessed. By then, winded and appalled and in an inexplicable way mesmerized, I could only watch him. I have never seen anything like that display of tireless malevolence before or since, and it seemed incredible that so much violent force and emotion should be directed at me, at me—a nobody, an invisible ghost girl, a former house maid who all her life kept to herself and whose only desire was for a quiet place of her own.

"Someone will see the smoke," I commented calmly. "They'll come to see what's wrong and I'll tell them everything. There won't be a place for you to hide." I could already see someone coming, a lone rider, and knew even at that distance who it was, knew the horse and the rider not so much by sight as by heart.

Fletcher looked over his shoulder, then quickly and awkwardly pulled himself up on his own mount, a man uncomfortable in the saddle and looking ungainly, like a sailor looks on land. Somehow he knew who the rider was, too.

"You do just that. You tell him everything. You send him straight to me. I'll be waiting for him. But tell him to watch his back, girlie, cause he ain't met a man like me before. I got my own rules." He rode off behind the cabin and down the ridge and was out of sight.

I went inside and with a blanket in one hand began to beat out the flames that remained. No great conflagration but several small blazes and a lot of damage. Almost everything wooden was charred. The books that hadn't burned were in shreds, glass was shattered, tins knocked and dented and even split open. Spilled flour and pickle brine and spring peas soaked into the rug, the pungent odor of burning wool filled the room, and over it all wafted the reek of kerosene.

I heard John Thomas calling my name from a distance, even before he threw himself off his horse, heard his racing steps across the yard and turned to see him stop in the doorway, take an uncomprehending look around the room, and then bring his gaze back to me.

"What happened here, Hope? What happened? I saw the smoke. Are you all right?"

I slowly looked all around me and said more calmly than I would have thought possible, "Yes, I'm all right. I don't think it's as bad as it looks."

My tone and my demeanor must have startled him because he stood there a moment studying my face before he came inside. Then, not bothering to respond to my absurd answer, he took the blanket from me—in fact, that beautiful sunset blanket I had once intended his parents to have—and said quietly, "Go outside, Hope." When I didn't move, he repeated very firmly, "Go wait for me outside while I finish putting out what's left of the fire."

I went to stand next to the garden, looking sadly at the sunflowers, their large decapitated heads forlornly littering the ground. I fingered the delicate tomato plants, now unrecognizable, and the beans ripped from trellises, picked up what ears of corn could be salvaged, touched pepper plants broken off at the root and squash blossoms that would not recover from the trampling. Still, the potatoes, the onions, and the carrots were safe below ground so I supposed I could eat those all winter. I was a good cook. I could do a lot with potatoes.

As I wandered the garden, my mind was racing, trying to decide what to tell John Thomas. What would he accept from me? What would he believe? What could I possibly say that would be believable? Even the truth had the ring of fiction. I was determined not to give Ivan Fletcher the opportunity to truly hurt me. It was what Lou Davis had said all along, what I had begun to figure out the night of the box social: Home had very little to do with place, even this place, this place of my own I had waited for my whole life. I'd start again or I wouldn't. That remained to be seen. This place was just a building; this spot just a garden. All that really mattered to me was that John Thomas Davis was alive. Only John was irreplaceable. He was the only home I would ever need.

He finally stepped outside, grimy with dirt and smoke, and took me by both shoulders, staring hard at my face. "What in the name of heaven happened here? If I didn't think about you every minute of every day, if I didn't wonder what you're doing and ride the edge of your property like a lovesick schoolboy hoping to catch a glimpse of you, I'd never have seen the smoke."

I opened my mouth to answer and a surprising thing happened. Out of nowhere, unexpected and unplanned, but certainly not unrehearsed, with no warning and no preamble, I said, "I want to tell you about my mother."

He looked at me as if I were a lunatic, and I can't blame him. I admit I was caught a little off guard by the words myself. "What?"

By then it seemed the most sensible, normal thing to say and I repeated, "I want to tell you about my mother, John. It's important."

He had a completely mystified look on his face as if I were a madwoman stranger he'd just met, as if he didn't understand a word I was saying, which was probably true. He said my name in a soothing voice, and I believe he thought I'd lost my mind, that I'd had my senses temporarily interrupted.

But then he said, not in a soothing tone, "You're hurt."

"I'm not hurt," I responded as bewildered as he. "A little shaken up but not hurt."

He was staring at the stain of blood that had soaked through my shirt, and I looked down at it, too, horrified at the wound's betrayal and trying not to show my panic.

"Let me see," he ordered, and I heard his mother in the firm tone of his voice.

"It's nothing. I told you before I hurt my shoulder. It's from that."

"That's not your shoulder." John spoke grimly and repeated, "Let me see."

I truly panicked then, absolutely certain he must not see the reopened wound but not knowing how to stop the inevitable from happening.

"Hope, I'd never touch you without your permission and I'd never hurt you, but one way or the other I'm going to see what's making you bleed like that, so why don't you save both of us time and embarrassment and a lot of trouble and show me?"

I had come to a dead end. At that moment the house and the garden didn't matter. The money and the waste of my summer's work seemed insignificant. Because this was far worse than all of that together. I could have written the scene because I knew how it would play out. I knew what his face would look like and what the tone of his voice would be, and I knew exactly what he would do when he saw that F cut into my left breast. The only thing I didn't know was how to keep the dreaded moment from happening.

I took one more look at his face, now as stern and as set as chiseled rock, nothing soothing or soft to be found in him anywhere, and slowly began to unbutton my shirt. Methodically, button by button with hands that didn't tremble one little bit, I unfastened it completely. Then I stood there, chin jutting out, daring him to do more because I wasn't going to.

He took the dare and with hands that did tremble, just a little bit, tentatively pushed the shirt off my left shoulder and my chemise to the side. I felt exposed and vulnerable to him but loving him as I did, I wasn't afraid or shy or embarrassed. I was just scared, and not of him but for him. As scared as I had ever been.

The wound looked uglier than it really was because it had torn open along the straight edge of the letter and oozed a dark viscous blood. This morning when I had changed the dressing, I'd been pleased with the way the injury was healing, but now seeing it through his eyes, the cuts looked atrocious, a flaming red and puffy F, the skin puckered and still raw around the three incisions.

I kept my gaze fixed on his face, and from the puzzled look in his eyes, I don't think he could at first understand and then believe what he saw. I watched him take it in, watched the progression of emotions cross his face. It was so foreign and inconceivable to him that anyone could even think of such a depraved act, let alone execute it, that at first sight his face went blank as he tried to make sense of what he saw.

My poor dear, I thought lovingly, if you lived to be a hundred you could never understand a man like Ivan Fletcher. You're different species and you live on different planets.

Finally he asked incredulously, "Did someone take a knife to you?" His finger gently followed the outline of the letter on my skin.

Without touching him, I felt him change, watched his eyes darken and his initial uncomprehending expression turn to something icy and still, everything about him suddenly frozen. I shrugged back into my shirt and buttoned it quickly.

"Who did that to you, Hope?"

"What does it matter?" I asked in return. "It doesn't hurt any more and it will heal. You can't make it disappear. You can't do anything to change the memory or the fact that it happened. It was horrible, but it's over, and all I want to do now is forget that it happened. Please respect that."

"Forget that it happened?" he repeated incredulously. "Do you think that's something I'd forget? Someone did that to you and you think I'd just forget about it?" He was genuinely flabbergasted by the idea.

"Yes. I'm asking you to do just that. If you respected me and my wishes, you would."

He took one step toward me and enveloped me in his arms, not kissing me, just holding me so close I had to put a hand between my injured breast and him to keep the force of his embrace from doing further harm.

"Respect you? I love and respect everything about you. I've loved you from the moment you stepped outside and asked if you had mud on your face. From the moment you slipped on the wagon step and laughed at yourself and promised you wouldn't step on my toes, from that moment I knew you were the only woman there would ever be for me."

I pushed away so I could look up into his face.

"Then do this one thing, John. Do it for me. Forget you saw this. I admit it was terrible, but you can't go back in time. You can't make it not have happened. All you can do now is make matters worse."

"This is about that man from the social, isn't it? The one who frightened you. My father told me his name."

"Ivan Fletcher." At the flare of rage in his eyes as he matched the name with the wound, I took hold of the lapel of his shirt with my right hand and said urgently, "Listen. Listen to me, John Thomas. I know this man. I know how he thinks and you don't. You can't, thank God. He wants to hurt you because he knows that's the worst thing he could do to me. Do you want to know how I know him or why?"

"No, not now, and only if you want to tell me later. That won't matter or change how I feel. You had a life before you met me, and I don't care what it was. I only care about you now."

At those words I felt so full of regret, so vain and stupid and foolish that I could have wailed out loud. I should have known that's what he would say and how he would react. All the time I had been worrying about how my past would affect my future, John Thomas had only cared about the here and now. How I wished I would have trusted him with the truth from the start! If I had done that, none of this would have happened. Secrets build walls, Lou once told me, and oh, she was right! She was so very right.

"This is all my fault," I cried, "and more violence won't make it right! I'm begging you, John, let it go. I'll never ask you for anything again, I swear. Just do this one thing for me, for us. We can tell the authorities and let them handle it, but you need to let it go."

"My darling girl, you've lived here how long now and you still don't understand us, do you? You sure don't understand me. Do you really think that a man could hold you down and carve his letter on you, and I'd stop in to report it to the constable and then go about my business and forget about it as if it never happened? Maybe that's what you're used to in San Francisco, but that's not how we are here. I am my father's son, and I thought you understood what that meant. I can't do what you're asking."

"You won't."

"No, don't you see? I can't. I just can't."

He kissed me then, not passionately but lightly and tenderly, as one would kiss a photograph of someone dearly loved or a precious and prized memento brought out to warm memory, barely touching me with his lips.

"If something happens to you, I will never forgive you," I whispered.

"Nothing's going to happen to me. I promise. When I come back, I'll build you a new house and we'll plant a new garden, and then you can tell me all about your mother and anybody else in your family you feel like discussing. But first I have some business to tend to."

He took one more look around the yard and then down at me, no longer any anger or outrage on his face, nothing tender or loving either, a blank face with eyes as gray as gun metal, almost a stranger. Without any further word or glance, he mounted and left, headed toward Laramie and leaving me standing in the yard watching him disappear in the distance.

Because I'd been vain and afraid, I had started something that I believed would end in grief and tragedy. How could I stay behind and wait to read about it in the paper? John Thomas might accuse me of not really understanding him, but I could level the same accusation in return if he thought I was a woman who would patiently sit at home waiting for news.

I went inside and grabbed the rifle and a piece of unburned cloth to stuff inside my shirt against the bleeding wound. Then, spurred on by fear and foreboding, I followed the Wildflower cross-country, sometimes walking, sometimes running, to find Fergus.

It wasn't until I saw Fergus's expression that I realized what a sight I must be: rifle in hand, a blood stain on my chest, my hair wild and unrestrained, my face smudged with soot.

"I'm all right," I told him, brushing away his concerns. "Really. But I have to get into Laramie fast. Can I borrow your horse, Fergus? I'll bring her back, I promise."

"Have you ever ridden before?"

"No, but how hard can it be? I drove a wagon team once and was told I had good hands for that. This is important, Fergus. It's John Thomas. I have to get to Laramie."

He didn't continue to question after my panting explanation but brought out the horse he used to draw his wagon, threw on a small saddle that was nothing like the big saddles I was used to seeing, and added bridle and reins.

"This is the only saddle I've got. It's not been used in many years, but you're a little thing and it will do. Lucy's a good animal, gentle and patient. She won't go very fast, but she won't throw you either. Don't pull too hard on her mouth. She's not used to it, and she'll do what you want without a need for force."

Fergus boosted me up into the saddle, slid my rifle into a casing that he wrapped around the small saddle horn, and placed the reins in my hands.

"Just hold on, Hope, and try to get a feel for the rhythm of the ride. Lucy's a lady and she'll take care of you."

"Thank you, Fergus. I won't forget this."

The ride was bumpy and several times I felt close to toppling right out of the saddle, but despite her age and docile temperament, Lucy at a trot was faster than I would have been on my bicycle. She saved even more time because, just as the crow flies, we were able to cut across grassland where there was no road. If the trip had been any longer, it would have grown much more uncomfortable because my bottom always seemed to be going down when Lucy was coming up, and with my skirts bunched up, the inside of my legs began to chafe against Lucy's side.

But although my mental pictures of a confrontation between Fletcher and John Thomas made the journey seem endless, the trip really didn't take as long as I had feared. I thought that in the future I might actually learn to enjoy riding, enjoy the height and the power of the animal—as long as it wasn't any more threatening than old Lucy, of course—and that feeling of being connected to it. But I would enjoy the experience only if John Thomas taught me, if I could ride next to him and never lose sight of him. Otherwise there would be no joy in riding, no joy in anything at all.

I came into Laramie from the north, then turned west on Grand. I remembered that Becca Wagner had once commented about a bad element in town, especially along Grand. No doubt Ivan Fletcher's habitat. I slid off Lucy, thinking there had to be a more refined way of dismounting than sliding off the animal's back, landing off balance on my feet, and falling gracelessly on my behind. Someday John Thomas could show me how to do that, too. He was inextricably bound up with everything in both my present and my future, and I was determined not to lose him.

I pulled the rifle out of the case and then just stood there with no idea where to go or what to do next. For a woman who had planned her future practically from childhood, who thought things through step by step, who set goals and worked toward those goals single-mindedly allowing no distractions, I was completely at a loss. At that moment and in that place I had no plan at all. I was just a bedraggled young woman who refused to be left behind.

Grand Street was quiet. I could see the white-peaked mountains in the distance and across First Street the train tracks and the platform onto which I had stepped almost six months earlier, a different girl then, a girl who thought she could order life around and make demands of it without paying a price for the arrogance, a girl unloving and unloved. Now I knew better. Fergus was right: Joy and grief were two sides of a coin and no matter what happened, with the right person no regrets for either side. All of life is a balance.

Grand Street was the kind of area that came to life at night, full of honky-tonk racket, piano music and laughter and all the noises associated with the bawdier side of business. I could see a bar, a rooming house, and a saloon all in a row. The name of the saloon struck a memory. Hadn't Ivan Fletcher said something about the Gaslight Saloon, something about setting up business on the second floor there? And hadn't the body of Tony Rubio been found in an alley off Grand?

I started quickly down the street when the door of the Gaslight crashed open and a man came hurtling out, flung backwards and landing on his side in the street. I heard no other sounds, no voices and no traffic, so the crash of the door and the thud of the man's body were startling in the stillness. As if we'd been given a common signal, the few pedestrians present all turned and looked at the man lying in the street. I remained at a distance, but even from where I stood I saw a second man stride through the open doorway, close behind the first. Two men fighting and I would have known either of them anywhere.

Ivan Fletcher lay on the ground and John Thomas stood over him, breathing hard enough that even from a distance I could see his chest rising and falling. I walked closer, watching, thinking, planning what needed to be done. Fletcher reached out with both hands and tried to jerk John's feet out from under him, but John kicked out at him instead, backed up, reached down, and lifted Fletcher upright by his shirt. He hit him once, hard, right in the face so that blood spurted, then pushed him backwards. Fletcher kept his balance and stumbled away as John Thomas relentlessly pursued him. I could see the bright blood streaming from Fletcher's nose. The spectacle held no glamour and no glory. It was bloody and primitive, two animals fighting and goring, all the years of civilization and progress stripped away with only the grunts and sodden thuds of flesh meeting flesh remaining. The sight was sickening, but it was also of my doing and I had only myself to blame for the carnage, so I stepped closer, stood very still, and raised the rifle to my shoulder.

A brief, strong breeze swirled down the street, blew against my face, whipped my skirts around my feet, and stirred an eddy of dust up in front of me, but I would not be distracted again. It was August and warm. Sweat beaded on my forehead and along my upper lip, but still I waited, immobile and unwavering. I would not hesitate and make the same mistake twice, and certainly not twice in the same day. Too much was at stake.

Fletcher lay on the ground unconscious, or so it looked, and John Thomas bent down next to him, the other man's shirt bunched in his hand to lift him off the ground. I could see in John's posture that he wanted to hit him again, wanted to keep hitting him, wanted to hurt him.

"Enough, my darling," I said aloud, "Stop now."

As if he'd heard me, John Thomas let Fletcher fall back to the ground untouched, the body dead weight and not moving.

John looked down at him for a long minute, his hands clenching and unclenching at his sides. Then he turned his back to Fletcher's limp body and crouched to pick up his hat from the street. He paused there a moment staring at the ground, and I saw his broad shoulders rise and fall from a great breath.

It's over, I thought, but I felt no relief and I didn't relax. Instead, I kept the gun at my shoulder, poised and ready for something nameless and certain.

Behind me I heard the running footsteps of more than one person and heard a man call John Thomas's name, call it desperately and furiously. I saw why the caller's voice held panic. As John Thomas crouched there, catching his breath and dusting off his hat, his broad back unprotected and exposed, Ivan Fletcher, in one smooth, deadly motion pulled the knife from his boot, that same knife I believed I would see in my dreams for all my life. With a cat-like spring he was up on both feet and leaping forward, his left arm angled to encircle John Thomas's neck and yank back his head, the knife in his right hand ready for a sweeping slash across his throat. Fletcher was propelled with such deadly intention that I believe the force of the knife would have taken John's head off.

"Your mistake," I said out loud and pulled the trigger.

For a very brief moment it seemed that time literally stood still, Fletcher in mid-spring, John half turned toward him, only then sensing danger, everyone around me motionless, even the wind and the dust quiet. But that queer moment quickly passed.

Ivan Fletcher never knew who or what killed him. One moment he was driving forward with the knife, ready to kill, lusting for the feel of the blade as it entered flesh and tore across bone and muscle, and the next moment he was nothing, a lifeless sack instead of a man, with a hole in his chest just starting to show red. To my shame I suppose, I felt worse when I killed the coyote. I have never wasted one moment of regret for that man's death. Not one, not ever, not then, not now.

I put the gun down, my hand still around the barrel and the stock resting against the ground, and began to tremble, not at what I'd done but at what I had almost lost, everything that was life to me, everything that was home. Only then did I turn to see who was behind me, but I already knew. John Thomas's father, still breathing heavily, met my look.

"You were right," I told him. "Sometimes you have to take advantage of the moment or you could lose out on everything."

John Rock Davis's eyes narrowed in thought as he tried to place the comment he'd shared at Katherine's party, and I could tell the exact moment when he recalled the conversation. His smile started in his eyes, and then, in the incredibly sweet, rich way his son had inherited, warmth and light stole across his face like sunrise on a mountain, changed the dark, severe look that had been there just a moment before into something wonderful.

John Thomas will look exactly like that in thirty years, I thought, and please God, let me be right beside him the whole time. Let him love me with the same faithful and unabashed devotion this man carries for Lou. I thought there was a good chance for it. 'I'm my father's son,' John Thomas had told me.

I let the rifle fall and turned to see John Thomas striding purposefully toward me, so focused on me that it seemed he saw nothing else. I went toward him, too, and we met in the middle of the street, the two of us standing there as if a crowd hadn't gathered around the body and the local law officer weren't staring at me.

"What did you do?" John Thomas asked me, disbelief and pride warring in his tone.

I reached my one strong arm up to the back of his head and pulled his face down to mine.

"Did you think I'd let him hurt you?" I responded fiercely. "Did you?" And I kissed him longer and harder than he'd ever been kissed in his life.

After a while, my head resting against his chest, he spoke so quietly I almost didn't hear: "So you understand us after all, don't you?"

I understand you, I thought to myself, understand you so well that we might as well be one person. Why else would my body curve into yours just right and your chin rest just so against the top of my head and your arms fit perfectly around me? We were two parts of a puzzle that belonged together long before we ever met, two separate pieces just waiting to find each other and interlock and make the picture whole.

Chapter 13

After a while John's father came up to us and put his hand on his son's shoulder.

"You hold onto this woman, son. You never know when a good eye and a steady hand will come in handy." Something warm but unspoken passed between the two men before John Rock Davis continued, "I'll talk to the constable. Why don't the two of you go over to Becca's? You're both looking the worse for wear."

John Thomas had his arm around my shoulders as we walked.

"Do I look that bad?" he asked.

We stopped and I turned to face him, licking my thumb to brush away a small trickle of blood that had dried on the corner of his lip.

"You're a mess. You're going to have a nasty bruise along your cheekbone, your lip's already starting to swell, and I think your nose is crooked. At least I don't recall it had that exact slant before. Your father's right, John. The two of us together are a sight to scare children." Then I lifted up on my toes long enough to brush his lips lightly with mine. "I'd better do that now before your lip gets too swollen."

We started walking again, both of us slowing down inside and out almost in unison. I could feel my heartbeat settling back to normal and my breathing calm.

"If you think a swollen lip will keep me from kissing you, you're wrong. That would only make it feel better." And to give validity to his statement, he stopped beneath the overhang of the Albany Bar and Rooming House, nestled us as far back in the late afternoon shadows as we could get, and kissed me again.

"You know that my brother-in-law is a preacher, Hope. He could marry us. We could go to the house, and it would only take a few minutes, and then I wouldn't ever have to let you go again." John Thomas was very serious, his breathing hoarse and quick and his mouth, bruised as it was, lingering at the base of my throat before finding my lips again.

John's suggestion was a great temptation as we stood together in the shadows, both of us oblivious to anyone or anything but each other and a mutual love and need that surprised me with its physical intensity. We could do just what John Thomas suggested, with no need for anyone's permission or approval, both of us of age and I so sure that this was the right, the only man for me that we might already have been an old married couple. I could see into the future, although the present held enough promise for the time being.

"We could spend tonight at the Johnson Hotel, and tomorrow we could start building our home. Together. Why should we be apart any more?" The words whispered in my ear were powerful, and for a moment I was almost persuaded to say yes. But then I pulled back and took his arm to move him along the boardwalk.

"We can't do that, John Thomas. Your mother would never forgive me."

"You're not marrying my mother."

"Well,"—I laughed a little and rested my head for a moment against his arm as we walked—"that's not exactly true," and let him figure out what I meant.

Because as dear as this man was to me, as much as he was life and home for me, I had loved, even desired, his family first. The way his parents had sat so close together on the wagon seat the first day I'd arrived. The warm, rowdy kitchen conversations. Family pictures on the sideboard. Lou's embracing kindness that had gathered me in without question. The way Ben couldn't pass Becca without touching her. Katherine's instant fellowship. The look in John Rock Davis's eyes as he followed his wife's movements around the kitchen. Uncle Billy's fiddle that sang of family. I had loved all that first, and somehow in the middle of it, as an inevitable afterthought, I had lost my heart to this black-haired young man.

Someday I would try to make John Thomas understand what I meant in a way that wouldn't hurt his feelings, but first I needed to talk about something else.

Standing there on Ben and Becca's front porch, waiting for someone to answer our knock, I said one final time, "I want to tell you about my mother, John," and responding to the seriousness of my tone he answered, "I'll listen to whatever you want to say, but you don't have to tell me anything. There's nothing that will matter."

"It matters to me."

"I know it does. That's why I'll listen."

Then Becca opened the door, saw us, called Ben's name as she pulled us into the house, and we didn't have the chance to talk privately until much later.

The four of us sat around the Wagners' kitchen table, John Thomas soaking his hands in warm water and Epsom salts as we talked. The knuckles on both hands were skinned and swelling, and Becca thought the soaking might make them feel better. She could have been her mother bustling around the kitchen. Certainly she resembled her mother in face and figure but even more in her cool and practical attitude toward the two of us, arriving as we did, unannounced and in such a sorry state. Becca Wagner was the perfect minister's wife, unsurprised by circumstance and so warmly hospitable she might have been sitting and waiting expectantly for two such disheveled and exhausted visitors to appear on her doorstep.

John Thomas, of course, looked much worse than I. The bruises on his face were already coloring a prominent purple, and he walked stiffly from a blow to the ribs I was glad I hadn't seen and that he wouldn't talk about. Compared to him I looked prosaically normal, my new bandage comfortably hidden beneath one of Becca's shirtwaists. With my face washed and my hair pulled back, I felt human again, almost as if the last seven hours hadn't happened, as if I hadn't come face to face with a future without John Thomas and hadn't killed a man to keep that from happening.

Becca, with her mother's tact, helped me wash and bandage my wound without comment but on the way out of the room, she stopped and put her arms around me, saying in a voice close to tears, "I'm so sorry this happened. It must have been terrible for you and you all alone! I've already begun to think of you as a sister, and it makes me furious that someone would do such a terrible thing to you."

The gesture and the words touched me so that I couldn't speak, couldn't get anything by the big lump that had suddenly formed in my throat. Becca looked at my face and with a corner of her apron wiped away the tears pooling in my eyes, then dabbed at her own.

"We won't talk of it again," she declared and has stayed true to her word.

The chief of the constabulary came to talk to both John Thomas and me that same afternoon. I had to show him my wound, and when he saw it he stated simply, "I won't need to bother you any more, Miss Birdwell," a grim expression around his mouth and eyes.

I never heard about any charges being filed or any kind of formal investigation and never read a word in the *Boomerang* about what happened. The incident simply faded away, becoming a thing of the past even while it was still very much in my present. It remains a mystery to me what became of Ivan Fletcher's body, and there's a fine justice there, or if not justice, at least balance. My mother lies buried in a nameless grave in an unknown place. Why should he have any more than that?

After the constable left, Ben Wagner pushed away from the table, saying, "I think it's time for our daily walk, Becca." His wife looked at him blankly at first and then smiled.

"Of course, our daily walk," she repeated, rising too.

On the way out Ben put a hand on John's shoulder. "Do you feel better now, John?" He wasn't speaking about John Thomas's swollen hands or the bruise along the side of his face but about something else entirely.

John Thomas hesitated before responding, "I didn't do it to feel good, Ben, but it had to be done."

"Are you sure?" Instead of answering the question, John asked one of his own.

"Are you telling me you wouldn't have done the same?"

Ben looked over at his Becca waiting in the open doorway, her chestnut hair plaited into one large braid that fell over her shoulder and her eyes bluer than the late afternoon sky behind her. I saw Ben reflect on John Thomas's question, frowning a little at his thoughts as if they didn't please him before he squeezed John's shoulder with affection and understanding.

"No, I can't tell you that. I wish I could be sure, but I honestly can't say what I would have done."

I liked Ben Wagner very much at that moment, honest with himself and us, as human as the rest of us poor mortals and maybe more aware of it than most.

After they'd gone, I lifted John Thomas's hands from the basin and dried each one in a towel, handling them so gently they might have been delicate crystal. Then, because he just sat there dumbly and looked at me like I was the most beautiful thing he'd ever seen, I lifted one of his hands with both of mine and held it to my cheek.

"Stop looking at me like that," I said.

"Like what?"

"You know." Then I added, "Let's go sit in the parlor. I want to talk to you," and still not letting go of his hand, I led him into the next room. I sat him on the sofa and moved to the rocker across from him, sitting forward primly with my hands in my lap.

"I wish I'd done this weeks ago, but I was fearful and vain and foolish until it was almost too late. There's a power to truth I didn't understand and a power to love I didn't know about either. I want you just to listen to me and not say anything. Can you do that, John?"

"I can do whatever you want."

I thought there couldn't be a better man with a more loving heart than this one, and if he still wanted me after I finished talking, he would be stuck with me until we were both old and gray and toothless.

"I wasn't raised like you and your sisters and brother, John Thomas. I never knew what a family was like or how ordinary men and women acted together. I never saw it. My mother was unmarried and a prostitute. I'm not sure who my father was. I was raised in a bordello in the company of women who made satisfying men their business. One of my mother's customers didn't have any money to pay for her services, so he gave her the land grant that she passed on to me, and that's how I came to Wyoming."

At first I stumbled over the words, but once I began, I couldn't stop. I wanted him to know my mother as I had known her, not judge or condemn her, just know her. What good would judging do? She was gone and the past was past, and after all this I believed she had done the best she knew how, the best she could. I wanted to paint a picture for him so he could see Bea Birdwell as clearly in his mind's eye as I did in memory and dreams. I told John everything, described her charm and beauty, her early status and her eventual fall from privilege, her last days in a crib on Morton Street at the mercy of the cruelties and indignities of Ivan Fletcher, her despairing end from a drug overdose, the unknown, unmarked grave where she slept now, mourned and missed only by me.

"I was never ashamed of her or of myself, not really, until I came here, until I met your mother and your family and saw what it could have been like. I saw how crude and unnatural my life had been and I didn't want you to know. The contrast was so great, and I was afraid I'd disgust you. I should have trusted you. I know I was wrong. I'm so sorry." I fell silent then, the only sound in the room the ticking of the clock on the mantel.

"Am I allowed to speak now?" John asked. When I nodded, he leaned forward and said with great intensity, "If your mother were here now, if she walked into this room right now, I'd welcome her into our family like someone born into it, like I'd known her all my life. Because she brought you into the world. Because she gave me you. That's all that's important, Hope. Nothing else matters."

He said exactly the right thing, offered no platitudes, didn't judge her or make excuses for her, just accepted her as she was.

I heard the back door open and Becca's voice speaking unnaturally loudly to announce their return and knew I had only a moment.

My hands still in my lap, I raised my eyes to John's and said very clearly, "I've been waiting a long time for you, John Thomas Davis." And then because I had never said the words and he deserved to hear them, I added, "I love you, love you more than life," and knew it to be true.

We turned down the Wagners' offer for supper.

"I'd guess Mother's expecting us," John said. "By now she'll have heard all about what happened, and she'll want to see both of us to be sure we're each in one piece. Hope can stay with us a while. Mother will enjoy the company, and I won't complain about it either."

I stopped so abruptly as we walked out the door that he stumbled up against me.

"What?" he asked.

"I forgot about Lucy."

"Lucy who?" I smiled at his tentative tone. The poor man probably thought I'd just recalled another family member I needed to discuss.

"Lucy, Fergus's horse. I tied her to the rail somewhere on Grand Street or maybe it was on Second, I wasn't exactly paying attention, and she's been there for hours. Fergus will be sending out a search party looking for her, probably thinking I've turned into an ungrateful horse thief."

"Hope, are you telling me you rode a horse?"

"How did you think I followed you into town so quickly?"

"I don't know. On your bicycle, I guess."

"Only if it sprouted wings and flew like a bird. I needed to go across country where there wasn't a road and a bicycle sure wasn't right for that."

Memory and understanding brought a grin to John's face "As I recall, you promised me a pie if that circumstance ever occurred. Didn't you guarantee it would be the best pie I'd ever have?"

"My darling," I replied happily, "I'll make you a pie every day for the rest of our lives if that's what you want."

"I don't want a pie every day. I have something much better in mind," and he stopped halfway down the walk to turn me into his arms and show me exactly what that something was.

Chapter 14

We went straight to Lou after leaving Becca's house that day, I riding on Lucy next to John like I'd ridden horseback my whole life. After John Thomas came back from returning Fergus's horse, we all sat down for supper around the kitchen table. I thought Lou's eyes looked a little red, and I didn't want to picture her crying. The idea prompted sympathy tears just thinking about it, and because none of what happened would have happened had I been truthful from the outset, I felt guilty besides.

Later that evening I tried to tell Lou that and to say I was sorry, but she just raised her hand in a decisive way. I knew she would be right to scold me or at least express disappointment or displeasure in my behavior. I had jeopardized her family and purposefully lied to her after all, and while my heart sank at the idea, her reaction was understandable. She loved John Thomas, too, and I deserved a scold. I just hoped she would be able first to forgive me for endangering her son and then to tolerate me in the family, because John Thomas and I had already decided that I was definitely joining the family.

I don't know what I was thinking because instead of scolding, Lou put her hand to my cheek and said softly, "You're never to talk like that again, Hope. We're the ones blessed to have you in our lives. My son sat at our supper table tonight alive and the happiest I've ever seen him, all because of you. I can't ever thank you for that because language doesn't have the right words."

"You'll be a mother some day, God willing, and then you'll understand what I'm trying to say. You'll come into this family as much my daughter as if I had given birth to you, and you'll always belong here. This is your home and we're your family now."

Her forceful words and the regal lift of her head made her magnificent as she spoke with such passion, and I knew how John Rock Davis, Civil War veteran and man with a past, had come to love her. There wasn't the remotest possibility he could have resisted her even if he'd wanted to, not with that compelling force about her, the clear-eyed power of her character and will that said, Step aside or take hold and hang on, but don't you dare get in my way.

With the help of both his father and his friend and foreman, Sam Kincaid, John Thomas started building our house the very next day, but he wouldn't allow me to go back there or to see it until they finished.

"The cabin looks worse than I remembered," he admitted grimly, "and I don't want you to see it like that. I promise you'll be happy when we're done."

I suppose *building* didn't accurately describe John's activities because despite his intentions, he had to confess that the season was too far along for there to be time to get in much new construction.

"We'll never get a new house up before winter," he told me with apology, "so for the time being we're going to improve on what's there. The place will do for the two of us this winter, and then next spring I'll build you the house I promised. We'll need more room when the children come along anyway."

Children, I thought, finding the idea intriguing. I didn't know much about them and hadn't considered that far ahead. Of course, there would be children, little John Thomases running around, bringing home orphaned creatures, and slaying imaginary dragons. Just the thought made me smile.

Lou and her husband left for San Francisco early in September on an anniversary trip John Davis, Senior, had planned as a surprise for his wife.

"Stay at the Palace Hotel," I advised him when he asked, "and plan to eat at least one dinner at Delmonico's on Market Street, but be sure to take your life savings along with you because that's what it will cost to eat there. Don't miss Golden Gate Park and ride the streetcars as many times as you possibly can."

They visited just in time, before the earthquake of the next year leveled the city and turned its glitter to dust. I knew San Francisco was considered a magnificent and cosmopolitan city filled with the latest in fashion, luxury, invention, and design, but I found it mystifying that anyone would want to go there, even for a visit, when everything a person really needed for life and happiness was in Laramie, Wyoming.

While we waited for the train that would take them to San Francisco, Lou teased, "I promised John I wouldn't embarrass him by wearing men's pants while we're there," a remark that would have made a person laugh to hear it because she was dressed in the latest fashions for travel, her lustrous chestnut hair topped by a hat of blue silk with a curved feather that brushed charmingly against one cheek. Lou held on to her husband's arm and laughed up at him, excited about the trip, her complexion in high color and the last twenty-five years smoothed away. A simply beautiful woman.

John Rock Davis didn't say anything in return, just smiled down at her. He didn't possess the same transparency as John Thomas, and I never dared presume to read his mind, but at that moment I knew what he was thinking; he might as well have spoken the words aloud. Wear whatever strikes your fancy, his look said. There's not a man alive who wouldn't want to trade places with me.

While they were gone, Gus and I kept each other company in the big house, which suddenly seemed too enormous for comfort. John Thomas moved out to bunk with the hands until his parents returned.

"No use tempting fate," he told me. "We'll do what's right and have our wedding night in our own house."

I admit I was a little disappointed at John Thomas's self-control. Lou and John would be gone for two whole weeks and the necessity for waiting to be together escaped me, the wedding date was set, after all, but John Thomas gets funny ideas sometimes, and I'm still learning how to recognize when there's room for discussion and when I should just nod and sweetly say, "Yes, dear." I'm not an unintelligent woman, but I'm beginning to think I'll need longer than I thought to figure him out. I can be awfully smug about reading his mind, so I guess those times when John takes me completely by surprise are humbling and good for my character.

The first real snowfall of the season fell on our October wedding day. I rose early that morning, sat by the window in my room for a while, and watched the heavy white flakes fall gently from a sky the color of John Thomas's eyes.

"Here's that winter I planned for and worried about," I said to myself, and like a schoolgirl I traced my initials and then John Thomas's into the frost on the glass, surrounded them with a heart, and added an arrow for good measure. Isn't life something?

We left for the church around noon, and before two o'clock I was a wife. I wore a dress that I had stitched myself from rich satin the color of snow, the bodice high necked, covered in lace, and woven through with threads of deep green velvet ribbons. I had piled my wild curls on top of my head and threaded tiny sprigs of green pine through them. The look may sound silly, but the effect was exactly what I wanted, like the day, like the first snowfall blanketing the earth and covering everything except the tips of the evergreens.

I am a quiet woman and not likely to change, a woman not given to giddiness or easy conversation, a private woman who holds her deepest feelings inside in a way that is sometimes mistaken for ignorance or arrogance. I often wish I could be different, wish I had Becca's easy, compassionate friendliness or Lou's genuine goodness, both women able to make a person feel welcome and comfortable with naturally generous and uncomplicated gestures.

But I spent too many years as a child in a world of adults where I was neither seen nor heard, too many years wordlessly watching my mother's face for clues about how and when to speak, spent too much time on my own and alone, trusted only myself for too long, to be anything other than what I am. So on my wedding day no one could have suspected how my heart was beating to burst, how it was singing so loudly with joy that it threatened to drown out Ben Wagner's voice. But it was, it was, and even John Thomas didn't really understand until later, until that night when the two of us were finally alone in our own home and caught up in the ageless expression of love. Then and only then did he fully appreciate how deeply and how ardently I treasured that day.

John never built the new house he promised because I wouldn't let him. I saw no need to part with the old one and considered doing so to be unnecessary and ostentatious. Instead, he added a large room to the north side of the cabin and connected it with a door to the original main room that we converted into our kitchen. We sleep in the new room, a singed blanket of sunset colors draped across the foot of our bed. John Thomas enlarged the back workroom and added a stove so I could more comfortably do my weaving there. By the front door he carved windows and put in real glass, added a porch, tightened the logs of the original structure, filled in the gaps and papered the inside walls with wallpaper ordered from Chicago. When he put in solid wooden floors throughout, he never once reminded me of our earlier conversation: how I wouldn't allow him to help me, how I told him I would "hire" it done myself someday. One of the many reasons I love John Thomas Davis is that he doesn't have a mean-spirited bone in his body.

He and Sam Kincaid figured how to run water from the Wildflower into the kitchen through a pump on a sink. Despite their ingenuity, the pump is of little use in the dead of winter when the temperature sinks well below freezing. That small inconvenience doesn't matter. The snow offers water enough, and all winter we have more snow right outside our door than we could ever use.

John Thomas bought a real stove to replace the small line stove I had used for months, and before the ground froze, he dug a springhouse on the south side of the shed so we'd have a place to store root vegetables and meats. John insulated the privy for us and the shed for the chickens, finishing all that work in eight weeks. A man possessed.

I saw the renovated cabin the day before the wedding and stood speechless. Whirling in the middle of the kitchen, I clapped my hands, delighted and applauding his efforts.

"It's perfect!" I crowed. "Who ever would have thought I'd live in a place as grand as this?"

John watched my reaction carefully, like someone that gives a gift but worries it isn't suitable or valuable enough. I went and put my arms around him and buried my face against his chest.

"Thank you, John. No wonder I've hardly seen you in weeks. Why would we ever need more than this to be happy?"

"I don't even need this," he said, his wonderful smile tinged with relief. Then, after kissing me, he announced, "I only need one thing to be happy and I'm holding it right now."

"Your hat?" I asked innocently.

"Don't start, Miss Birdwell."

"Only Miss Birdwell for one more day unless you think we should put the wedding on hold while you work on the house a little longer." He gave a small groan and kissed me again.

"I couldn't stand to wait another day. As it is, I asked Ben if he'd mind hurrying the ceremony along tomorrow and skipping any unnecessary parts. The man in the moon is dancing so hard right now he's about worn out."

Thinking about it afterwards, I decided the ceremony had been a little speedier than I'd expected, so Ben must have had pity on John and taken his request to heart.

At the marriage celebration that followed, Uncle Billy played a bright, lilting tune on his fiddle to welcome me into the family, and only Katherine's absence shadowed the day. But she wrote her best wishes and we have been corresponding ever since.

Fergus, back through on his fall swing, came to the wedding. He had trimmed his beard and his hair, put on a smart green jacket and corduroy pants, and looked quite handsome.

I asked him who was watching the sheep during his afternoon absence. After all, I told him, my lambies were still in his flock and I had an interest in their well being. Fergus shrugged off the question.

"The good Lord can handle the woolies for a while," he stated firmly, and because we were standing at the back of the church at the time, I didn't think I should express any doubts about divine competence, especially when it came to being a shepherd. I had heard Ben cite several Biblical texts that proved God knew how to handle sheep.

After the ceremony I stood on tiptoe to whisper into his ear, "Thank you, Fergus." It wasn't for his company or his friendship or for the loan of Lucy that I was thanking him, and he knew it. It was for knowing right and wrong when I didn't, for not letting me make a mistake that would have eventually grieved us both, that would have robbed me of this happy day. Fergus put an arm around me and lifted me off my feet into a big hug.

"You're looking bonnie today, lass, so you must be happy. That's all I ever wanted for you. Once you said to me that you wished you could give me back what I lost. Well, in a way, with that look on your face, you've done just that. Now you've got a young man and a family all in one day."

Not long after our wedding I announced to John Thomas that I wanted to raise sheep. He had just come in from working all day, still red-faced from the cold, a cattleman born and bred, used to cows all his life, and had sat down unsuspecting to supper when I made my announcement.

"All right," he answered cautiously. "You've got 160 acres in your name, and if you're sure that's what you want, we'll do it."

I had been thinking about the idea for some time, so I responded confidently, "I'm sure, John. Why not? There's plenty of room, and it isn't true that cattle and sheep can't live together. I read where that's being done very successfully. We just have to do it right. We have the land," I added, stressing the word *we*, "and the beginning of a flock. There's a growing market for mutton and wool both south and west. Maybe in the spring we could talk to Fergus about it, maybe hire him on and put him in charge until we know what we're doing."

Which is exactly what we did.

Becca gave birth to a baby girl the first spring after our marriage. Lily Kate was born with a head of golden red hair and sparkling eyes. I found the baby enchanting. I hadn't had much to do with babies in my life, and I couldn't get enough of Lily Kate. On our first visit to see her, I hovered over the cradle, captivated by the baby's soft smell and feel, the little sounds she made, and the expressions on her face.

"She's so small," I said to Becca in awe. "Aren't you afraid you'll break her?"

"I was at first, but not any more. Lily Kate is sturdy and strong like all the Davis women."

Becca, still looking too pale, sat in the rocking chair nursing the baby. The delivery had been long and difficult, and for a while there had been unspoken fears for her and the baby's safety. While the doctor looked grave, Ben locked himself behind his study doors, then came out at peace and confident that everything would end all right. I don't know what special line he has to the Almighty, but Ben was right. Lily Kate was born healthy, and a tired Becca had been strong enough to hold her daughter in her arms right after birth.

At her first sight of Lily Kate, Lou's eyes glistened. "Here's our next generation, John," she announced, taking the baby in her arms, the glowing look on her face reminding me of the first time I'd seen Lou Davis more than a year ago in the Moss Dry Goods and General Store. "I believe this baby officially makes us a patriarch and a matriarch," and then she laughed at herself and at the look on her husband's face. As if he'd spoken, although he hadn't said a word, she added, "I know. I don't feel qualified for the title either."

That night I lay curved into my husband, my back against him and his arms around me, thinking about Lily Kate.

"John Thomas," I said, trying to nudge him awake. He was nearly asleep, poor man, and at my voice murmured something unintelligible in response. I turned in his arms, my face very close to his, and laid a hand against his cheek.

"John Thomas, wake up. This is important. I've been thinking, and I believe we need our own baby." The words brought him instantly awake.

"You already know that's fine with me," he replied, raising himself on one elbow to look at me, "and I thought we were working on that. I sure don't mind talking about the subject, and I don't have any argument with the idea or the effort, but just out of curiosity, why are you bringing up the topic at this particular moment?"

"I've been thinking about it a lot lately and I believe we need to get more serious about having a baby. I don't think it's enough for you and I to, you know, enjoy each other haphazardly. We need a plan."

I could see John's face above mine, the moonlight through the window behind him turning the tips of his tousled hair silver, grinning as if I hadn't made one of the most serious pronouncements of my life, as if my mind wasn't already spinning with plans for the baby and the baby's future.

"You know, darling," he drawled, laughter in his voice, "I couldn't agree more, and I have just the plan to make that baby happen." And while it wasn't exactly what I'd meant, John's plan worked perfectly. Our Jack was born nine months later.

John Rock Davis the Second, to be more accurate, but we slipped into Jack the first week he was born and it stuck.

"Too many Johns in the family could be confusing," I said, contentedly, "and Jack seems right for him."

Jack was born in January, the day after the worst blizzard of the season. Snow blew in drifts as high as the windows, and the landscape lay white wherever we looked. We couldn't get out and no one could get in, so when it was time, I pushed Jack out into the waiting hands of his father, who was better than any doctor or midwife I could have asked for. Between the two of us, we figured out what to do, and although John Thomas gets a little offended when I compare the two, I credit all those years spent pulling calves for his ability to birth a baby without hesitation. I sure didn't know the first thing about it. I teased him that maybe he should follow Katherine off to medical school, but the truth was that he stayed calm and strong for both of us and not shy about anything.

I wasn't shy either when the moment came, but modesty is the first thing lost when a baby's made the decision to be born. Lou tried to tell me what to expect, but the whole process was messier and more exhausting than I anticipated. Recalling Becca's prolonged suffering, we realized we had been blessed with an easy delivery. Jack came crying into the world only a few hours after I had the sign he was on his way.

John, Senior, Uncle Billy, and Sam Kincaid dug us out as soon as they could get over to us, but in a way I was sorry to see them arrive. There was something wonderful when it was just the three of us—John Thomas and the baby and I—in our own world, our own little family in our own little home.

John Thomas cleaned and dried Jack, then wrapped him in a blanket and handed him into my arms. As soon as I took Jack, my husband sat down abruptly next to the bed as if he were the one who had done all the work and had suddenly lost all his energy.

"He doesn't have much hair," I remarked at my first glimpse of the baby, making cooing noises at Jack like a woman bereft of her senses. Perhaps for a moment I was. I thought that this child who came out of my body in the most incredible way was perfect, with tiny fingers and toes, transparent blue-veined eyelids, long dark lashes, and skin as delicate as a butterfly's wing. I knew from experience that not everyone shared the parents' opinion about their baby's angelic appearance, but I honestly couldn't see how anyone would think our child wasn't absolutely perfect.

"He could win a prize for being so beautiful," I murmured in wonder. I pushed the blanket away from his face and looked over at John Thomas. "Look what we made, John. Isn't he something?"

At that moment, I saw tears in my husband's eyes. The bright morning sun shone through the snow piled against the windows and filled the room with a peculiar white light that made John's tears glisten.

He opened his mouth to say something but swallowed quickly instead of speaking, and I realized that emotion wouldn't allow any words.

I was filled with such a tenderness for him, for them both, that I reached for John Thomas's hand and brought it over to the baby, both our hands resting together on Jack's blanket so we could feel the slight rise and fall of our son's breathing.

"It's all right," I said to John Thomas, "I heard exactly what you said," and then I fell asleep. Later when I awoke, John Thomas still sat in the same place, tears gone, just sitting with his hands on his knees, looking at Jack and me. I don't think he had moved at all.

Lou tells me, always with an understanding smile, that I'm spoiling Jack. I suppose it's true, but I can't help it. I had no idea I could feel like this, so powerfully protective, so fiercely loving, emotion welling up from some deep part of me I never suspected was there. I recalled what Lou had said to me the day John Thomas had come home from his fight with Ivan Fletcher, how I would be a mother some day and only then understand what she was feeling. She was right. I'd do anything to keep this child safe, well, and happy. Sometimes I wonder if my mother ever felt the same way about me. I think now that she might have.

There are times when Jack cries and will not quiet that I bring him into bed with John Thomas and me. I'm told by wiser women than I that I'll regret doing so, but I don't see how that could be. I can't bear the idea that for even a moment my child might think he isn't loved or might fear he's been abandoned and is alone in the world.

The times I cherish most are when we nestle Jack between us, John Thomas and I on each side of him, our little pea in a protective pod, innocently content, cooing baby noises and snuggling safe, warm, and loved right where he belongs.

Our wedding picture hangs on the wall in our bedroom. In the photograph I wear a thoughtful look, too serious for the happy day and appearing more serene than I was. That woman seated in the picture looks confident and poised, but she's a stranger to me, a fair-haired stranger in a dress of white lace woven through with traces of dark velvet ribbons. The look in her eyes is only a quiet reflection of the joyful day, giving no hint of what was truly beating in her heart. Standing behind me, John Thomas looks serious and slightly bemused. Ignoring the photographer and his directions, John's eyes look down at me and his hand rests on my shoulder. My hand reaches up to cover his protectively.

Next to the wedding picture hangs the land deed my mother gave me years ago. I put the document behind glass and had John Thomas make a dignified wooden frame for it. Sometimes in the night as I'm sitting in bed with my back against the wall, Jack nursing at my breast, the moonlight reflects off the glass and the gleam reminds me of that sunny afternoon in Golden Gate Park.

I'm seventeen again, sitting on the park bench with my mother and she's handing me a folded, yellowed paper. I hear her speaking, eager to give me the only valuable thing she possesses, no mockery in her voice as she tries to say good-bye to me. But I'm so caught up in my future plans and the adventure of life, I don't realize that's what she's doing.

John Thomas, who rises before dawn and comes home after sunset every day, always intends to wake with Jack and me in the night but despite his good intentions, he sleeps soundly, and I never have the heart to rouse him. As usual, my husband lies with an arm flopped across some part of my body because even in sleep he needs to touch me and assure himself that I'm there. As if I would be anywhere but next to him. As if I had any other place of belonging, any other home.

Jack, with an appetite like his father's, suckles greedily at my breast where only the remnant of a scar shows. I'm glad the wound healed so completely that John Thomas no longer has to see it and remember, but even in the dark I can trace the faint outline of an F on my skin.

Memory is as close as a flash of moonlight.

"Here," my mother says as she hands me the worn, creased paper, more fanciful in her speech than I've ever heard her, saying goodbye with her own simple poetry. "Maybe this old deed will help you find your heart's desire."

I rearrange my son in my arms, then close my eyes and whisper softly into the darkness, whisper to my mother wherever she is, "You were the smart one after all, Mama, because that's exactly what that old deed found for me. How did you know?"

Jack gives a little hiccup and John Thomas's arm lies warm across my legs.

Heart's desire indeed.

Isn't life something?

Made in the USA
Coppell, TX
15 May 2021